A Wild MOOSE CHASE

A Wild MOOSE CHASE

Ken Tustin

Wild South Books
Dunedin, New Zealand

ISBN 0 9583723 0 6

Cover and inside front cover maps reproduced courtesy of the Hocken Library, University of Otago / Uare Taoka o Hakena Te Whare Wananga o Otago.

Cover photograph of Fiordland supplied courtesy of Fiordland Travel Ltd.
All other photographs by Ken and Marg Tustin, unless otherwise acknowledged.
Design by John Buchan Design Ltd., Dunedin
Printed by SNP Offset, Singapore

Contents

	Acknowledgments	vii
	Foreword by Philip Holden	viii
	Dedication	xii
	August 1996	1
1	Winter 1990 Moose 1900–1934	3
2	January–March 1967	13
3	1969–71	25
4	February–April 1972	32
5	December 1974–January 1975	46
6	January 1975	51
7	Deer 1909–79	57
8	February 1992 Moose sign	67
9	February–March 1992 May 1992	76
10	April 1994	84

11 April–May 1994 91

12 May 1994 102

13 August 1994 110

14 March–April 1995 114
October 1995

15 Moose hunts 1930s and 1950s 125
April 1995
August 1995

16 October, November 1995 138

17 March 1996 148
June 1996
July 1996

18 Fiordland living 165

19 August 1996 175

20 August 1996 182

21 September, October 1996 189
November–December 1996
April 1997

22 Conclusion 205

Epilogue, July 1997 218

Author's Note on Sources 220

Bibliography 221

Acknowledgments

Many people helped in gathering material for this book and most are mentioned within. They shared memories, diaries, written records and photographs. To them—and others unnamed—and to those who assisted us in recent years, I thank you all.

Bill Black deserves special mention not only for his flying but for so graciously repaying his debt.

Thanks too, to the estate of Denis Glover, for permission to reproduce part of the poem 'Sings Harry', and to Valerius Geist, for permission to reproduce the line drawings from his article, 'On the Behaviour of the North American Moose in British Columbia'.

Finally, I'm grateful to Max Quinn and Marg for comments on a draft of the text.

Foreword

Way back in the summer of 1963 I was a government hunter in the Kaweka Mountains, Hawkes Bay. Together with a bloke called Geoff Beale, I was given the rather thankless task of attempting to keep deer and other introduced wild animals under some measure of control. Great days, way back then.

On a blistering hot day in late January we were en route from the Manson Country, on the back of Ngamatea Station, to Kiwi Mouth Hut, located on the other side of the big Ngaruroro River.

Up on the open tops of the Manson we had camped out under canvas, seen deer a plenty, and were now looking forward to spending a night at a decent hut before heading out to the base camp at Kuripapango, on the inland route linking Napier and Taihape.

Once across the river, we tramped upstream. Soon the hut came into sight, smoke drifting into the still air from its tin chimney. Visitors were rare out here in those days.

In the hut were two young guys: an Englishman named Des, and Ken Tustin. They were also on the Forest Service payroll, cutting a track between here and another hut downriver. As this was a Sunday they were off duty.

Looking back, I recall Ken as a young man: slim, dark, good looking in a boyish way. He was obviously very much in his element in the hills. He had an open-sighted .303 rifle and, most evenings after work was over, would go out hunting. He had, he said proudly, already shot a few deer. The life Geoff and I were living fascinated him and his eager questions about deer and other aspects of the job came like a flurry of winter snowflakes, thick and fast.

Obviously the life of a government hunter wasn't suitable for just anyone. True, one had to be—or become—a good hunter; that was mandatory. But there were other requirements to be taken into account too: the right physical and mental approach; the ability to cope with living with oneself, perhaps for long periods, in a landscape oftentimes daunting.

So it was rare for me to actually encourage someone to become, of all things, a government hunter. Yet in this particular instance I could in young Ken Tustin read the right signs as clearly as antler rubbing on a pepperwood tree. Moreover, I did something positive about it.

Before we carried on to base camp next morning, I realised that I had warmed very much to Ken Tustin. He had, I later learned, lied about his age so that he could obtain this job during the long school holidays.

In recalling this incident in a letter to his publisher in 1997, Ken wrote 'I worshipped the professional hunters, and I'll never forget when Phil took me aside and told me "You'd make a good culler." To a school kid that was inspirational indeed!'

Four years would pass before I ran into Ken Tustin again. This time it was at the Forest Service base camp at Te Anau. Now, in the summer of 1967, he was tall and well-built. Moreover, he was working as a hunter in nearby Fiordland with the Forest and Range Experiment Station, a research section within the Forest Service. An ambition realised, you could say, because the FRES boys could also be considered government hunters. Precisely what Ken was doing there is something he will explain later on.

Like many others, I had long been interested in the story of moose in this country. Did they, or did they not still survive in southwest Fiordland?

I took my interest in moose a step further by including a chapter on that very question in my 1976 book, The Deer Hunters. The last part of that chapter covers an 'abridged' account of an FRES expedition to southwest Fiordland in 1972. The object of this exercise was to try and solve the moose mystery once and for all. Ken Tustin was a part of that research team and what I wrote was based on material he had already published which he generously allowed me to use.

In the August of 1986 I spent several days at Preservation Inlet as the guest of Allan Johnstone who, at that particular time, was in the process of establishing a hunting and fishing lodge. It is the closest to moose country I have ever been, to this day.

I was to be taken out of this wild and altogether magical area the same way I had been brought in: by Invercargill-based Hunter Hamilton in his Cherokee 140 amphibian aircraft.

It was a splendid Friday afternoon when we lifted off the unruffled waters of Preservation Inlet. Instead of flying directly to Invercargill, and as a special favour to me, Hunter suggested that I might like to see more of this very special and always intriguing part of the country.

'Over moose country?' I asked.

'Good as done!' Hunter replied with a big Southland grin.

And so for the first time I saw moose country. Saw it from a very low and very clear level, the Cherokee barely clearing the high peaks. It was a big, heavily forested region that held an instant and strangely arresting appeal.

There was Wet Jacket Arm, bigger than I had expected, snaking from the coast to the hinterland. And, yes, that had to be Herrick Creek spilling into it. Herrick Creek, as you will soon discover, was and is a very special place in the continuing saga of moose in this country.

Swinging back, we crossed Supper Cove, the Seaforth River merging with it.

But were there still moose in the country I had seen from above?

From what I have learned about moose, and given all the evidence we have to reflect on, I would say yes, there are moose still remaining in this country. But it would have to be a 'yes' with reservations. If they have somehow survived, then their numbers have to be very low. Yes, low enough to be classed as a remnant herd, an endangered species that has, despite all odds, somehow clung precariously to life from one never-say-die generation to the next in an environment most unsuitable for such as they.

Given the circumstances of how we first met way back in 1963, I feel privileged to have been asked to contribute a foreword to Ken's story. This is a remarkable, modern day odyssey about a rather unique individual and his dedicated search—spread over many years—to prove conclusively that moose still exist in what is arguably the most remote and inhospitable region in New Zealand.

Philip Holden
Queenstown
Spring 1997

For Margie

August 1996

Fiordland in midwinter. Soaked to the skin despite my parka, I was becoming very cold. Sometimes I wondered what I was doing here.

In the gathering dusk I hunted quietly, pushing gently through dripping pepperwood inside the edge of the swampy clearing. Then stopped again, alert and watchful. Still no sign of life. I wondered if my frozen fingers could still operate the video camera hanging from my neck, bulky and clumsy in its waterproof housing.

The sky was leaden—a week's rain had stopped only hours before. Dark forested slopes crowding the small valley disappeared into low cloud. In the grey light, upper Herrick Creek was bleak and uninviting. It was nearly dark. I shivered involuntarily. Time to give up for another day.

It was hard not to be disheartened after six tough days. But that wasn't unexpected—I'd been a month or more without seeing sign on other trips. And the occasional encounter with red deer reassured me that my hunting technique was OK.

My little tent was only a short distance away, and with it some modest comfort. A final look around, a shrug to myself. Careless of noise now, I crossed the creek, knee-deep and icy, and headed home, squelching across the swampy ground.

I followed the side of the stream along the clearing's edge to avoid the deep swamp, for here the ground was higher and the travelling easier. Some deer had used the same path recently—their tracks were clear in the wet sand. A hind with last season's calf, I guessed from the size of the marks.

Then, at the clearing's end, where the stream disappeared back into heavy bush among big boulders green with moss, I noticed another set of tracks. Quite different. Crisp and clear in the mud. Big, splayed hoofprints. Large, slotted, dewclaw imprints.

Rain and cold were forgotten! My heart hammered. At last! And so fresh! The animal wasn't far away. Maybe it had heard me with those big ears, or caught my scent, and ghosted off. There was no time to search today, but tomorrow was another chance, and the day after, and the day after that–

Moose footprints! Moose! A New Zealand moose had walked here only a few hours before.

1

Winter 1990

Marg followed me into the garage.

'It'll be here somewhere,' I said, 'Probably under the bench with all my old forestry stuff.'

We shifted the lawn mower and the battery trolley for starting the helicopter, a box of wire strainers and rusty possum traps, an old ice axe and some battered nailed boots. 'Here we go.'

A pile of dusty cardboard boxes, labelled with felt-marker pen in my untidy hand. Marg read some of the labels out loud.

'Diaries, 1964 to 1979. Himalayan Tahr Field Notes and Observation Records. Flight Manuals and Aircraft Handling Notes.'

It was like excavating my past.

'Try this one,' I said, dragging out Tahr and Chamois Skulls: Material for Demonstrating Aging.

We opened the lid.

'Yep. Here it is.' I pulled the treasure out, rattling the other bony contents of the box, blew some dust off it, and held it out to her.

'So that's your moose antler,' she said, clearly disappointed.

'Not any bloody old moose,' I responded defensively. 'A New Zealand moose! From Dusky Sound.'

'I expected something bigger, being a moose, and, well, more flattened.'

'This one's been cast by a three-year-old bull,' I explained. 'They don't become palmate until they're older. New Zealand moose never had big antlers anyway.'

'There were very few ever shot here,' I added. 'I can think of only three trophy heads which were ever mounted. The last one was in 1952.'

'That's a long time ago,' Marg said thoughtfully. 'When were you searching for them?'

'In the 1970s. When I worked for the Forest Research Institute. Before I went flying. That was twenty years ago now. We found sign, and this antler, but never saw a moose.'

We walked back to the house with the small antler and I talked of those earlier days.

'Moose. Here in New Zealand,' Marg mused. 'Isn't that fantastic? Do you think they're still down there?'

'I'm not sure. I doubt it somehow. Things weren't going too well for them. But I love the place. Fiordland is superb. I'll take you there sometime.'

'Pour me a wine,' I suggested, back by the fire, 'and I'll tell you what I know, but it could take a while.'

'I've got a while,' she replied, settling back in her chair, glass in hand.

We didn't realise until much later that this moment marked the beginning of another long, long hunt.

'Well, Once Upon a Time,' I began, trying not to sound too corny, 'it was decided that New Zealand should have many types of Big Game

Animals. The Largest and the Grandest was to be the Moose, and two liberations were made...'

1900–1934

Even if Hokitika residents had missed out on local gossip, nobody picking up the 'West Coast' Times on 20 February 1900 could fail to note the stern warning:

> Notice Re Canadian Moose.
>
> The Canadian Moose recently imported at great expense by the Government of this Colony, having been liberated in the vicinity of the Hokitika Gorge, all persons are cautioned against interfering with or disturbing, or with any manner injuring such animals, and any person found so offending will be prosecuted with the utmost rigor of the law.
>
> By Order.

The story of moose in New Zealand was about to begin.

Two years earlier, negotiations between New Zealand's Native Minister, Sir James Carroll, and the Premier of Canada had resulted in the capture of 14 young moose by the Hudson Bay Company, destined for shipment to New Zealand.

Early in the voyage from Vancouver to Sydney, in January 1900, the steamship 'Aorangi' ran into serious trouble in a violent four day storm. Ten of the moose died and their carcasses were thrown overboard. Their caretaker, Archibald McDonald, begged the ship's captain to change the housing of the four still alive, and the moose were shifted from forward in the ship to a mail room and cabin between the saloon passengers' and officers' cabins. They survived the remainder of the voyage.

After transfer in Sydney, the four moose arrived in Wellington on 8 February 1900. They were taken to Lane's stables in Molesworth Street for a couple of days.

'They were as tame as pet ponies,' wrote T. E. Donne from the Government Tourist Department, 'and when I offered one of them a biscuit all four wanted it, and their attentions became quite embarrassing.'

Donne's interest was understandable, for he was responsible for many liberations of game birds and animals, which he later detailed in his 1924 book, 'The Game Animals of New Zealand'. But in 1900, he probably did not foresee he would be involved with moose again ten years on.

From Wellington the moose were shipped by coastal steamer to Greymouth, railed to Hokitika, and temporarily kept in stables. Horse-drawn drays took them a further 30 kilometres to a specially built enclosure on the property of Mr Dedrich, near the Hokitika Gorge, where they were kept to acclimatise to local food. On 19 February 1900, they were finally released.

Two bulls and one cow promptly disappeared up the Hokitika Gorge. A few accounts exist of the survival of at least one of these until about 1903. The second cow remained semi-tame and stayed around the back of Doughboy, near Vine Creek, for 14 years. She was an occasional visitor to the settlement of Koiterangi, where she bemused the residents and terrorised strangers. More than one prospector abandoned his equipment and fled to spend an uncomfortable night up a cabbage tree with the bewildered cow hanging around below, still looking for biscuits.

Westland's attempt to establish a herd of moose for trophy hunting had failed. Prime Minister Dick Seddon, who had taken a personal interest in the project, would have been disappointed. After all, the Coast had been his constituency.

With the first moose liberation unsuccessful, a second was subsequently authorised by then Prime Minister Sir Joseph Ward, who was also Minister of the Tourist Department. Canadian authorities cooperated: 17 moose calves were captured in the winter snows around Alberta and Saskatchewan in 1909. They were hand-reared at Good Hope, and then at what is now Elk Island National Park, on a diet of cows' milk, brush and saplings. Ten of them—six females and four males—were finally sent to Banff. Under the care of Fred Moorehouse, a New Zealand Tourist Department inspector, the moose were railed to Vancouver, crated individually, and shipped. They survived a rough trip, finally arriving in Wellington via Hobart on 2 February 1910—'in the pink of condition and without a scratch or a mark', Moorehouse wrote proudly to his boss, T. E. Donne.

At Wellington the moose were kept in quarantine at Somes Island for nearly two months while their liberation site was argued. Finally, back in their crates, they were shipped to Bluff on the 'Moana', transferred to the government steamer 'Hinemoa', and released at Supper Cove, Dusky Sound, on 6 April 1910. The calves were only about ten months old, but already stood chest-high to their handlers.

'They were very tame when we landed them,' wrote C.M. Baird in a letter to Robin Francis Smith, '...[but] not very pleased with the location as some...returned to their crates until we upended them...'

With the trauma of shipment and handling, the unfamiliar surroundings of Fiordland and the ferocious sandflies, the young moose could hardly be blamed for seeking refuge in their familiar crates. However, a squabble developed between two animals outside the upended crates, in which they reared up, swiping at each other with their forefeet. So Moorehouse, who had nursed his charges safely halfway across the world, was obliged to report to Donne that one female had had her leg broken at the shoulder. Nonetheless, the second liberation of moose had taken place: the animals were now free in the New Zealand wild. And what a wild it was.

Even with modern air transport, Dusky Sound is a difficult place to get to; in the first half of the century it was much more remote. As in the case of other, comparable, releases, the moose were protected by law, their wellbeing keenly followed by their custodians, the Southland Acclimatisation Society and the government. But there were few opportunities to learn how the moose had adapted to their new surroundings, and not many records exist of the establishment of the Fiordland herd. Of those that do, some are contradictory and a number are puzzling. Written reports came from commissioned investigators, visitors to the sounds, or, later, from licensed hunters. Authorities sometimes granted 'prospecting' licences outside the normal designated 'blocks' to some hunters, in which case a trophy was permitted and the fee waived in exchange for a written report from the hunters on their observations. It was a good way to keep tabs on herd dispersal.

There was an early casualty: one moose was shot at the liberation site within a few days or weeks of the herd being released, apparently by fisherman Noel Bragg. Tom West, himself a fisherman and a relative of Bragg, recalls having heard that a young female just 'walked right up to him'. The incident, never documented, seems quite well known among the fishing community. Bragg 'didn't realise what it was', but, 'got hell for it from his old man'.

The 'Southland Times' reported in December 1912 that miners had seen footprints of both adult and young moose at Supper Cove. It was the first indication that moose were breeding. But it was March 1921 before the first official efforts reported on the status of the wapiti herd further north and of the moose at Dusky Sound. Fred Moorehouse returned to the area in the ketch 'Britannia' with a representative from the Southland Acclimatisation Society and a photographer. At the head of Wet Jacket Arm they 'found the first moose tracks, also trees that had been barked, and ferns that had been eaten'. The following day at Supper Cove they noted 'well-beaten tracks...along the banks of the Seaforth'. From here they travelled as far as Loch Maree, at one stage disturbing two beasts they believed to be a cow and her calf, and observing 'tracks and eaten bushes...in great numbers'. From the boat at Supper Cove in the late evening light, they saw animals which they concluded were moose. Moose 'are now well established in this locality', Moorehouse concluded in his report.

Early in 1923 the Southland Acclimatisation Society's own ranger, Charles Evans, undertook a similar survey on Harry Roderique's boat, 'Waterlily'. He was reported as finding moose sign from the head of Gaer Arm in Bradshaw Sound, far to the north, to the Richard Burn, well south of Dusky Sound, as well as in many places within Dusky Sound and Wet Jacket Arm. Viewed in today's light, the findings further afield seem suspect. However, at Supper Cove two moose—a young bull and a cow—broke from the bush as the boat approached, and stood on the beach only 40 metres away before swimming across the Seaforth River. Their hesitation was fortunate for Charles Evans, for he was rewarded with the first photograph of moose in New Zealand.

On the basis of Evans' report, the Southland Acclimatisation Society applied to the government and was granted approval to issue the first two licences for moose hunting. For the not insubstantial fee of £30, 'to be divided between the Society and the Tourist Department', one trophy head was permitted for each licence, and the season fixed between the dates of 24 March and 31 May 1923. Viv Donald and Les Murrell hunted that season, but the only moose seen was a cow.

The following season, 1924, another two licences were issued, one being taken by Eddie Herrick and the other by Colin Deans. Neither party saw moose, although they found sign and picked up cast antlers in the Seaforth area, and between them explored other parts of Dusky Sound and Wet Jacket Arm. Ranger Evans accompanied the two hunters, who travelled together on the ketch 'Rakiura'. Evans' report a year earlier had suggested moose were both widespread and abundant, but Herrick's guide, the knowledgeable Jim Muir, commented wryly to the press on the party's return to Bluff that the numbers were not what they had been led to believe. Herrick recommended that no further hunting should take place until more was known about the moose herd. It is a measure of the respect in which he was held that no further blocks were offered until 1931.

Invercargill resident Geoffrey Todd was on a scenic cruise on the 'Waterlily' in February 1925. The vessel anchored at Supper Cove one evening, and from the deck next morning two strange creatures could be seen on the beach. A dinghy was launched, and as it approached the shore 'both animals trotted up towards us, showing no fear'. The two cow moose then swam across the flooded Seaforth, trailing wakes 'that would have done credit to a speedboat' and leaving behind two incredulous boatmen, and Todd with the second photograph of wild New Zealand moose.

In May of 1927, well-known Fiordland boatman, bushman and hunting guide Les Murrell was commissioned by the government to report on the moose. He and his brother Burton searched Wet Jacket Arm and the Henry Burn, finding no sign, and continued looking up the Seaforth Valley. Above Loch Maree they watched two young bulls for 15 minutes, Burton finally flushing them from the scrub with a few well-aimed rocks while Les took two photographs of them standing in the river. They were both in good condition, about four and five years old, with heads of 12 and 14 points. The next day the two brothers saw a cow moose crossing the Seaforth.

Three years earlier Les Murrell had surmised that the moose population numbered 'between 80–100' animals, but he now revised his estimate: 'I am convinced that the herd is small...the tracks of only ten animals were observed. I would place the number of moose between 20 and 30 and that is optimistic.' He added, 'I have reason to believe from remains found...that the original herd suffered a few casualties in the first years. This has vitally affected the increase.' Like Herrick, he recommended that no further block licences be issued for at least five years.

New Zealand's first legal moose trophy fell to Hawke's Bay gentleman farmer Eddie Herrick in March 1929. Operating on a prospecting licence with his guide, Jim Muir, the two men spent a difficult five weeks hunting before they disturbed a big, black-bodied moose on the far edge of a swampy clearing. Muir signalled it was a bull as the animal moved away, and the boom from Herrick's .350 echoed around the steep slopes of the lower Seaforth. The moose collapsed in the sedges and fernery and the two men hurried forward. The bull was an old one, 'in low condition and well past his prime', Herrick wrote of his slightly disappointing trophy. The teeth were very worn; it was possibly even one of the original Canadian releasees. The antlers had ten points but lacked significant palmation. Nevertheless, they were a better pair than the eight cast ones they had picked up in the course of their extensive search of the Seaforth and many tributaries, and although they had seen five other moose, this was the only one resembling a trophy. In his report to the Minister of Internal Affairs on the state of the herd, Herrick noted that moose 'appear to be more plentiful than they were during my previous visit [1924], at the same time I do not consider they have done remarkably well'. He expressed concern about the numbers of red deer in the area and the damage they were doing to the forest.

Newspapers of the time extolled Herrick's skill and perseverance. Headlines read 'New Zealand's First Moose Head'; 'Moose Hunting – Good Head Secured – The First In New Zealand'; and 'First Head Secured – The Trackless Fiordland'. Herrick's own typewritten account of the hunt modestly notes: 'Luck plays the biggest part of the game, hunting for Moose in New Zealand'.

It wasn't until 1933 that licences for moose blocks were again taken up, although prospecting blocks were approved in some years, and in the 1931 and 1932 seasons blocks were offered for sale but no applications received.

The last season of licensed hunting for moose was in 1934. This was because things had changed by now for all introduced game animals. Eddie Herrick's misgivings about the health of the country's forest areas had long been echoed throughout New Zealand. Efforts by the acclimatisation societies to cull deer in order to limit numbers, enhance antler quality and avoid the mounting criticism had proven futile. The debate eventually came to a head at the Deer Menace Conference of 9 May 1930, and led to legislation which removed all protection from game animals and the acclimatisation societies' power of jurisdiction over them. These animals were now classed as pests, and an active campaign for their destruction began, administered by the Department of Internal Affairs. Red deer were the main problem, and Internal Affairs' Wildlife Branch began employing teams of government hunters, the hardy bunch known as deer-cullers. A new era in wild animal management had begun—not with a bang, but with a fusillade.

2

January-March 1967

Hired guns they might have been, but the New Zealand deer-cullers of the 1930s to the 1960s were Kiwi style: woollen shirts, oilskin parkas and muddy boots, and usually no horses. In the late 1960s I was one of them, and in early January 1967, a bloke called Andy Leigh and I found ourselves labouring under heavy packs as we walked the four hours to Clark Hut in the upper Grebe Valley. The old beech slab hut was to be our main base for the next few months of hunting the forested mountainlands bordering Fiordland, south of Lake Manapouri.

I had spent the previous year in Wellington at Victoria University, completing a Bachelor of Science in zoology and ecology. Under a Forest Service professional staff training scheme, I was to begin study for a further degree in Canada the following August. I was more or less on track for a career in animal ecology, specialising in New Zealand's introduced wild animals. They had long been a problem in many places, and there were still new areas where populations were flowing into virgin terrain, their numbers limited only by food, to the detriment of the habitat. There seemed to be no easy solutions, and few efforts had been made to study the animals themselves; I envisaged a fascinating future for myself.

Between university years, as part of the training scheme, I worked for the Forest and Range Experiment Station, a branch of the Forest

Research Institute, based in Rangiora. At the F&RES I became a summer-season hunter for Graeme Caughley. Caughley was a brilliant scientist, shortly to become a population ecologist of worldwide renown. Along with a handful of others—some students like myself—I had spent the two previous summers among the Rakaia and Rangitata headwaters, shooting tahr and chamois for demographic study data. In brief, our role was to shoot animals from the populations being researched, not taking tail tokens like our deer-culler counterparts, but examining each kill for specific biological information. Some data can be obtained only from dead animals. Researching wild mammals in New Zealand was unique, since their pest status permitted sampling without restraints. To do the same in other countries would be unthinkable.

Research, mountains, wild animals—it was an intoxicating brew for a fledgling ecologist, but working under Graeme Caughley was something special. His wapiti red deer hybridisation project, a study investigating the extent to which red deer and wapiti were interbreeding in the wild, ran for the summer of 1966–67. Unlike today, little was known about such matters, as deer farming had not yet become established. The study's results would contribute real information to a sticky confrontation looming between recreational hunters and the government on wapiti management in Fiordland.

Andy Leigh and I were one of several teams whose job was to shoot and autopsy female deer from two areas: the Stuart and Franklin Mountain sample, which would include pure wapiti, red deer and any hybrids; and the Grebe, where hinds would be pure red deer. Some skulls were to be collected from both areas. A third skull-measurement sample would come from America, consisting of pure wapiti that I would measure from museum collections in Montana. The analysis was Graeme Caughley's problem; Andy and I had to shoot as many deer as possible for him. He told us 400 females was the minimum useful number.

Elwyn Green, in charge of logistics, walked in with us to stay the first few days. We would meet him again at the end of the season, on 15 March. Since November we had been hunting wapiti in the Fiord country behind Lake Te Anau, but this was different. It was red deer country.

Elwyn left, and Andy and I spent the first month hunting around the upper Grebe and its Florence and Jaquiery tributaries. We camped together most nights but hunted alone during the days. Between us we shot six to eight hinds on a good day, filling out autopsy data for each on a preprinted card. It was pretty simple: a few tape measurements, the weights of some organs taken with a small spring scale, and reproductive information, which was important and the reason for the female-only sampling. Half a jawbone was also taken from each specimen and fixed with a numbered metal tag for subsequent aging.

After a month the pile of jawbones outside Clark Hut was still too small. For some time we had been waiting impatiently for better weather so that we could venture over the hill—a very large and steep one—to Lake Roe, where a deer bonanza supposedly awaited us.

The remote part of Fiordland we called the Lake Roe area lies to the western side of the 1700-metre-high ridge which makes up the Merrie Range. It is a kind of elevated, stepped wilderness—unusual in Fiordland—where a number of big river catchments have their headwaters: the Hauroko Burn and Lake Hauroko to the south; the Long Burn and Long Sound not far to the southwest. The area towers above the huge Seaforth River valley flowing westward to Dusky Sound. It is granite country, ringed with cirque basins, steep and benched, dotted with tarns and covered in tussock, alpine scrubland and occasional small stands of beech.

Elwyn was convinced this wild and distant place had deer running around in 'great thundering mobs'. His information came from an old character he had run into in the Te Anau pub, who claimed to have shot there for the Department of Internal Affairs in the early 1950s. It was probably the last time the area had been visited.

More deer. We needed that. But there was another reason we were itching to get to Lake Roe. And that was moose.

The Seaforth Valley had been the centre of the small moose herd which had flourished in the 1930s. As far as we knew, it was 15 years since one had been shot, but others had been photographed at the time, and 15 years is within the life span of a moose. Graeme Caughley was fascinated by the moose story and his enthusiasm spread easily to us. It was only because he could not be there himself that he had instructed us not to waste time looking for them. The Seaforth Valley. Moose. It was a tantalising thought.

Elwyn organised airdrops of supplies for Clark Hut and our tent camps at the Florence and Jaquiery forks, at the same time throwing out 10 days' worth at Lake Roe. Food supplies were divided into 25-kilogram loads in straw-packed chaff sacks with two small parachutes on each to slow the fall. These were tossed out from a height of 100 metres, usually by an airsick crew member, through the open doorway of a Dominie biplane piloted by Bill Black or Gary Cruickshank. The state of the crew member determined drop accuracy.

With our food supply in place at Lake Roe, it remained only for us to get there. We spent a miserable and unrewarding week waiting out weather in a fly camp at the head of the Jaquiery. Finally, in marginal conditions and with our food running out, we made the trip. It was a tough 12-hour slog, made difficult by wind so strong that we were on our hands and knees in some places, despite heavy packs. Elwyn had given us a tobacco-packet drawing of the site of the old cullers' camp and the airdrop location. We finally found the camp site in the gathering darkness: stones from a long disused fireplace, scraps of canvas and rusting tins. It was the only place around suitable for a camp. Another search revealed widely scattered chaff sacks with our next ten days' food—Elwyn must have been pretty crook by that stage.

We slit one open, prised out a bent tin of corned beef and some fragments of service biscuits, and collapsed gratefully into sleeping bags in a quickly pitched tent. We had picked up three hinds on the way but there was no sign of any thundering mobs. Perhaps they were sheltering from the wind.

About an hour after dark the first spatters of rain started. Within a short time it was pouring. We began to regret making such a hasty camp. Outside the ground was awash, and the floor of the tent was soon flooded. We crawled around in the dark, confined space, gathering possessions and heaping them above the water. Soon sleeping bags were squelching below waist level; we sat up, shivering, trying to keep the upper part of them slightly drier. It was a long night.

It was still pouring at daylight but now thick fog reduced visibility to a few metres. We pulled on wet clothes and, with nowhere to escape to, set about organising a better camp. We emptied out the tent and re-erected it on a thick beech-branch bed. Within a few hours we had constructed a rough fly from parachutes and sacks and set it up on beech poles over the fireplace area. Finding stems long enough was a problem, as only small stands of gnarled beech were to be found in the vicinity. We wrestled bits of firewood from these same trees, which they gave up reluctantly. Eventually we coaxed a tiny fire into life by using a candle to ignite it then taking turns fanning it with tin plates. The first brew of tea we had managed since leaving the Jaquiery 30 hours earlier was a major triumph.

While one struggled with the fire, the other gathered the strewn airdrop sacks. Opening airdrops can be exciting—each item adds to your standard of living. The quality of goods is a measure of the concern felt for you by those residing comfortably far away, and a good field officer will put in a few treats for the lads. We fumbled wet sacks with cold fingers. Apart from a brief Christmas spell we had already been on hardtack for two months.

Unfortunately for us, Elwyn had fallen in love with a lady traveller passing through Te Anau, and his mind was definitely not on the job. How could he so quickly have forgotten his own days at the front line? There was no rice, a staple whose absence was puzzling. There was flour, but no yeast, baking powder or salt; the six kilograms of butter and two-kilo tin of peanut butter would be tough going without any bread. In any case, kea had got into the butter through the sacking and plastic, as they were inclined to do, and their incision had let three weeks' Fiordland rain into a vast stack of macaroni, probably there in place of rice. This now resembled a half-sack of gib-stopping mix with the remains of sugar packets soggily floating in it. There were tins of creamed corn everywhere and a few of baked beans, spaghetti and peas, but (predictably by that stage) no canned fruit, nor any can opener to get into any of them. Condensed milk, tea, powdered milk, six packets of dripping. A large mound of service biscuits had shattered into powder—they would make good porridge. Plenty of candles, but no matches (dry matches being more precious than gold, we had been careful to provide our own anyway). There were 150 rounds of .303 ammunition for me, presumably to help level the thundering mobs, but nothing for Andy's .270 (another omission his suspicions had fortunately made him anticipate). Some toilet paper would have been nice, even just a little, for there is nothing better for keeping telescopic rifle sights useable in wet conditions.

Had we missed a vital sack? No. The tobacco packet read four bags. Shivering on sodden bedding, rain hammering on our flimsy tent, dripping scrub and tussock barely visible outside in the swirling fog, we froze with cold but burned with indignation. Like kids at Christmas finding the bloody old aunts and uncles had only sent colouring-in books we already had.

There are few things less inviting than a wet sleeping bag. A dry one is the one retreat which makes all other discomforts acceptable. With all our clothing wet and not enough firewood to warm up on, darkness came on gloomily. We sat up in our soggy bags with teeth chattering, shovelling spoonfuls of cold baked beans from bent tins. We retold our life histories, reshot every deer, rediscovered the moose and devised a thousand slow and painful tortures for Elwyn. The rain continued.

On about day four rain turned to snow, covering the saturated ground in an ankle-deep layer of frozen slush, making our hurried excursions into the fog for more firewood particularly unpleasant. By day six further rain had cleared most of the snow. Andy's method of drying gear using body heat was making progress. A small family of weka made themselves at home with us. We entertained them with dinners of Elwyn's dripping, thinking better-conditioned birds might be a good investment.

On day seven we awoke to the fearful screeching of kea. It was 4.00 a.m., still dark, and—kea aside—strangely quiet. The rain—stopped? A look outside confirmed it: stars. Stars! We got dressed immediately.

Heading off in different directions, we left camp, leaving all our gear draped over surrounding shrubbery. It was our first real look at this superb part of Fiordland. Liberated at last, in warm sunshine and drying clothing, in open country with magnificent views in every direction; we relished the marvellous feeling of freedom. The hunting was slightly disappointing, however. Surprisingly, deer were few and wary. Hinds were scattered in twos and threes, usually close to scrub cover. Stags, mostly solitary and in late velvet, were in the more open country. Working around them was difficult; getting it wrong meant they would spook nearby hinds. By the day's end I had shot only nine, Andy six. We didn't care. Being out and about was enough, and the absence of thundering mobs was temporarily forgiven. Back at camp kea had scattered our clothing but most of it had managed to dry. We collapsed, exhausted, into comfortable bedding, content at last and with new stories to tell.

The pattern of hunting over the next week or so was similar. The kea, which had grown in number to 14, would begin screeching an hour before daylight. We would get up as the noise became unbearable. Most days we tallied ten or a dozen deer between us, usually hunting alone. One memorable day we worked a duet in an alpine basin and shot 26 before splitting up for another eight, making 34 for the day. Sometimes it rained part of the day, but we had a dry camp to return to. There were two haunting problems, though: food was getting short, and the kea were becoming destructive.

Kea are loveable birds in small doses, but every day we would come back to find something tipped over, wrecked, ripped or missing. And our tolerance of the morning cacophony was wearing thin. Whereas earlier we had simply cursed and thrown small stones, which they would adroitly dodge and ignore, we now collected larger missiles and aimed them with spite. Each morning the birds were busy in the space under our makeshift fly scattering tins, plates, food and other household effects. It couldn't go on.

Andy snapped first. The screaming started one morning as usual. A heavy flop as one bird landed on the fly ridgepole and marched its length. A brief, tense silence, then a fearsome ripping as beak shredded nylon. A pause. More screams. Another flop. Another rip. Andy exploded from his bag with a curse and crashed out through the tent door. I heard him fumbling for a stick. More derisive screams from the kea. Pause. Thump. A slither as one slid down the fly. Thump. Thump.

'Take that you bastard!'

Andy's voice dripped with venom. Thump. He returned to his sleeping bag, breathing heavily. Nothing was said. I was trying to contain my laughter but was cautious about becoming victim number two. Eventually I heard a snort and snigger from Andy, and we both burst out laughing.

It was the beginning of a brief war. At first we tried hanging the dead kea at the crime scene as a reminder to the others that they had overstepped the mark. It failed. Tent-ripping had caught on. We made an example of an adult bird who seemed to be a leader. It made no difference. Finally, one morning, along with the screeching, came a sudden rip and a green head peered inquisitively through holes in both tent and fly. It was the last straw. We both leapt from bed. There was a thunder of shots; the smell of cordite wafted over the camp. Six kea lay dead. The rest disappeared.

To help overcome the guilt in the silence which followed, we decided we should at least recycle the carcasses. Andy skinned four and I boiled them up. It turned out to be a waste of precious firewood and we threw the lot over the bank.

The lack of a can opener meant that tins of food had to be opened by sheath knife. Not wanting to take the edge off mine, I made a habit of surreptitiously using Andy's for the purpose. That lasted until one day I returned with a quicker-than-normal load of firewood for camp and found him looking up sheepishly from a half-opened tin with my precious knife stuck in it. Unfortunately I could not get through my speech of outraged indignation without dissolving in laughter.

Building a fire was a constant battle, with only a little dracophyllum scrub in addition to the stunted old beeches available for fuel. We made a practice of drying the next day's wood over the fire the night before. On one occasion I had all our spare firewood layered carefully over a tiny blaze and Andy's only spare socks drying on top, along with my own. During a moment's inattention the fire, which up until then had shown no enthusiasm, suddenly burst into life. Too late! The socks—the most priceless of items—were ruined. A wince. A shrug. There was nothing to say.

We were working hard each day, always walking; climbing and descending, struggling through thick scrub or sidling steep tussock faces most days for 12 hours or more, with the inevitable sweating. We learned that the omission of salt from the supplies was serious; we developed an insatiable craving for it and each night both of us suffered terrible cramps which remained unrelieved until our return to the Grebe.

By March we had stared into the Seaforth Valley 1200 metres below for long enough. We had enough deer to salve our consciences over leaving for part of a week to get a taste of Moose Country, but it had to be immediately, for time was running out and the remaining food was mostly rubbish. A moose? We could be lucky. Nobody we knew had travelled the Seaforth for more than a decade.

We planned an early start for the long descent through the bush. By evening, an ominous black line appeared to the west, and around midnight the showers turned into a deluge. By morning, rain had turned to sleet, sleet to snow, and soon this was calf-deep. Frozen fog came and went.

It stayed that way for seven days. Lack of food became a problem when venison ran out. For day after day we lived on a glug of creamed corn mixed into a flour paste and fried in butter. It is now 30 years later and I still cringe at tinned creamed corn.

When the weather finally cleared, snow was still thick on the ground, but we were starving. Our lust for the Seaforth and moose had evaporated. It was time to go. We packed up belongings and wet tentage, divided the heap of jawbones between us and trudged off, probably to the relief of the weka family. We had to clear the Merrie Range tops, 600 metres above, before we could drop into the Jaquiery to food, safety and a decent camp. Below us lay the Seaforth, misty, still, green and gloomy.

Any secrets it held would have to wait for another time. Kicking steps in the snow we shut our minds to the long day ahead.

Back on the eastern side of the range the weather was better. There was still a week to go before the end of the season and we were 30 deer short. We split up and met at Clark Hut again late on March 15. Elwyn was there, pacing around anxiously, sure that something serious had happened. We were three days overdue, he told us. Overdue? That was news. We'd taken some pride from working until the last day. We checked our diaries. Aha! Here was the problem. We had both given February 31 days.

But the season was over and Caughley had his tally. The next day we walked out to where Elwyn's Land Rover awaited us at the road end.

'One day I'm going to get to that Seaforth,' I told Andy as we left the Grebe behind, 'and have a look for those moose.'

And I did.

Back at the sleepy little township of Manapouri there was a new sound in the air. Tim Wallis's helicopter, a Hiller UH–12E, departed noisily each morning at dawn to hunt the surrounding hills. In an inspired move, this businessman/entrepreneur/hunter/sawmiller and now pilot had seized the opportunity of turning a pest into a marketable resource. Deer were now being shot on remote hillsides from helicopters and their carcasses recovered for export as game meat to European countries. The fledgling operation of two years earlier was now becoming very efficient, as Elwyn and I learned. We teamed up with

Wallis and his crew for ten days, working with them at the remote staging points, and sometimes in the helicopter, as we collected red deer skulls for the last part of Graeme Caughley's project. During that time the helicopter crew shot and recovered more deer than Andy and I had managed all season. Instead of shivering in some remote campsite, fanning a weak fire with a tin plate at the end of each day, we were having a few beers and playing pool in the Manapouri pub. It was not hard to sense that dramatic changes to the deer situation were imminent. I was about to leave for two years' study in Canada, and wondered how things might be when I got back.

3
1969-71

The Forest and Range Experiment Station was still based at Rangiora when I returned from Canada in June 1969 and took up a position there on the scientific staff, although it was about to shift to the Canterbury University campus in Christchurch. About 25 scientists and 40 support staff worked in various disciplines around the theme of mountainland management and ecology. I was part of the Animal Ecology Section, and my first job was an assessment of wallaby control problems in the hills behind Waimate.

Two years of study had earned me a Bachelor of Science in Forestry from the University of British Columbia, biased towards wildlife rather than commerce, and got me hungry for mountains and bush again. The first Sunday after my return I dusted off the old .303 and, with Mike Barnett, an old shooting buddy from the Caughley times, took to the hills behind Rangiora for a day's hunt.

It was wonderful to be sidling along a bush edge again at first light. We split up after a couple of hours and bush-hunted the beech forest. I shot a hind and yearling in a broadleaf gully, and shortly afterwards heard a single shot from Mike. We spent most of the day carrying the carcasses out to Mike's car, arriving sweaty, bloody and exhausted but extremely happy. Back at Rangiora by midafternoon, we exchanged my two deer and the medium-sized stag that Mike had shot for $78 at the Game Meat Depot. It was the first time I had sold any deer. My public-service annual salary was $2700, the tax-free $39 for my share of our kill had won me the best part of a week's wages. The possibilities of hunting for a sideline revenue began to dawn on me. I had sometimes thought about learning to fly. Maybe here was a chance to fund it, one hobby paying for the other.

We sat on the steps of his flat in the sun, boots off, with a couple of bottles of cold beer.

'Thanks Mike, that was a good day.'

'That's nothing,' Mike said. 'Wait until spring when they're paying really good money for antlers in velvet.'

'Yeah?' I was really interested now.

'Welcome back to New Zealand.'

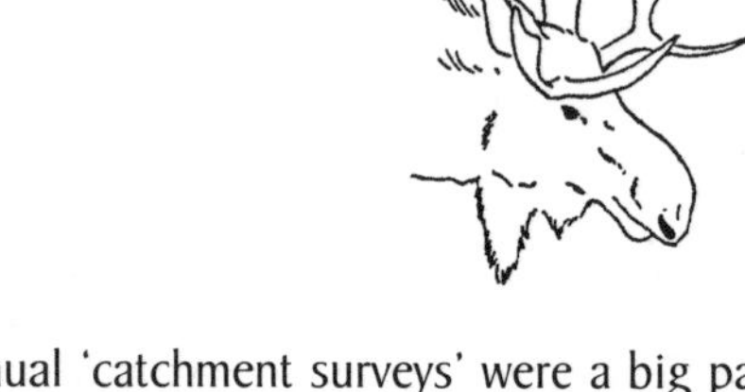

Annual 'catchment surveys' were a big part of the work carried out by the F&RES. These were ecological investigations into areas of mountain country involving the combined efforts of forest, alpine grassland and wild animal ecologists. The reports produced described the botanical composition of an area, often for the first time, along with the current distribution and density of wild animals, especially deer. Since deer eat plants, relating trends in the health of various plant communities to animal occupation history and current densities was an essential aspect of the reports. These data would form fundamental baseline information and a yardstick for changes.

Catchment surveys were massive exercises. They were carried out using teams of university students, such as botanists-in-training, supervised by the professional scientists of the group. Field teams spent the entire summer in the bush.

During the 1969–70 season the area under study was northern Fiordland, an enormous piece of wilderness behind Lake Te Anau, including the western fiord country stretching from Charles Sound nearly to Milford. Chris Challies and I were responsible for the wild animal part of the survey, my work being in the field, Chris's being to take autopsy data from an experimental helicopter shoot of deer and wapiti from Caswell Sound. Our results would dovetail with the vegetation studies.

The survey area was an interesting and varied one. The central part was occupied by wapiti, while red deer were present throughout most of the range in varying numbers, and the two species were hybridising to a large extent in some places. Some of the western sounds had been occupied by wapiti for 65 years, while the north was still being colonised. In the Murchison Mountains, hunting as a means of deer control was taking place to protect takahe habitat, and possums were present in a few areas.

With colleagues from the plant world, I spent five months in Fiordland gathering data, then Chris and I, with others, spent another fortnight working on Tim Wallis's ship 'Ranginui', a coastal trader converted into a support vessel for the helicopter recovery of wild venison. Bill Black was now flying the Hiller. He and his crew were delivering deer for export and research at the rate of 100 carcasses a day. No wonder deer-population sampling was no longer carried out on foot.

After the field work came the task of writing up. This wasn't so much fun, but was considerably easier on the body.

I needed information on animal colonisation history in Fiordland to help the botanists interpret vegetation changes. I travelled to Wellington and for a week tracked through old records from government departments, acclimatisation society files, newspapers and sporting publications such as the 'Fishing and Shooting Gazette'. Along with early wapiti and deer records were occasional references to Fiordland moose. I carefully separated these, and by the time I left for Rangiora my Moose File was already three centimetres thick.

My interest in New Zealand moose had been sharpened by the Canadian experience; it was a smouldering spark, waiting for a breeze. The breeze came sooner—and blew stronger—than I might have expected.

In mid-April 1971 I happened to be at the Forest Service base in Te Anau when the door burst open and Gary Cruickshank raced in.

'Jump in!' he said, indicating his Land Rover. 'Spunky Anderson's shot a moose and the float plane will be here in a few minutes.'

We leapt into the vehicle. On the way Gary explained he was on duty for Southern Scenic and had stopped at their flight office to check any radio calls for upcoming flights for the float plane he operated for them. At that time Te Anau-based meat-hunters—deer-shooters supplying the game-meat industry—were operating around many of the southern lakes and coastlines. Most had an 'agent' from a game-meat packing house to whom they sold their venison. In return for their business, agents kept in touch by radio, organised float planes to pick up deer carcasses when there was sufficient for a load, purchased and sent in groceries and fuel, and so on.

That morning there had been traffic on the radio, and Gary had chanced to overhear a conversation which went something like:

'Did you hear Spunky shot a Big One?'

'Big one? How big?'

'Well, the hindquarters weighed 200 pounds.'

'You're kidding.'

'It was an M-O-O-S-E.'

We stopped at the waterfront as the float plane taxied across the lake and drifted to a stop at the wharf. It was full of deer but no one knew anything about moose. Gordon Anderson, or Spunky as he was known, was at that time a professional deer-hunter. For this purpose he operated a jet-boat from Beach Harbour in Breaksea Sound, and his permitted block included both the Breaksea and Wet Jacket Arm areas. He was a secretive person who did not enjoy publicity, nor did he have good relations with the staff of the Fiordland National Park board, although that was usual among the hunting fraternity. He was a hard worker and a skilled hunter.

For a week rumours abounded about Anderson's moose, making all the newspapers and even national television. When he finally flew out from his bush camp, a small crowd of expectant locals and reporters were waiting. Ignoring their questions he brushed them aside and disappeared.

'Knowing Spunky,' Gary Cruickshank recalled later, 'it was exactly as I would have expected. He panicked at the publicity. He was scared the park would close the area and he'd lose his block. So he decided to get rid of the evidence and deny everything.'

About a week later a reporter cornered him in a pub and somehow coaxed a comment from him. 'I was just hunting through the bush when I heard some grunts,' he was reported as saying. 'I followed the noise and saw a bull moose and a cow.' He described the bull as 'weighing about 900 pounds and having antlers with 21 points and a spread of about four feet', which hints at more than a live-animal sighting. As to whether he'd shot it, Anderson had 'no comment'.

This was to be his only statement. No remains from the incident came to light, and with Anderson's determined silence adding nothing, few people believed he had shot a moose or even seen one. Those close to him—his occasional workmates, his agent, and even his brother, Brian, who sometimes hunted with him—were left guessing, and still are to this day.

Years later, Gary, who knew Gordon Anderson well from earlier days when they both worked at the Mataura freezing works, was having a beer with a much more relaxed Spunky. In a discussion on the merits of various rifles, Spunky volunteered the events of that time: he had been hunting 'in the creek with the lake' (Herrick Creek) in Wet Jacket Arm and heard an animal calling. He had stalked towards the noise to find a cow moose with her calf, and, as he watched, these had been joined by a bull. He had shot the bull through the throat with his .243, and it had collapsed. The other two animals had hung around for a time before making off.

'Spunky had probably never read a book in his life,' Gary commented to me, 'but the detailed description of the animals, of their behaviour, vocalisation, and the group composition at the time of the rut, all ring true.' Gary believes Spunky did indeed shoot his moose. Whatever happened to the head and antlers may take time to emerge: unfortunately Gordon Anderson is no longer alive.

Whether or not Gordon Anderson had seen or shot a moose quickly became irrelevant. A major ripple of interest about New Zealand moose swept the country. People were asking questions about them, but the last record of any being seen was from 1952, nearly 20 years before. Few Fiordland National Park staff, in whose area the mystery rested, had been anywhere near Dusky Sound. There was no park interest in moose. They shared the status of 'noxious animal' along with all the other wild ungulates, and should, accordingly, be eliminated. Embarrassed by shortcomings in knowledge about an animal they had presumed no longer existed, the National Parks Authority demanded a survey by the Forest Service, which took responsibility for all noxious animal issues. Southland Conservancy Forest Service, not to be drawn into a sticky one, neatly passed the buck to the F&RES.

Jack Holloway was director of the F&RES. Brandishing my Moose File, and acting as though I already had the survey half done, I marched into Jack's office and landed the job.

4

February-April 1972

I gripped the cold railing with trembling hands, eyes streaming and unfocused on the distant horizon, face ash-white and clammy. Occasionally, in the misted-over window behind me, colleagues' faces appeared, showing a mixture of concern and distaste. With knotted stomach and careless of the flying spray, I wished for a kindly wave to suck me into the heaving grey sea, where I would slide into blissful oblivion. Hilton would be in charge, but first he would have to fill in 20 forms, five copies of each, explaining my death to the Public Service. I hoped they would be short of carbon paper. I clung on grimly, but the thought helped.

Finally 'Miss Akaroa' slid into the calmer waters of Acheron Passage. Not long after, somewhat watery-kneed, I was helping the lads unload 10 days' worth of food and fuel at Cascade Cove on the southern side of Dusky Sound. The Moose Survey was under way! From this depot we had to search Resolution Island, the smaller islands of Dusky and the land behind Cascade. The unloading completed, George Burnaby turned his boat for Supper Cove, at the head of the sound, 30 kilometres away.

Supper Cove! This was where it had started—the liberation point for moose in Fiordland. The hum of the engine, the rush of water under the bow, the rocks, headlands and forest gliding past in the still evening light; a long-held dream was rapidly becoming reality. But it took only a glance at the landscape to realise what an awesome task we had set ourselves, and it was hard not to feel intimidated.

At Supper Cove we found a newly completed hut and boatshed, complete with a three-and-a-half-metre aluminium boat. That would be useful. This was to be our main base. We carried a month's food to shore. From here we would search the Seaforth Valley and its tributaries. And we would pack supplies up to another new hut at Loch Maree, five hours' journey upstream, for upper-valley searches.

With daylight now fading, the boat headed back up the sound into Sportsmen's Cove, the sheltered anchorage at Cooper Island. We stopped for the night, leaving another 10-day drop with fuel for the boats.

I was happy with our crew: Jim Hilton was an up-and-coming member of the scientific staff at the F&RES; Nige Prickett, now an anthropologist, was another of Graeme Caughley's hunters and an old university friend; and Les Stanley was taking time out from running the deer-control programme in the Murchison Mountains. At times we were to be assisted by national park rangers or deerstalkers coming in by float plane on short trips, once the moose search was under way.

Our final drop-off next morning was Herrick Creek in Wet Jacket Arm. We would build a tent camp here. It was centrally sited in the sound with an overland route through to Dusky. Our equipment for the next two months made a fair pile on the beach: 12-gallon fuel drums; cases of tins (sans creamed corn); tentage; black plastic sheets for a camp fly; billies; camp oven; axes; shovel; rifles and fishing gear; a four-metre aluminium dinghy and nine-horsepower outboard; packs with personal gear; and perishables packed in galvanised rubbish tins.

It was early February, 1972. We would be picked up from Supper Cove mid-April. We had a long time to search.

'Miss Akaroa' backed off. With a whine from her engine, a puff of blue smoke and a swirl of water, she surged back up the sound. A wave from George. Silence. Only the slap of water from an incoming tide. The call of a weka. We were here, alone now, and The Hunt was on.

It is fair to say that none of us was familiar with moose-on-the-hoof sign, although Jim and I had read all we could find on the subject. But we knew about deer, and the ensuing search for moose started as a systematic combing of each area for animal sign that was not characteristic of red deer, as well as sign that matched our expectations of moose.

During the 11 weeks that followed we searched valleys, slopes, terraces, basins, swamps, beaches, clearings, tops, slips, riverbeds, faces, flats, saddles, hummocks, benches, guts, gorges, creeks and waterfalls.

Weather was generally good in early February, but turned during March, at one stage raining 24 consecutive days. Terrain imposed other limits, and sea conditions often frustrated our efforts in the undersized dinghy. But, little by little, the map filled in as we worked our way through the Wet Jacket catchments, the Seaforth Valley and its tributaries, the smaller islands and parts of Resolution Island, back to the Seaforth, back to Wet Jacket, back to the more promising places we had searched earlier—and so it went.

We had some frights in the dinghy. One day Nige and I tried to go round the seaward side of Anchor Island and suddenly found ourselves in a huge southwesterly swell rolling in between Five Fingers Peninsula and South Point. We lost sight of land in the troughs, and were too terrified to turn for fear of broaching. In this direction the next stop was Australia. Eventually, somehow, we got the boat back to the shelter of the Seal Islands, shaken and considerably wiser.

Les didn't scare easily, but one day he and Jim got caught coming out of Goose Cove on Resolution Island after a desperately wet, nine-day fly camp. Nige and I were waiting for them in pouring rain at Duck Cove so we could return together to base at Cascade. They arrived white-faced, Les with a long-forgotten cigarette, extinguished by spray 40 minutes earlier, still clamped in his mouth. They had taken the boat out to test the conditions and, unable to turn back, were forced to slog round the coast in squally winds and a wicked chop.

We had known that finding moose in this vast and often unkind place would not be easy. After all, if there were more than just a few, someone, sometime, would have seen them. There was a good possibility we would find nothing at all. To avoid going nuts or becoming insanely obsessive, we supplemented our searching with hobby interests. Nige and Jim were birdlife experts, and under their guidance we kept careful records, hoping our observations would form a useful modern survey to compare with those from Cook's visit in 1773, or the more detailed accounts from 100 years later when Richard Henry lived in the outer sounds. Slogging through wet bush day after day, it was good therapy to have more than one purpose there.

Our supply of stores required us to shoot meat and, in most places, it was not too hard to kill a deer every few days. Les was our most expert hunter. But we also kept record of each deer sighting and carefully noted the time spent searching, travelling or hunting each day. The purpose was to end up with a simple index of relative deer density that could link with forest types or geographical areas. During 735 hours of field time,

660 deer found their way into our grubby notebooks.

Fishing was fun but also necessary for a reasonable standard of living. When fish were biting, camp needs could be met in five minutes. If not, it was a great way to recuperate from tough times ashore. We enjoyed many hours serenely floating about in the still waterways with a line overboard, safe from sandflies, reflecting on ways to increase our chances of finding moose, or wondering what we would do if one swam past.

There was a small hut at Cascade Cove, placed there years before as a marine emergency shelter. It was big enough for two people and a lot better than our little tents, since clothing could dry there. We patched it up and it became Home at that end of the sound. Les found an empty 44-gallon drum abandoned by a fishing expedition and manufactured a bath from it using an old axe head and a stone. During daytime there were too many sandflies to use it, but at night we would build a fire underneath and heat water for the luxury of a hot soak. One of my most enduring memories of the survey was relaxing in that bath one night. A tremendous thunderstorm was roaring to the north beyond Resolution Island, lighting up the ragged skyline with vivid flashes. Visible in the strobe light and joining in the din, a pair of kiwi strode boldly around the camp, shrieking.

Nige and I spent a few days late in the survey around the historic sites used by earlier residents of Dusky Sound, in a landscape which had remained unchanged. Signs of Maori occupation I found particularly fascinating; our aluminium dinghy now wobbled and clanked where totara canoes had once rested. But early Maori, Cook and the other seafarers—Henry, Docherty and the like—were lucky they didn't have to go thrashing about in the wet shrubbery looking for moose.

Near the end of February, after many false alarms, the first suspected moose sign was reported. It was in the Bessie Burn, towards the upper

Probably the first photograph of wild New Zealand moose. Taken by Charles Evans from a dinghy at Supper Cove, Dusky Sound in 1923.
Weekly Press, 15 February 1923, Courtesy of the Canterbury Museum.

Burton Murrell threw some rocks to flush these two bull moose into the river. His brother Les took the photograph. Seaforth River, 1927. Weekly Press, 30 July 1927.

The first bull moose (above) shot under licence and the successful hunter, Eddie Herrick. Lower Seaforth Valley, 1929. The bull was 'well past its prime' and may have been one of the original releasees. Herrick also claimed the only other moose shot under licence (left) in 1934, in the creek that now bears his name. Courtesy of the Herrick family.

Fishermen occasionally shot moose over earlier years. This young bull was taken near Supper Cover by Gordie Cowie, 1950. Courtesy of the late G. Cowie and G. Copland.

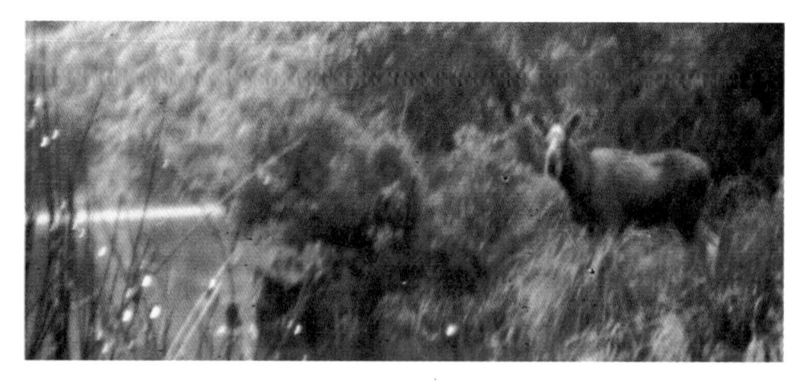

Max Curtis stalked this cow moose around the lake in Herrick Creek, 1952. Courtesy of the late M. Curtis.

Jim Mackintosh poses with the cow moose he shot at Herrick Creek, 1951. Courtesy of the late J. Mackintosh.

'It was HUGE... I thought it was a bull.' A snap shot in the bush and Robin Francis Smith was left lamenting for having shot a cow moose. Henry Burn, 1951. Courtesy of R.V. Francis Smith.

Robin Francis Smith crawled through Herrick Creek and took 14 photographs of this cow moose; this was the best print. For 45 years it has been the last confirmed moose sighting, 1952. Courtesy of R.V. Francis Smith.

It may have been the excitement or the slow speed of early colour film but Robin Francis Smith could not keep the shake out of this historic and probably the only colour photograph in existence of a New Zealand moose. Percy Lyes with his trophy, Herrick Creek, 1952, for years considered to be the last moose shot in New Zealand.

Andy Leigh and me at Clark Hut, Grebe Valley, 1967.

Hunting around Lake Roe, Fiordland, close to moose country, 1967.

Hunting for game meat from helicopters dramatically lowered deer numbers to a fraction of earlier densities: (from top left) Shooting... Recovery of carcasses to a 'gut heap'; Peter Brown waits for a load of deer.
Bill Black lifts off with a load in Alpine Helicopter's Hiller UH–12E...
and delivers it to the 'Ranginui'. 1970

The 1972 moose survey team at Herrick Creek camp: Nige Prickett, myself, Jim Hilton and Les Stanley.

The top clearing of Herrick Creek in 1972. All forest plants palatable to deer are hedged from browsing, clearing grasses trimmed by red deer. There is little food for all, especially moose.

Seaforth. We all revisited the area next day and debated the find on the spot. Twigs more than a centimetre thick had been taken from broadleaf and fuchsia trees from over two and a half metres above ground level—too high for deer, even on tiptoe. The disturbance was not recent—many shoots had since resprouted—but prior to that find we had been quick to reject any sign that could possibly have been made by some other agent. This, however, was not storm damage or anything else we could think of. The arguments continued by candlelight late into the night at Loch Maree hut. It just had to be moose. But the trail was cold.

I had long promised myself a nostalgic return to Lake Roe. The prospect of the trip was an exciting alternative to another discouraging day of searching wet bush for moose sign. One day dawned fine and Jim and I left Loch Maree at daylight. Breaking out above bushline over the Seaforth was superb, the weather was perfect and the traverse along the familiar tops was like a homecoming. But at the site of our old campsite, bright and new and barely completed, was now a Park hut. Our fireplace was visible not far from one corner of it, and some of the beech poles we had so laboriously cut with Andy's tomahawk were still in place. The affectionate memories I had nursed of our privations there only five years earlier evaporated. We returned to Loch Maree after a long day, Jim bemused and me, disappointed and dejected, wishing I had never made the trip.

Nearly another month passed exhaustingly. Red deer, yes—we found quite a few in places—but still no sure sign of moose. The lads were becoming exasperated, and no wonder: gut-wrenching effort, pack-carrying, wet fly camps, mud. The Bessie Burn sign was all we had found and it was too old to be definitive. Niggling doubts remained. We were beginning to question our judgment. There was more than one 'What the **** are we doing here?'

One day Jim and I were heading back to the Seaforth from Herrick

Creek overland. Midway, in the Henry Burn at the bottom of an ancient slip, we were stopped by a browse line on a stand of fuchsia, too high to have been made by deer. It was similar to but a lot clearer than the one we had seen in the Bessie Burn. We discussed it for some time, taking a few photos. Moose? It had to be. But our confidence had been eroded by nearly two months without finding anything positive, and we left in a dither of indecision.

A week later Jim and I were returning to Herrick Creek via the same route. Again we stopped to examine the browse line. It could only have been made by moose. Where were they?

Half an hour later we found out. Two kilometres upstream, for the very first time, we discovered fresh browsing sign! Fuchsia bushes had been ripped down and wrecked; branches broken and stripped from finger-tip height above ground; stems, two to three centimetres thick, bitten through. Suddenly all doubts evaporated as we understood what we were seeing. It was clear. A New Zealand moose had been here only a few days before.

It was a quantum development. Moose were alive in 1972. We now had to build on this find to achieve something useful from our survey, but time was running out. We continued over the saddle into Herrick Creek with new heart.

As we descended, we picked up more sign here and there, similar to that we had already seen but becoming progressively fresher. Had the animal completed the same journey? At the top of the lake a clump of fuchsia was newly demolished, the ground littered with stripped branches, the leaves bruised and in tatters. The sign was only hours old, maybe less. This time there were also hoofprints, big and clear in the firm mud, so very different from those of red deer. We dropped our packs and carefully sneaked around until dark, disturbing a few deer and giving ourselves some heart-stopping moments, but the moose—obviously not far away—was not to be seen. We stumbled into camp after nightfall, exhausted but rejoicing. We had made contact.

First light found us back there. More sign. More stalking. More deer. No moose. But we were beginning to see where she (we decided it was a cow) had been, what she had eaten, even where she had rested. At last we were beginning to learn something. And each lesson made us more alert for another. We stalked the area carefully, slowly, quietly, with total concentration. Once, when a pigeon launched explosively into the air on singing wings alongside my head, my heart stopped. By midafternoon we had run out of ideas.

That evening the others turned up, having boated round from Supper Cove. We told them of our discovery, and we all made our way up the valley next morning. It seemed that a sighting was imminent.

'What do we do if we see it?'

'Shoot the bugger,' suggested Les, who was good at that sort of thing.

'No,' I said firmly. 'A sighting will be enough. Especially with a good description. But twenty golden splondahs to whoever gets a photo of her.'

By now the moose had shifted and was residing somewhere in the big seral forest faces above and downstream of the lake. The place was littered with her feeding sign and her hoofprints were everywhere. We spread out up the slope and 'drove' the face, all very quietly, meeting at the lake. We put up seven deer, but no moose. We reformed and drove back the other way, finding her footprints overlapping ours. Then we split up, each taking a different line, hunting intuitively. Apart from continually running into those with similar ideas, and the odd deer, we came up with nothing. By the middle of the afternoon we seemed to have exhausted all possibilities, so returned to camp and went fishing. Two came back for last light, hunting and watching until dark. Nothing.

It was not easy work: there were rain showers and shifting winds, the terrain was rough and broken and difficult to move stealthily in. The moose continued to keep out of sight, although I swear I disturbed her on two occasions—the bedding place was warm, and I found hoofprints still filling with water. Both times I smelt the animal—not the pungent, musky-sweet smell of red deer, but something, well, more goat-like. It became hard to believe the cunning old girl could evade us throughout all our efforts yet remain in the area. By now her tracking and ours, along with that of the deer in the area, were hopelessly interwoven. How could four seasoned hunters miss a 400 kilogram moose? The answer was simple: very easily indeed.

We continued searching over the next few days, increasingly frustrated and still without success. There were only days to go now. Jim and Les tired of hunting the Herrick Creek faces and tried somewhere different, another search of two promising-looking valleys which run into Wet Jacket Arm from the north, near Oke Island. They were scouting around for something to tie the boat to inside the forest edge, when Jim noticed part of an antler half-buried in the moss and pulled it free. It had belonged to a young moose! They triumphantly brought it back to camp at the end of the day.

It was a great find. Like all the deer family, bull moose cast their antlers annually, around September–October, and regrow them over summer, each year larger than before. By April they are ready for display and combat during the rut. Even where stags are numerous, finding cast antlers is not too common because they are chewed by other deer and forest rodents, presumably for their calcium.

The antler's owner had been a young bull going on four years old. We reckoned it had lain on the ground about two years—certainly not more than five. Unless it was the animal Gordon Anderson had shot—if he had indeed done such a thing—the bull was almost certainly still alive. We knew a sceptic would argue that there were no moose because we had not seen one, that the other sign was merely interpretative and therefore questionable. But with Jim's find we had skeletal evidence, undisputedly from a moose, that dated from quite recently. At the very least, the survey had updated the continued presence of moose by 20 years.

We had one more day, and there were camps in Dusky Sound to pack up and gear to recover. The weather, never good, changed for the worse. We tried another drive on the fuchsia faces where our Lady of the Lake still resided, probably laughing her head off. It failed. We pulled down most of the Herrick Creek camp for an early departure next day.

Near evening I undertook one last desperate solo hunt. It was raining steadily but, for once, there was no wind. I was slipping quietly through some lacebark, about to turn for home, when I caught a flutter of movement 100 metres ahead. I froze. Slowly, slowly, I dropped to the ground and inched towards the place, keeping under cover. It took 20 minutes to cross the first 40 metres, slithering on my chest in the moss and mud. Still the flash of movement. Dark, greyish coat? Yes! But, unable to see, unwilling to crane upward for fear of being seen, I couldn't understand what the animal was doing. Finally, the remaining distance was only 40 metres. I could hear it easily—a rhythmic slurping that left me puzzled. I slowly raised my head, heart thumping. A young red stag, rolling around in a mud wallow, sensed my presence and stood up.

We left Wet Jacket Arm in the boat, leaving the camp gear ready for collection, packed up the Cascade and Sportsmen's Coves camps, and carried on to Supper Cove. Nige and Les went up to Loch Maree for a final search of the upper Seaforth and Kenneth Burn and to bring back some tentage. Meanwhile Jim and I hunted some of the better areas, confident of not overlooking moose sign now our powers of recognition had improved. In those last few days we found more browsing, and some tracking, in six more places. Had we missed them earlier? We doubted that. Where had the animals been? I don't know. But the seral forest slips on the south side of the sound near Cooper Island had recently had a moose resident, and so had a site in Shark Cove. I had a near contact at the mouth of the Henry Burn, where Jim had reported fresh browsing the day before.

Just before dark, on 13 April, George Burnaby's 'Miss Akaroa' tied up at Supper Cove. The search was over.

We boated around next day, picking up camps, enjoying the stress-free ride in George's big boat and eating all his fresh food. Last stop was Herrick Creek, where the temptation to abandon ship for one last look for our moose was almost overwhelming. We could imagine her watching, hoof-to-nose and tongue out, to make sure we really were leaving.

As we glided back up the sound I reflected on our trip. Eleven weeks of effort. We were tired. Our clothes were in tatters and rancid from being continually wet. We looked forward to the comforts of home. If there was one regret, it was the feeling of unfinished business. We had failed to see a moose.

In most respects, however, the lack of a sighting was incidental. We could answer most of the questions the survey had set out to resolve. Most important was that moose survived in Fiordland. Numbers were small but exactly how many could only be guessed. We had found recent sign in seven places, suggesting the existence of at least that many individuals. All things considered, I reckoned it was unlikely there were more than 25 moose in the Dusky Sound and Wet Jacket Arm catchments. But there was also no reason to suppose that moose were limited to this area. As early as 1932 a bull was seen 60 kilometres southeast of the liberation point at Papatotara, near Tuatapere. Closer to the main herd, but east of the divide, was the cow Les Murrell saw twice in the upper Spey Valley.

We were now reasonably knowledgeable about moose forage and feeding behaviour in New Zealand bush. It was easy to understand the animal's position was precarious because food was short—five decades of red deer presence had seen to that. The main advantage moose had over red deer was their higher reach, yet moose were progressively destroying their own food supply through their destructive method of browsing. Plants like fuchsia, three- and five-finger, pate, broadleaf and lacebark simply do not respond to browsing with vigorous regrowth like their North American counterparts, such as willow and poplar. And New Zealand has no equivalent of the aquatic plants which make up a big part of moose summer diet in the northern hemisphere. Furthermore, many seral forest plants in New Zealand are deciduous—what, then, about winter feed? Plants which provided quality bark and twigs in any quantity seemed rare in this eaten-out forest.

Although red deer numbers were not incredibly high overall, big numbers did frequent the three plant communities which were most productive: alpine tussock, small areas of valley-bottom grassland, and seral forest. But moose mouthparts and stature meant they were unable to feed on either tussock or grassland, and obliged them to share the seral forest with the voracious deer. Under the forest canopy, everywhere, there was such a depleted understorey of palatable plants we often wondered how a moose could find the 25 kilograms or more of greenstuffs it needed each day to support that big body.

What about calf survival? Moose calves, the same size as adult red deer, would be in direct competition for food but, unlike their competitors, unable to graze. And were moose numbers sufficient for finding one another for breeding? Were we merely looking at a few survivors, below the threshold number to sustain a population, on their inevitable slide towards extinction? There were as many questions as answers—but you need good information even to ask questions.

What was the future for moose? We could expect everyone to ask that. Well, one thing was clear: only a drastic reduction in deer numbers would restore the understorey of plants. Without that, forage would remain so limited that continued survival of New Zealand moose was doubtful. Yet there seemed no force powerful enough to achieve that in the forests of Fiordland. Or was there?

'Miss Akaroa' was just short of Acheron Passage when another, much larger, vessel swung into Wet Jacket Arm. It was Alpine Helicopter's 'Ranginui'. Wild venison recovery in the remote southern sounds was only economically feasible with ship support. As the 'Ranginui' drew closer we could see a helicopter parked on the flight deck, and rows of gutted deer hanging on rails underneath.

The two vessels slowed. A row of faces along the 'Ranginui's' rail looked down at us. I immediately recognised Bill Black, Jim Kane and Peter Brown, with whom we had worked on the northern Fiordland survey.

'How d'you go?' Blackie called. Our moose survey was well known.

'Not too bad,' I answered cheerfully.

'If there'd been moose here, we'd have seen 'em,' Blackie stated, then added reasonably, 'But I'll tell you what. If you prove to me they're still around, I'll give you a dozen of beer.'

There is nothing quite like 70 days in the bush to turn thoughts towards the benefits of civilisation. High on priorities ranked a cool beer or two. Now here was a great break: I sensed 12 easy ones.

'OK,' I said. I reached up and we shook hands on it.

'Well, did *you* see any?'

'No, but—'

'There, I told *ya*. How d'you know they're there?'

I explained.

'Bullshit,' insisted Blackie.

I persisted, but nothing would convince him. He needed us to have seen a moose, dead or alive. He thought he could maybe forgive No Photograph, but nothing else was enough, and he was unmoved by any description of sign, or even the fact that our treasured moose antler could not have fallen off a red stag. As far as he was concerned, the beer was his, and that was that.

We sailed on.

I was a bit taken aback. There was clearly a misunderstanding about what constituted acceptable evidence. Blackie had been so adamant I owed him the beer that the transaction took place, and I left a case on his doorstep in Te Anau. I thought he was being a bit tough but I considered it a loan, which I would take great delight in taking back from him shortly afterwards, with interest. I did not know then that his scepticism was shared by most New Zealanders. Anyway, I had already thought of a plan to win my dozen back.

5

December 1974-January 1975

Following our 1972 moose survey I got a fair ribbing from friends and colleagues, and even from the press, about our lack of a moose sighting. Most of it was light-hearted, but it surprised me how many people could not believe that large animals like moose could continue to exist without being seen. The last definitive evidence was a bull shot 20 years before; moose were undoubtedly extinct and only exhibitionists or fantasyland folk could think otherwise. That sort of mystery simply could not persist in modern New Zealand. Few people understood the solitary nature of moose and their wariness in a forest, or had much idea about conditions in Fiordland.

An editorial in the 'Christchurch Press' drew parallels between our efforts and those of A.A. Milne's Pooh Bear and Piglet, on the track of Woozles, circling a copse of larch in the snow and peering at the growing number of footprints with increasing apprehension. It did not help when I told a reporter just how close we had been to seeing a moose and let go that I believed I had even smelt one. That was enough to be reported widely, to the great mirth of my friends, who went about loudly sniffing and snuffling like foraging hedgehogs for weeks whenever I walked into a room.

But it was my dissatisfaction over a job not quite complete—rather than the need to recapture some pride and soothe a tortured soul, or, for that matter, to recover the beer I had lent Blackie—that haunted me in the years that followed.

Almost three years later I wrangled some leave and, with a colleague from work, Jan Webster, headed back to finish the job. It was mid-December, 1974, when we pulled away from the wharf at West Arm in Doubtful Sound for the trip south to Dusky. We had managed to hitch a ride on the Fiordland National Park board's newly acquired vessel, 'Renown', due to pick up some scientists from Breaksea Island. It was not too far from Supper Cove for a largish boat, and the park staff kindly offered their service.

Things were looking good: I had borrowed an outboard; we could use the park's dinghy at Supper Cove; we were provisioned for a month; even the weather was perfect. I had a very firm plan to build on the experience we had won so hard three years before and focus our efforts only on the 'good moose country' – the seral forest areas at the eastern end of both Dusky Sound and Wet Jacket Arm. We unloaded our gear on the beach in front of Supper Cove hut and waved off the 'Renown'. The next month was ours.

This was the only time I ever considered shooting a moose if I saw one, and I took my new .270. However, once at Supper Cove I put it aside. Killing a creature to prove it still lives? That was nonsense. A photo would be more challenging and keep my conscience from prickling.

Incredibly, we picked up almost where the earlier survey had left off. Within a week we had found moose sign—some of it fresh—in similar places, and in a few others besides. On one occasion I was looking for the stand of fuchsia Jim Hilton and I had found freshly browsed near the mouth of the Henry Burn when I disturbed animals feeding on the same patch. They had caught my scent, or heard me, and slipped away. Two sets of tracks marked where they had filed up the opposite bank just seconds before. Splattered water still balled in the dry sand. I studied the marks closely and concluded they had been left by a cow and calf. It was the first time I had been sure that a moose had a youngster at foot, and it was a significant find. That calves were still being born said a lot about the resilience of the herd.

We tried everything over the next few days to find them again, but no amount of careful stalking brought success. However, we found where a moose had walked 100 metres along the Seaforth track—in fact, did so three days running. There was not much tramper traffic in those days, but that a bunch of Girl Guides could rediscover moose in Fiordland before we did was a horrifying possibility.

Wherever there was moose sign we hunted, sometimes for days on end, but without success. We found only red deer, and if numbers had been reduced at higher levels by helicopter hunting, it seemed that densities were pretty much unchanged in valley-floor areas.

The weather was not always as good as it had promised at the outset, and one 'fine' day we took ten days' supplies round to Wet Jacket Arm. It was a trip which started OK but became spooky when Acheron Passage turned on a brisk wind from one direction and the tide flowed the opposite way. There were some anxious moments, and a long wait, before we resumed.

Herrick Creek was much as the moose survey team had left it a few years before, but without the resident moose at the lower end. We picked up a spot of old sign in the upper clearings, but nothing worth chasing up. After a few nights in the upper valley we returned, and used the boat to scout other tributary valleys. At the head of Wet Jacket Arm one morning we found tracks so fresh that the incoming tide had yet to erase them, then spent a day trying to find the originator, but the moose had disappeared and there was no feeding sign nearby to suggest it had lingered. We found similar sign near Oke Island, where Jim had discovered the cast antler, but there was so little forage for animals there it was hard to know even where to start hunting, and after half a day we gave up.

The weather changed, food ran out, and we boated back to Supper Cove in heavy rain on a flat sea. We had added a few extra marks to the map but still not seen a moose.

In early January we worked the lower Seaforth and tributaries up as far as Loch Maree, and repeatedly hunted the areas where we had found sign before. We took the boat up to Shark Cove and the two big seral forest slips near Cooper Island. All had been used by moose earlier that season, but it seemed none was still home.

One mid-January afternoon, after a few days away, we returned to Supper Cove hut. I rigged the aerial on our borrowed radio and called Te Anau for news of our pick-up. A few phone calls were made at the other end and we discovered it was set for that evening. We packed up frantically, and at about 8.00 p.m. the 'Renown' came round the point and cruised up to the beach, in a hurry and hoping to pull out immediately for Bluff. We piled our gear aboard, and she backed off, turned, and headed westward up Dusky Sound. Our 1975 expedition was over.

Back at the Forest Research Institute my work had become increasingly focused on Himalayan tahr. There were two main aspects to the research. One was a behaviour study which required living alone in a tiny hut, mid-slope in a tributary valley of the Godley River, north of Mount Cook. About 30 tahr lived on a bluff opposite. I sat with my eyes glued to binoculars for about ten days each month for two and a half years—270 days in total—recording the range use, daily and seasonal activity and social behaviour of the animals. The second aspect involved working closely over the winter months with helicopter operators who were now hunting tahr for game-meat export as deer numbers thinned. Tahr, being a bluff-dwelling, open-country animal, were very exposed to airborne hunting, especially over winter, when they were confined by snow and their presence was readily given away by tracking. What was happening to deer over the course of two decades was taking place within a few winters among tahr. I collected demographic material and some rumen samples from carcasses, and took particular interest in the dramatic changes in numbers, wondering how low densities would become. I could expect the next few years to yield valuable information on how wild-animal populations coped with extraordinarily heavy exploitation.

When I was not in the field for my job, I hunted for fun and money. Fellow scientist Ian James and I teamed up, paid for an old Land Rover, put ourselves through the necessary training to obtain private pilots' licences, bought a quaint little aeroplane (a Bolkow 208, for $3600), and started building houses for ourselves, all largely on the proceeds from deer-hunting. Over long, bitter winter nights in my hut in the Godley, dressed in all my clothes and inside two sleeping bags, I killed time by studying for a commercial pilot's licence by correspondence, never dreaming that one day I would actually use it. I also wanted to write a history of moose in New Zealand, and took every chance to gather information for it—so my Moose File was growing steadily fatter. I was determined that I wouldn't give up until I'd seen a real one.

6

January 1975

Tracing the progress of the moose herd through written records becomes difficult after the end of licensed hunting in 1934. There was no longer an interested administration encouraging exploration and requiring reports, nor the formal structure of hunting privileges through the block-application system. In earlier years the return of each block-holder from his hunt had been eagerly awaited and reported by the press, but such ambushes by reporters could now be avoided. Most hunters prefer keeping hard-won information to themselves.

Newspapers sometimes carried snippets, but these were frustrating in their brevity. For example, the 'Southland Times' of 13 September 1935 had a note on a trip to the Dusky Sound area by R. and B. Martin. According to the paper the pair saw axis deer, red deer in large numbers, and four moose, one of which—a cow—was shot.

With their power now gone the acclimatisation societies could only watch, often with dismay, as their precious trophy herds came under the gun. The 1938 annual report of the Southland society noted rather acidly regarding moose that 'government deer killing parties are at present operating on this herd and, consequently, no stalking parties have been out this season. No reports are to hand as to the number killed.'

That was a little unfair, for the Department of Internal Affairs' campaigns were targeting deer. The men, however, were itching for a crack at a moose. Under Bill Chisholm, who would later become well known for his management of Molesworth Station, they operated briefly in early 1938. When the boat 'Matai' dropped them off at Supper Cove, the engine noise must have disturbed a moose, for they found sign fresh on the ground. A few days later, Chisholm, Ivan Murdoch and another—possibly Jack Collins—were hunting in Waterfall Creek, the small catchment running north from Supper Cove, attempting to drive the valley. Chisholm glimpsed the black shape of a young bull moose and snapped off a shot. He wounded it badly, but the three men were unable to find it. A few years later, apparently, Ivan Murdoch returned and found the remains close to the area they had searched.

The skilled professionals hunted the Seaforth area for six weeks. Chisholm reckoned there were 'probably up to 40 moose in the area', but although they noted sign in many places they were frustrated in their efforts to sight any. Chisholm told me that a bull, cow and calf were living above Loch Maree at one time, leaving sign so recent that 'water was trickling into tracks'. But only Murdoch saw another moose—the quick flash of a cow in Roa Stream. Hoping to shoot one, he had hunted her for three days, resorting to stalking in bare feet.

It was the only season Internal Affairs shooters operated in the Seaforth, but they continued shooting in the mountains to the southeast until the Forest Service took over noxious animal control in 1956. Their tally for the 1937–38 season in the southern blocks, of which the Seaforth was part, was 8400 deer killed.

The Department of Internal Affairs' records of its Monowai Area have little to say about moose until the 1947–48 season report, in which Ken Miers notes to the Queenstown office that 'two were seen by Messrs Kershaw and Mills on a clearing in the Roa Stream', and 'this year [1948] a Mr F.G. Williamson of Bluff reports seeing two in the Seaforth Valley'.

From time to time written records I searched on moose history contained vague references to sightings, and the occasional shooting, of moose by fishermen. For example, the Southland Acclimatisation Society annual report for 1936 notes: 'several cows have been shot by fishermen during the summer months, but no heads have been reported', while the 1937 report states: 'fishing parties advise the animals still exist in the area around Dusky Sound'. There were similar murmurings in the 'Southland Times'.

Obviously the fishing community had some moose stories to tell. I was keen to add a page or two to the records before the tales were lost, so in January 1975 I decided to take some leave and make a short trip to Invercargill and Bluff. Workmates were discouraging. Fishing folk were a law unto themselves, they said, who were suspicious of strangers. I, of course, was the worst variety of stranger: a Public Servant. They would tell me nothing. I would be wasting my time. That seemed likely, but I went anyway.

My father's brother's first wife had a relative in the fishing industry, so, clutching this tenuous thread as an introduction, I drove to Invercargill. I pulled up outside Southland By-Products Ltd, went inside and introduced myself—somewhat nervously—to the manager, Charlie King.

Over the next few days I lost any apprehension about fishing people being unhelpful. Charlie's list of names quickly snowballed. With many of the folk I spoke to, any moose stories they had heard were as vague as my own, but in such cases they willingly referred me on to others. Of course, many old-timers had died, but some families have fished the southern waters for generations and all manner of stories, fishing and otherwise, are passed on as family folklore.

There was a risk of excluding a good record, or doubling up on another, when the passing years had blurred dates or when slightly different versions of the same incident had evolved. Some stories could have gathered a little embellishment while the record at its heart remained intact. Many could never be verified. Others, however, were clearly first-hand accounts, many could be crosschecked, and some were real gems.

Tom West told me of a time—he wasn't sure of the date, but recalled it was 'in the codding days'—when his brother Carl (Charlie) and Norman Roderique were following some big tracks up the Seaforth at Supper Cove. Charlie carried the rifle, a .318 Ross, but had only .303 ammunition for it. They reached a spot where the animal had been browsing, but it was so high above ground level they became a bit apprehensive, considering their light weaponry, and headed back to their dinghy. Meantime, however, the moose had circled behind them, swum the river and was climbing out on the far side. Charlie shot at it, to their amazement wounding it mortally. They towed the carcass back to their boat with the dinghy. It was a pregnant cow, and I later saw the slink (unborn calf) skin, which they kept as a memento and which is still in the possession of the Roderique family. From another source I found out that the date of that incident was November 1935.

Tommy and Bill Ryan told of a cow being shot while it was swimming in the water at Supper Cove by Jack Pratt, from the vessel 'Aurora', sometime 'shortly after the outbreak of the war'. This incident was referred to by others. At that time fishing crews sometimes boated to the Seaforth to shoot swans, they added. The last time these two had heard of a moose being killed was around 1948, when another cow was shot at the Seaforth mouth by a fisherman named Birnson, off a Riverton-based boat.

Frank Williamson's name cropped up often, and I pursued the item from the 1948 Internal Affairs report. After the war there was a profitable trade in deerskins. Williamson and his brother, Mark, along with Charlie West, did some shooting together around Dusky Sound, where deer were abundant. Tom West, the Ryan brothers and Kes Roderique had all heard of a moose—Roderique thought two—being shot at Supper Cove by Frank and Charlie. This tallied with Ken Mier's note on the 1947–48 season.

Although I never met Gordon Cowie, his friend Maurice Beale told me his story, and Gordon kindly sent me two photographs of the young bull moose they had shot in November 1950. Their boat, out of Riverton, was at Supper Cove when a moose was seen on the beach. All three crew fired at it, then went ashore. There was fresh blood where the moose had stood. Next day Gordon and Eric Johnstone went inland in search of the animal, travelling up the lower Henry Burn for some distance but finding nothing. On the way back, Gordon, who was walking behind, suddenly noticed the animal and shot it with his .303. It was a young bull, with antler stubs in early velvet. The shots fired from the boat, Maurice thought, must have been 'long range', for the moose had only a flesh wound from them low in one back leg. The two continued back to the boat and returned with the owner, Gardie Copland, to butcher the moose and take a few photographs.

Mick Fowler had seen moose on two occasions. The first sighting was of a cow about halfway along Wet Jacket Arm. The crew of his boat watched it swimming and then leave the water. The date? He wasn't sure—possibly about 1948 he thought initially—but then remembered they had had a rendezvous with the amphibian aircraft which was flying out fish for them on one of its earliest flights. Since the amphibian service started in 1951, that dated the record nicely. On the second occasion he had seen a cow and calf standing on the beach at what is now Herrick Creek, sometime around 1954.

Old Bill 'Two Ton' Johnson at Bluff had been around a long time. He told me he had sometimes heard fishing folk talk of moose, but was not too interested himself. However, he added, about five years earlier (making it the late 1960s), he had been in a dory with another bloke at the end of Five Fingers Peninsula. They had looked up to see an animal standing, watching them, only 30 metres away. It was, he said, a 'red deer–moose cross'. It had the 'hooked' nose of a moose, was grey in colour, very much bigger than a deer, but had red deer antlers, 'not big palmated ones'. What Johnson did not realise was that he had just given me a perfect description of a three- or four-year-old bull moose.

Maybe fishing people, as a group, do appear to be a closed community. In the unforgiving workplace they have chosen, they are driven by seasons and tides, long trips away and shared dangers. That makes people tough, resourceful and independent. I have nothing but respect for the people that fish the Fiordland coast.

Many tales remained to be told, but the folk I had spoken with were interested, helpful, and often hilarious. I drove back to Rangiora with a full notebook and a light heart.

7

Deer 1909-79

No story of moose in Dusky Sound can be told without recounting the history of deer there for, far more than any other influence, the presence of red deer has dominated the fortunes of moose.

A liberation of red deer was made at Supper Cove in 1909, the year before the ten moose were set free, but involved only two hinds and a stag. It is questionable whether these were the ancestors of the populations that followed. The closest point at which deer were otherwise released was at The Monument, Lake Manapouri, where four liberations took place between 1901 and 1910, at least two of them involving ten hinds. Around the same period were others at Lake Hauroko and in the Lillburn Valley, near Tuatapere. Five axis deer were also turned out at Supper Cove in 1908.

The earliest record of red deer in the Seaforth valley I have found comes from a scrap of sign seen at Supper Cove in 1926, suggesting the 1909 liberation was a failure. Only a year later, in 1927, Les Murrell reported deer there as 'fairly numerous'. By 1929 Eddie Herrick reported with some alarm that deer 'are in this locality in large numbers' and that some parts of the bush were 'absolutely eaten bare by Red Deer, and not a Green blade of shrub or Fern is left'.

This is a typical scenario of the irruptive increases that followed red deer invasion, repeated all over New Zealand as populations surged into a 'supermarket' environment without the northern hemisphere checks of winter or predators. From liberation points deer spread like ripples from stones cast into a pool, their radiation distorted only by local geography. Nationally the dispersal rate averaged 1.6 kilometres per year, but in many areas this was greatly exceeded. At first, numbers expanded 25–30 per cent annually, usually peaking 15–25 years after the first females had found their way into a new area. Then, as forest edibles began to disappear, animal health suffered. Deer lived shorter lives and bred later. Fawn mortality increased especially dramatically, until few survived their first year. Sometimes an event such as a particularly hard winter would trigger mass starvation, although usually the effects were more subtle. With recruitment near zero and mortality high, population numbers plummeted. The forest—already modified but temporarily free of overwhelming populations—then staged the beginning of a recovery. Deer survivors benefited; the beginnings of an equilibrium were in place.

One hunter, Jim Shaw, regularly tried his luck hunting for moose in the Seaforth with his friends. Shaw told Gary Cruickshank that around 1951 deer were so plentiful he could shoot one every 100 metres, but they were small and in poor condition. A year or two later he could not find even one for camp meat.

In Dusky Sound deer invaded northwards and westwards. Resolution Island was without deer in the late 1940s, but less than 20 years later had suffered the explosive increase and subsequent lull and slump in numbers. There was no mystery—the forest was overgrazed and deer simply ran out of food.

Axis deer may have lasted until the early 1960s, when there were a few possible sightings by good observers, but to my knowledge no confirmed specimen was ever shot during this herd's short history. They had succumbed to what ecologists call competitive exclusion—the elimination of one species by another with broader survival skills over a shared resource. It was a textbook case. That moose did not follow them is remarkable.

The shooting campaigns of Internal Affairs—with no disrespect to their hunters, who slogged their hearts out—probably only prolonged the population crash. The numbers of deer shot give some idea of densities. Mike Soper shot in the Grebe Valley area in 1944; he told me his best for a day was 30 kills. Archie Clark was top tally man; his best was 50, and in total he shot 1400 deer that season. But despite such efforts the scale of the problem was insoluble. When the Forest Service took over wild animal control after 1956, efforts were focused on priority areas only. The Monowai block was not one of them.

It was commerce, rather than anything the government could think of, which changed the picture, not only for Fiordland but for all of New Zealand. Until the mid-1960s, a short period of hunting for deerskins in the years after World War II had been the only significant trade involving deer-killing. This had made inroads to deer numbers locally in some places, but the Fiordland sounds were too remote and drying and transporting the skins from there too difficult; there were much easier places to hunt. But things were about to change.

That change was helicopters. In the two decades from the mid-1960s, the appearance of these machines profoundly altered the status of wild deer in New Zealand. As international markets for wild venison developed, the skilful use of helicopters in the hands of a few hardy—if somewhat cavalier—individuals changed deer numbers virtually overnight, a quantum turnaround the government had been agonising over how to achieve for 50 years. Officialdom stood back—at first mildly bemused, then increasingly alarmed—as their half-century-old empires came under threat and the public servant's worst imaginable nightmare—being ignored—evolved. For the helicopter companies asked them for nothing, and the deer problem was being solved without their collective wisdom, consent, finances or, often, even their knowledge.

The early days of the deer industry resembled a high-tech gold rush, with all the attendant drama, innovation, daring and, not infrequently, tragedy. Fortunes were made, lost, then made again.

At the time of our 1972 moose survey, commercial hunting from helicopters had been operating for only three seasons in the southern sounds, taking 1000–1400 deer each year from the area we had searched for moose. That was already making a big dent in deer numbers on the alpine grassland tops, which were usually very attractive to deer, for we noted that only four per cent of the 663 deer we saw were to be found there.

It was a different story in the impoverished forest below. We found 70 per cent of our deer in valley-bottom clearings or seral forest. These two plant communities are often adjacent and, as a forest type, are disproportionately represented in the upper Seaforth and eastern end of Wet Jacket Arm. In the upper Seaforth we averaged a sighting of one deer for every 30 minutes' walking. Here slips and rockfall are simply functions of the steeper country: a cycle of landslides occurs at the forest–granite interface as shallow-rooted vegetation is released under its own weight every few hundred years. Seral forest and native grassland are early colonists of these disturbed sites. Many of the plants that make up these communities experience a vigorous annual growth flush, and such areas, especially, sustained deer (and moose) during the long history of animal occupation after the original forest lost its understorey.

In contrast was the less elevated, more rolling country towards the western end of the sounds, along the coast to the southwest and on the islands. In this stable landscape the forest is predominantly a beech/podocarp mix. With the understorey removed by browsing, productivity was very low indeed and consequently it supported few deer. Here it took us nearly two and a half hours' travelling time, on average, before a single deer was seen—a five-fold difference from the east.

Ask any experienced Fiordland hunters where they are most successful in this area and they will tell you in the clearings, slips and 'greens' (the seral forest). Our simple data put a figure on what they instinctively know.

By 1972 helicopter operations had become very efficient. Bill Black's Hiller had a crew of three, with Jim Kane shooting and Peter Brown as gutter.

'Once we shot 130 in an hour on a single face in the head of Breaksea [Sound],' Bill told me, 'and then spent the rest of the day carrying them out. My best day was 182. We used to average 10 deer an hour. That was finding them, shooting, picking up, gutting and taking them out. That lasted for five years. The best I ever did was a load for the 'Ranginui' in four days, that's 500 deer in 45 hours of flying.' Archie Clark's seasonal tally was being surpassed every few weeks by a single helicopter, but there were more.

The 'Ranginui' had only chilling facilities, not freezing, so was committed to sail every seven or eight days to discharge its load of carcasses at Milford or Bluff. A load was 600 deer from the south, around 500 from the Dusky Sound area, or 400-odd from Doubtful, where the deer were larger. This showed that colonisation had progressed from south to north in the western sounds and that Doubtful Sound was the most recently occupied.

The pressure on deer continued. The 'Ranginui' was replaced for a season by the 'Hotonui', capable of working three helicopters and with a capacity of 4500 carcasses, which it stored blast-frozen so that it was no longer necessary to run to port every week. But deer numbers were falling, helicopters needed to range more widely for their kills, and ships were expensive. Alpine Helicopters replaced the ships with a single Bell 206B Jet Ranger helicopter. With his new aircraft Bill Black's operation now became one of flying out fuel, supporting four Hillers and transporting their kills to waiting trucks at the nearest road end. He handled 200 deer on a normal day towards the mid-1970s.

As deer numbers began to fall, prices rose. In 1965 buyers were paying 33 cents per kilogram, and a good-sized hind of 40 kilograms in dressed weight would yield $13. By 1973, at $2.10 per kilogram, the same animal was worth $84. Alpine Helicopters' operating monopoly in Fiordland National Park lasted until the mid-1970s, when the park authorities finally yielded to pressure for other companies to be allowed to hunt. By the end of the 1970s, Waiau airfield at Te Anau on a day of bad weather looked like a nesting colony of Hughes 300s. On a fine day it was empty, with the lads all out hunting. Deer numbers, of course, fell steadily.

By this time another development had taken place. Markets for wild venison—especially West Germany—had been receiving exports of about 100,000 deer carcasses annually for some years. With falling deer numbers, those markets were under threat. An enterprising farming group resisted the pressures of a wary and pedantic Forest Service and began to farm deer, not only to sustain the existing markets but also to expand into countries whose health regulations permitted only farm-killed animals. By necessity, these new deer farms were stocked with wild-caught deer. Helicopter operators, already being squeezed by fewer deer, fierce competition, new tax laws and now falling prices for meat, seized this new opportunity with alacrity.

If the early years of aerial shooting were a gold rush, then the new era of live-capture had the explosive intensity and innovation of war. Deer values rocketed, and although the period was marked by wildly fluctuating prices, at its peak a good wild-caught hind was worth over $2500. With deer at that price, a helicopter could afford to range a long way, for a long time, recover few animals and still remain a very economical business.

Things were not so different for deer in Fiordland: instead of being chased around by a Hiller or two armed with FN .308s, they were now pursued by a fleet of 20 or more Hughes 300s and the bigger, snappier turbine Hughes 500s, which charged around with net guns, persevering until the deer were worried into open country from scrubland or even forest cover. Once shepherded into a suitable spot, a harassed deer would suffer the indignity of having a net blown over it, a shooter jump on it and tie its legs and, within minutes, being wrapped in a canvas carry-bag ready for the ride to town. Goodbye Fiordland! The view from the farm would not be so good, but it was better than ending up alongside boiled potatoes and sauerkraut at some faraway feast.

Incredibly skilled, their livelihood at stake and with a persistence bordering on fanaticism, helicopter crews hounded every corner of Fiordland. When the prices for live deer waned—as they did frequently throughout the next few years—the airborne hunters turned to shooting for meat. This time they shot not only the tops and clearings, but the slips, the scrubland, the creek beds and through the trees in the low-canopy forests. Deer numbers, already a fraction of earlier times, continued to fall.

If life was dangerous for deer in the 1970s, it was much worse for tahr. Helicopter hunting reduced tahr numbers from 30–40,000 at the beginning of the decade to less than 2000 by the end, with most of the killing happening over the three heavy snow winters of 1973–75. When the economics of low returns stopped the game-meat helicopters from operating, the Forest Service continued with search-and-destroy missions in the eastern Alps. It became difficult to find a tahr, even from a helicopter. Within the Forest Service there were mumblings about the 30 animals being 'protected' in my study area.

At Lilybank Station one day, on my way home from couple of weeks' tahr observations, I was bailed up by a reporter. What were my views on the tahr problem? he asked. I told him that, since there were hardly any tahr, there was hardly any problem.

'What about tahr management then? Is it possible?'

At the time hunters were protesting about the Forest Service's control efforts being 'overzealous'. It was a hot issue in South Canterbury.

'Of course management is possible,' I replied. 'You need to be able to count animals, manipulate their numbers, and have a good idea of their effect on habitat. And we can do all three—maybe not perfectly, but enough.'

The resulting article came out a few days later in the 'Timaru Herald'. The Director-General of Forests, Malcolm Conway, was furious. I was summoned to his office in Wellington for a dressing-down. His job was Policy, he told me grimly. Mine was Science. And I had better stick to Science.

I returned to Christchurch, indignant and fuming at the broadside which, probably naively, I saw as a conflict between Truth and Politics. It was obviously more convenient for those in charge of Politics that the Forest Service continue to have a tahr problem, whatever the real situation. It was not until years later that I recognised that this event was a turning point in my career.

By 1979 I had worked as an ecologist at the Forest Research Institute for ten years. I had been steadily gaining seniority, though I suspect this was due rather more to staff attrition than to talent on my part. The future was looking comfortable. Then, to the astonishment and horror of my parents and many of my colleagues, I borrowed some money, cashed in my government superannuation, got myself a helicopter licence, sold my house and, on my 35th birthday, joined the lolly scramble. The period that followed was wonderful, exhilarating, and scary.

Older than most beginners, but a very junior helicopter pilot, I nervously hovered the little Hughes 300 onto the recently modified flight deck of the 'Ranginui', which was moored against Cooper Island in the familiar landscape of Dusky Sound. Barry Eaton, newly employed, bravely held the shooter's seat, probably wishing he had stuck to his job as a mechanic and part-time hunter. Alpine Helicopters' Tim Wallis, obviously short of pilots in those heady bum's-rush days, had kindly given me a job.

The 'Ranginui' was back in service as a static base for live-deer capture. Her presence provided Alpine's helicopters operating west of the divide a haven, refuelling base and drop-off point for newly captured deer so that they did not have to run the all-too-frequent gauntlet of bad weather back to Te Anau. It also permitted an extra 30 minutes' flight in western areas at daybreak and nightfall, the two best times of the day for hunting. The flight deck accommodated two helicopters, and there were comfortable rooms for both men and deer, the latter being temporarily held below deck—thanks to an ingenious lift system—in darkened 'motels' until their trip to Te Anau and on to farms.

Barry and I stayed only a short time since we were bound for Haast, but I relished the return to Dusky Sound. One day, when it was too wet for flying, I rowed the ship's dinghy to the big forested slips near Cooper Island. We had found moose browse there in 1972 and again in 1975. This time I did not find any moose sign, but there was no deer sign either, and the forest was already beginning to recover.

8

February 1992
Moose sign

Within six months it seemed my flirtation with helicopters was over. Deer prices fell to less than $250 for a live hind and I was an early victim of the cost-cutting that followed. With too few skills to be a very marketable pilot, I was suddenly looking at a future which had turned a little shaky.

With the proceeds from the sale of my Rangiora house I had purchased another on a small block of land, in Wanaka. I loved the area and was desperate to hang on to the property if at all possible. Wanaka local Dave Richardson and I joined forces, fishing for eels in his jet-boat, trapping possums for their skins, and bush-hunting deer along the Haast road. I was tempted by an offer to continue my tahr study by turning the research into a thesis for a higher degree at Lincoln University. I hesitated—before deciding I had left academia for a Different Life, and turned the opportunity down. A few days later, trying to skin frozen possums around the frosty clearings in the Wills Valley near Makarora, I pondered the wisdom of my decision.

The following summer I had a job flying a Hughes 500 for tourist and geological-exploration work at Makarora. It was a brief but perfect reintroduction to commercial helicopter flying, still in my beloved mountains. And there was an unexpected bonus: Marg Campbell, still restless from a two-year overseas trip, was working at Makarora too. Marg's down-to-earth manner and wry humour were a delight, and we quickly became good friends. Her brothers still ran the family sheep and deer farm at Clinton. She had deer of her own, she told me. I could picture my Wanaka property, newly fenced, home to great thundering mobs of tame deer.

'How many?' I asked eagerly.

'Three,' she replied.

We married two years later, and Marg shifted her deer—now five of them—to Wanaka. The helicopter pilot market picked up again and, little by little, I learned my new trade. I flew on seismic work throughout Taranaki, and in the hills behind Gisborne and Te Anau for the Alpine-Whirlwide-Helicopter Line group of companies, and on all manner of jobs—from heliskiing to catching wild goats—out of Wanaka. Betweentimes I had three summers in Antarctica, flying as expedition support for the Italian Antarctica research programme with Nelson-based Helicopters (NZ). That company then picked up seismic contracts in Burma, and for 18 months I commuted monthly, working in jungle areas along the upper Chindwin River in the northwest of the country and living in Burmese villages. It was wonderful stuff. My only regret was that Marg was left at home.

Late in 1991 the Burma contracts came to an end. After all those alternate months apart, Marg and I planned a nostalgic summer of camping and tramping in places I loved from earlier times. Fiordland came first: we started at Lake Roe and spent two delightful weeks there. It was too short. We bought an inflatable boat and a small outboard, packed up for a month and went to live in Wet Jacket Arm.

Bill Black, now flying an AS 350B Squirrel helicopter, dropped us at the beach at Herrick Creek on a drizzly afternoon in February 1992. He took off again and we shifted our gear above the high tide mark. Everything about the place looked similar to how I had left it 15 years before—until I stepped inside the forest. Under the canopy the changes were staggering: the relatively short period with reduced deer numbers had already produced a forest thick with regenerating trees and shrubs, ferns and epiphytes, vines, creepers and ground cover. If New Zealand forests have often been labelled delicate, this one had shown itself remarkably resilient. I could not help thinking that it probably resembled the bush of the early 1920s, shortly after moose and other deer species were released. The plant supermarket was returning. The recovery would have many consequences for birdlife and other forest inhabitants. Deer populations, too, would begin to bounce back, but now a potent system of hunting and harvest existed which could be manipulated to ensure that the scales remained tilted in the forest's favour.

There was another—totally unexpected—presence among the new generation of saplings proliferating around our camp site. A stand of pate had been neatly broken at chest level, its tops stripped of leaves and left dangling, now dead. It was the work of a moose—I had no doubts about that. With rising excitement I explained the signs to Marg.

Moose survival had been against the odds: they had come through the period of critical food shortages. For 50 years they had shared a progressively decreasing food source with the adaptable red deer, severely disadvantaged by their specialised mouthparts and behaviour. But the seemingly impossible had happened: even in the deep forest deer numbers had been decimated by helicopter hunters, and the bush was recovering. Now, provided there were more than just a few surviving, the period ahead looked very comfortable for moose. Perhaps their only advantage—little more than half a metre's reach by an uplifted neck—is all that had prevented them from joining axis deer in oblivion.

It was Marg's first time in the sounds. She was clearly enchanted with the place. I had hoped it would be so, because there was an unresolved issue, and we could end up being there for some while. In the meantime, I hoped Bill Black had not forgotten about that beer.

Where do you start looking for moose? The problem is similar to searching for one of a dozen mice living in a few square kilometres of rough scrubland. However, historical records provide likely boundaries, and within these moose advertise their presence. Moose sign differs from that of red deer, reflecting the animals' size, strength, skeletal differences and peculiar behaviour.

It takes only common sense, good observation and a little botany to identify the local equivalents of North American moose food. When Marg and I hunt for moose we begin by searching the greens—the seral forest areas—where the favourite foods of New Zealand moose predominate. The plants we rate as favourites, in roughly descending order, are three- and five-finger, pate, fuchsia, broadleaf, mahoe and lacebark. Moose browse many other species, of course, but these seem to form the bulk of their diet. They are usually prolific on old slip sites, but are also abundant along the edges of clearings, under regenerating storm-damaged areas and along some coastlines. We call them indicator species, as a quick inspection of them in an area will reveal if a moose has fed there in recent times. They are the New Zealand equivalents of the willows, aspens, birches, alders, maples, dogwoods, elderberries and others which occupy similar sites in the moose's North American habitat, and which owe their abundance there more to fire or logging than slips.

Moose are large, inelegant creatures, disproportionately long and lanky in the leg, short and thick in the body, with distinctive humped shoulders and a short neck. They are tall animals. If you are of average stature for an adult man, the shoulder height of an adult moose will be slightly above your head. If you raise an arm and extend your fingers, your fingertips will be about 15 centimetres below the point—at around two and three quarter metres' height—which is within easy reach of a browsing moose. In contrast, the shoulder height of a red deer will be around your waist level, and a browsing deer, with neck extended, will reach only as high as your head, or about two metres up. Moose make use of this height advantage when browsing, thereby giving away their presence.

The height at which they browse, however, is not the only evidence moose leave on the bush. A moose's head is long—even horse-like at first glance—but unlike horses, moose (and deer) have no upper incisors. Their nose is more bulbous and their lips more mobile than those of deer, and they use their prehensile upper lip to great effect in a way which is easily discernible on Fiordland food plants. Recognising this distinctive feeding sign is another way of telling that a moose has been there, while being able to age it may tell you that the animal is still nearby.

Like red deer, moose feed by taking mouthfuls of leaves from the ends of twigs and branches. Unlike deer, however, they often feed by reaching up, grasping a branch in the mouth, and stripping it of leaves with a sideways motion of the head. The branch is often left broken and bruised, especially the lower surfaces, and with a tatter of leaf remains. Moose sometimes concentrate on a particular tree: characteristic sign, especially on fuchsia, is a main stem, still upright, with stubs of broken branches two to six centimetres in diameter to above fingertip height of an upstretched arm, while the ground beneath is littered with stripped branches.

Red deer numbers have been decimated in recent times, and in many places an understorey of saplings now exists. If these are around two metres high, a feeding moose may grasp the entire stem at about what is our waist or chest height, snap it with a circular motion of its head, and deftly strip the leaves from the upper part of the plant. We have noted that pate in particular lends itself to this behaviour, and sometimes have come across quite large areas where most plants have been so taken, the upper part left hanging, battered but still attached. The degree to which the leaf remains have dessicated gives a good clue as to how recently the area has been browsed.

In contrast to the manner in which moose grasp branches to feed, red deer tend only to nip terminal shoots, which they break off with a nod of their head, and they take only small stems. Moose can easily cut stems of up to three centimetres in diameter on the softer species like three- and five-finger, and sometimes we have found branches four to six centimetres in diameter crushed to splinters between powerful molars. Others appear to have been broken purely for sport.

Occasionally we have found larger saplings which have been straddled or walked down by moose, their canopy foliage browsed—another feeding behaviour not demonstrated by deer. Many pate saplings three to four metres high and up to ten centimetres in diameter around our camp in Herrick Creek were fed upon in this way during the winters of 1991 and 1995.

Moose frequently eat bark from upright stems of plants, even when greenery is readily available. We have noticed this particularly on pate, but also on many minor species, like some of the small-leaved coprosmas, marble-leaf and similar plants which grow into bushes two or three metres high around swampy clearings. With many of the minor species, it is hard to see what food value moose derive from this practice. Barking is conspicuous when fresh, appearing bright white in the dark bush, but ages quickly to become indistinct. Day-old barking on pate and three-finger found in August was hard to recognise by October.

Moose are totally at home in water and can swim long distances with ease. Aquatic plants make up a large proportion of the summer food of moose in North America. Moose even dive for these plants there, being able to hold their breath for up to 30 seconds while doing so—a remarkable feat for a member of the deer family. In New Zealand the large areas of swampy country in the Seaforth valley lent weight to its choice as a liberation site, it being known that moose liked swamps. They do so in North America, however, mainly because of the food available there, both in and around the water. New Zealand has no equivalent of these aquatic plants, and other plant species here which enjoy swampy conditions and semi-open country—sedges, hook grass, manuka, kanuka, and many small-leaved coprosmas and similar shrubs—are not particularly palatable. In Fiordland, then, while water is no barrier to moose movement, it does not seem to be of any great attraction. However, around many swampy clearings there are often good stands of seral forest, attractive to both red deer and moose, and these same clearings often contain short grasses and other small plants which make them particularly attractive to deer.

Footprints of moose are not always easy to identify, partly because of the soft, often muddy or vegetated conditions of the forest floor, but also because the print size is not as large as might be expected from an animal weighing 400 to 550 kilograms. Moreover, finding good prints to measure is difficult because the hindfoot imprint overlaps that of the forefoot in normal gait. However, the foot structure of moose is less upright than that of deer—probably an adaptation to soft underfoot conditions—and a moose's dewclaw imprints show on a firm surface whereas a deer's do not. A moose's forefeet are larger than its hindfeet; with red deer it is the other way round. Prints we believe to have been made by moose, in firm mud, measure around 90 to 125 millimetres by 85 millimetres, excluding the dewclaw mark. They conform to those of the forefoot trophies I have measured, from the cow shot by Jim Mackintosh and the first of Eddie Herrick's bulls. The largest, we are sure, was made by a bull, for there was fresh antler rubbing nearby.

We have been cautious about using dropping size as a definitive means of identifying moose presence, since both moose and deer range in size from small young to large adults, and because both species share the same food source. However, at the large end of the scale, and associated with other characteristic moose sign, we have found pellets too big to have been deposited by even the largest red stag.

A major reason why moose are such poor competitors with red deer—and which has nearly resulted in their demise—is that they do not have the ability to feed easily from short-growing plants. Their prehensile lips are not made for short growth, and with their short neck and comparatively long legs moose cannot reach ground level without spreading their forefeet or awkwardly 'kneeling'. In the New Zealand forest, therefore, moose are purely browsing animals, while red deer are both browsers and efficient grazers.

There are not many moose in the Dusky Sound/Wet Jacket Arm area of Fiordland. You may have to walk a long way, search a large area and stay for a long time to find sign of one. Sometimes that might be discouraging. Marg and I have found that if the lack of success of such single-minded searching becomes disheartening, a pause to reflect on other reasons for being there can be just as compelling. And for us, there are many. Some are wildlife-oriented, others historic, exploratory or personal. But all of them keep us returning to this magnificent but moody wilderness. Perhaps it is this affection and feeling of rare privilege that some people would call spiritual.

9

February-March 1992

I cut off the outboard and let our small dinghy bump into the shore. Behind us Wet Jacket Arm was misty grey. Bush-covered ridges rose steeply from a calm sea into ragged patches of low cloud. Rain fell steadily, big drops pocking the flat water and plastering our hair on our faces. I glanced at Marg. It wasn't much of a day to go hunting.

'Let's give it a couple of hours,' I suggested.

'We might as well, now that we're here,' Marg agreed.

Wet and stiff from the cold trip, we clambered awkwardly onto slippery rocks. I tied the bowline to an overhanging fuchsia. The tide was receding; the boat would be safe.

We climbed the bank and pushed into the bush through dripping, shoulder-high ferns and clawing small-leaved shrubs. It was surprisingly dark inside the forest.

The slope was an ancient slip. A huge fan of recent forest covered its boulder-strewn slopes, with ribs of older beeches running down the less disturbed ridges. It was a good place for animals.

We began our search, slithering through the sodden forest, sometimes climbing high to follow deer leads or natural routes, other times dropping back almost to the shoreline. We picked our way over monstrous rocks, moss-covered and saturated, overgrown with thickets of wineberry, fuchsia, mahoe, pate, lacebark and a thousand ferns. Rain rattled on our parkas, and bigger drops spattered us from the tangle above, spreading cold fingers inside our clothing. But any discomfort was short-lived in the excitement of discovery. Every so often, here it was again—unmistakable!

'There's been more browsing over here on this broadleaf,' Marg called, 'and more here—and here.'

For the second time we had found sign of moose. This place had access only via the water, but that was not a problem for the big animals. The browsing may have been six months old, but I had a growing feeling that there wasn't just a single survivor.

It was time to go. Soaked, cold, but pleased with ourselves, we turned for home. Six kilometres down the sound was our tent, the luxury of dry clothes, a warm fire and hot coffee with rum.

The rain eased over the last half-day. In the evening I took the radio from our tent, cradled it under my parka, and sloshed down the muddy trail to the water's edge where we had slung the aerial. Westward up Wet Jacket Arm the sky seemed lighter, but another rain squall was working its way down in probing grey fingers. I hurried to avoid a soaking, fixing the tiny wires with both hands, the sandflies making the most of this brief period to gorge themselves on my neck, temples and scalp unhindered. A tomtit fluttered cheerfully nearby. OK. All set.

'102 Te Anau, this is Alpine Portable. Do you read? Over.'

A moment later Carol Brown's voice came in clearly from her very different world.

'Alpine Portable, 102. Read you loud and clear Kenneth. How're you going over there?'

'Yeah, fine thanks Carol. Been pretty wet here. Any messages for us and do you have a forecast? Over.'

'No messages Ken. Forecast looks like it's going to come right overnight with a southerly change tomorrow and you should get a couple of good days coming up.'

That was grand news. We had been here for three weeks but it had rained every day of the last two, most of it medium-to-steady, up to 60 millimetres daily. In tent life that means nothing is dry. Fiordland sunlight is a special event; the prospect of some of it was very cheering.

'Alpine Portable, 104. Copy?'

A new voice. It was Dennis Egerton from his home in Arrowtown. Dennis was a colleague, friend and rival from earlier days, now a pilot with Helicopter Line in Queenstown.

'Egerton! How are you?' It was our usual greeting.

'Tustin! Yeah good. Hey, I'll be through your way tomorrow if the weather's OK. I'll drop in. Anything you need in there? Where's your camp?'

That was easy.

'OK Dennis, bring a newspaper and a bottle of whisky. We're at the mouth of Herrick Creek in Wet Jacket.'

'Yeah, got that. Maybe see you tomorrow. Cheers. 104 out.'

Wind ruffled the water in the sound. New, heavy drops of rain took hold. I unhooked the radio from the tutu bush and raced up the track to our tent with the news for Marg.

The Hughes 500 settled briskly with a rush of wind, scattering leaves and drying clothes. It throttled back and finally shut down to the mix of silence and bellbirds. Dennis climbed from the cockpit with a laconic grin and a bottle of 'Wilson's' wrapped in the 'Otago Daily Times'. He had obviously not expected to find us in such good heart after three wet weeks in the bush, lacking only news and, well, a wee dram or two for the evenings. We rehung our clothes and lunched on freshly baked camp-oven bread and Marg's tomato and garlic pasta.

We knew Dennis well enough to realise he wouldn't be able to resist asking what we were up to.

'OK, Tustins! What on earth are you two doing here?'

Maybe it was the unexpected company, or Dennis's thoughtfulness with the whisky, but I forgot my natural wariness.

'Egerton, follow me for five minutes and I'll show you something.'

We walked to some places close to camp where six months earlier a moose had spent a few weeks. I pointed to the sign we had recognised, describing the characteristic nature of moose feeding behaviour, so different from that of red deer, which Dennis, being a hunter, knew well. I told him about moose history in the area. He was fascinated. We walked back to camp.

Dennis's interest in moose was that of any Southland outdoors person—but with a difference. He and his older brother, Peter, and the three adult occupants of a Grumman Wigeon amphibian, believed they had seen one in 1964. As youngsters, they had been taken on a flight around the southern sounds with their dad, a well-known wapiti hunter. Flying down Herrick Creek at about 1500 feet, in deteriorating weather, they had seen a solitary 'big, black animal' standing in the shallows at the northern end of the lake. But the weather was closing in—there were no second chances—and the aircraft returned to Te Anau with its excited passengers. 'It could only have been a moose,' they later recalled. It was a schoolboy's dream.

Dennis, understandably, had been musing. He broke the silence. Unexpectedly he said:

'Y'know Tustin, this'd make an amazing film.'

Dennis had always been pretty enterprising. That idea was about as far as you could get from my thoughts, but I realised he was serious and I back-pedalled hurriedly.

'Whoa. Hang on a minute Dennis. This sign we've shown you isn't for broadcasting. So please, please keep it to yourself. It's a very private hobby for us. Don't tell anyone about this. OK? If you do, it'd be the same as me telling other people about your gold-mining spot.'

I hoped I had got through.

We spent an enjoyable hour catching up on news, and had the paper still to read. The 500 wound up again and Dennis roared off towards Queenstown, leaving us with a vague feeling of uneasiness about a film.

May 1992

Laos was not a place we had heard much about. After the Vietnam War a communist regime had taken over and borders had been closed. Now, with the Russians fleeing, the doors were creaking open again—just a crack. Western businesses which might help develop the country were being warily admitted. Through their Australian subsidiary, Helicopters (NZ) had taken up the challenge of starting a helicopter charter business there. They needed staff. We were really excited: if I was accepted, we could both go and share an adventure for a change.

I applied as a pilot and got the job but, at the last minute, ended up as the manager as well. Marg and I were to live in the capital, Vientiane, developing the operation with Lao staff, and using other New Zealand pilots and engineers on six-weekly tours to fly and service the aircraft if things got busy, much as we had done in Burma. We were to start with two Squirrel helicopters still in Singapore from the Burma operation.

It was hard to find out anything about Laos but Marg ordered a book through the Wanaka library. It arrived, and we lit the fire at home early one evening before sitting down to read and talk about it.

The phone rang. I recognised the voice.

'Egerton! How are you?'

'Tustin! Good. Off to Laos eh? Well, good luck. From what I hear you'll need it! Hey, I was talking to Michael Stedman from the Natural History unit the other day and I mentioned to him what you and Margie were doing in Wet Jacket. All the moose stuff you showed me—'

'Dennis! You didn't!' I was horrified.

'Yeah, but wait a minute. Like I told you, it'd make a great film and he agreed. But they won't—definitely won't—consider doing it without your approval. Anyway, a guy from Natural History, Neil Harraway, is going to ring you in about thirty minutes.'

I told Marg. There were more than a few dark mutterings. After some discussion we agreed that if the Natural History unit was about to make a documentary on moose, there were two courses of action: either we distanced ourselves from the project to protect our privacy, or we should get involved and support it 100 per cent. Maybe it was a matter of pride, but the thought of a serious documentary on moose without any input from us was just too unpalatable, so the second option seemed the only real choice.

Neil Harraway rang and I explained our wariness, which he understood. We agreed to meet and talk about it, and a few days later the three of us were sitting at our Tarras tea shop rendezvous. Neil was knowledgeable, affable, and paid for the coffee. He took our word that moose continued to survive in Fiordland and confirmed the unit's interest in filming a search of the wilderness there. It dawned on us that that meant A Photograph.

An image of a New Zealand moose on film—however it was achieved—would guarantee the success of the project. It was a monumental challenge, too exciting to ignore. Previous experience warned it would be incredibly difficult, but Neil wasn't daunted. He was enthusiastic about finding an animal using hi-tech equipment, even thermal-imaging devices from helicopters. I wasn't so sure, preferring to increase our efforts on foot, which would be more satisfying as well as give them something to film. Neil suggested fixed cameras operating on a trip system, which sounded like a good idea. I was keen on making the documentary a history as well as a hunt, which would not be hard as I already had the material at my fingertips.

Within an hour we had an arrangement. Natural History would send a lone cameraman into Fiordland on our next trip. He would stay about a week. They would pay our transport and food. After this reconnaissance they would decide if the moose story was worthy of a film.

We felt uneasy about the exposure, but stuck with our resolution to back the film venture as best we could. Reassuring was the professionalism of the Natural History unit. Their 'Wild South' films on wilderness and wildlife were legend.

Marg and I were leaving for Asia in a week. We told Neil we would save our leave, return to New Zealand in autumn 1994, and spend a month in Wet Jacket Arm to resume our hunt for moose. The cameraman assigned to the moose project had not been to Fiordland before, Neil explained, but he had overwintered in Antarctica and worked in other remote places. Neil was sure we would like him. His name was Max Quinn.

10

April 1994

Our overloaded Subaru eased into the driveway of Bill Black's hangar in Te Anau. The car was crammed with tentage, food, our deflated inflatable boat, the outboard motor, fuel, and countless other items for a month in Fiordland, although everything had been carefully pared to ensure it would fit inside a Squirrel helicopter, along with the third passenger we had yet to meet. I had spoken to Max Quinn on the phone and he sounded OK, but we were a little wary.

Max would accompany us for our first week. After that it would be Decision Time re the moose film. We weren't too concerned about the outcome. If it worked, fine, we would support Natural History in making the best possible job of it. If not, well, it hadn't been our idea anyway. But we had longed for the trip back to Wet Jacket Arm to pick up the moose trail again. The dozen beer Bill Black and I had laid bets on in 1972 would surely now, with interest, have turned into a very large bottle of Glenfiddich. I looked forward to claiming it from him. All we needed was a photograph of a moose.

Marg and I were jet-lagged from our return from Asia. Laos had been exciting and colourful, but exhausting. We now had a busy four-helicopter operation there. It was not an easy place to live in at that time, what with curfews, checkpoints, security paranoia, language problems, rust, dust, heat and all-too-often suspect food and water. Newspapers, books and magazines were banned. Sometimes our helicopters were shot at. The mere thought of the Fiordland sounds was a tonic.

A blue minivan turned onto the concrete pad. A tall figure unwound from behind the front seat. Lanky, even gangling, the bespectacled Max with his boyish grin was instantly likeable. Before a word had been spoken we were at ease with him.

The weather looked appalling. Grey rain hung over the mountains west of Lakes Te Anau and Manapouri. Blackie frowned at it; he thought he could get us into Wet Jacket, but did we really want to go in those conditions? The alternative was sitting out the bad weather in town. It seemed unlikely a moose would stroll into the Te Anau pub on a wet Monday afternoon, so we loaded up the helicopter and took off.

True to his promise, Blackie finally touched down at our camp site of two years before, but only after an uneasy roundabout route through driving rain and hills thick with mist. Sticking to our plan, we unloaded all the gear except three packs while Blackie kept the helicopter running, covering the pile with a tarpaulin and weighing the corners down with stones. Back in the helicopter, we continued through the murk to beyond the valley head and landed in a soggy clearing. We climbed out with our packs. A wave, and the helicopter was gone.

Only the noise of rain broke the silence. We struggled into parkas we should have put on earlier. Mist hung low and gusts of wind shook the beeches, bringing fusillades of heavy drops. We swung packs onto backs, and squelched up through shoulder-high scrub towards the saddle, already soaked. The dry rock was high in the bush somewhere to our right. With nightfall not far away and the ground awash it was no time to be far from shelter, but I couldn't recognise anything. Thirty minutes later, increasingly alarmed, I dropped my pack to search unencumbered, leaving Max and Marg shivering under the dubious shelter of a big kamahi. After five long minutes I glimpsed the grey rock wall through the mist among the trees above. Thankfully I turned back for the others. It was 20 years since I had been there.

We peeled off sodden clothes 15 minutes later. I lit a fire from dry wood stacked in the shelter of the rock overhang, wondering if I had been its last visitor. Rain poured down only a few metres away, and curtains of water from the face above at one end; we were living behind a waterfall. A billy held out on a stick filled in four seconds, but beside the rock it was relatively dry. The billy boiled, and over mugs of tea we talked of moose, of Antarctica, where Max had been recently, of our time in Laos, more of moose, of films and of things to come. It was hard to believe only a few hours before we had been in such different surroundings.

By morning there was no change in the weather. Rain slanted through the saddle, and even the ridge opposite, not far away, was invisible. With no sign of it breaking we had a choice of staying in relative comfort with little food, or gritting our teeth and slugging it out down to the main camp, six hours' travel away. I had hoped for weather fine enough for a leisurely trip traversing the length of the valley. We would have had a good chance of crossing signs of moose if any were resident, and could have followed up later with a clear plan of attack. But we would learn nothing waiting at the dry rock. We decided to go and make the best of it.

For his recce Max carried a Hi-8 video camera in a waterproof housing. For reasons of quality, any filming he did with it could only be used as small inserts in the final documentary. He had five days, he told us, then he would float-plane back to civilisation, but would return with a few troops and better equipment if there was a story here. We hoped he did not expect to find a moose immediately.

Getting wet is part of life in Fiordland. We pulled on yesterday's clothes, shouldered our packs and slithered through the steepening bush alongside the gorge which would take us to upper Herrick Creek. An hour later we were pushing through pepperwood around the swampy clearings. At one place I came face-to-face with a red deer hind. She froze only five metres away, puzzled by the apparition appearing in her backyard, while I hoped the others were close enough behind to see her. But she bounded off just as a very bedraggled Max and Marg came into view. We pressed on in driving rain.

A short time later I crossed the creek and pulled myself up the bank among waist-high ferns to a tangle of gnarled fuchsia and wineberry. A tattered lacebark dangled a metre away, its stem crushed and bent. The ground was littered with twigs and bruised leaves. A few metres further on another had been wrecked, snapped off from upstretched-fingertip height, with surrounding branchlets up to thumb-thickness cropped. I stood there stunned, waiting for the others to catch up.

'You bloody tin-bum,' I said to Max as he heaved himself alongside. 'We've just missed a moose.'

It was no time to go hunting, but I pointed out to Max the characteristic browse signature of the big animal. He took some video footage of it. We searched briefly for footprints, but conditions underfoot were too wet for finding the distinctive hoofmarks. It didn't matter. There was no mistaking this sign, only a few hours old, perhaps less. Maybe we had disturbed the animal? Max was very matter-of-fact, probably not realising our luck. Contact on Day Two! A perfect start for our trip. I grinned at Marg, hair plastered all over her cheerful face, and got a beam with a wink back. But we still had a long way to go, so picked up our packs again, aware that we were maybe being watched—or at least listened to—by our new friend.

The second gorge required a long climb under a beech canopy through dripping, shoulder-high fern, but beyond saturation there is no wetter. Then came a traverse and a prolonged, steep drop to the lower valley. It was another hour to the lake. The going had been reasonably open in the 1970s, but now we had to force our way through thickets of regenerating plants. I was preoccupied, unsure whether I could recall the difficult route round the lake.

At the lake grey rain swept across the water and cold gusty squalls chopped up the surface and shook the trees. We were cold and tired. I was especially anxious about Max, who was beginning to stumble with exhaustion. We had a quick pause for a handful of raisins, but it was too cold to stop. The true right side of the lake was a possible alternative route, but it would cost us an extra two hours of nightmare travel and two deep river crossings, too prolonged and risky an undertaking for our party.

We struggled among big moss-covered boulders under a sprawling fuchsia canopy, then clambered through bush. I dropped my pack again for a solo recce, then, after some anxious moments, recognised the way: a greasy green rockface with enough water pouring down it to qualify as a waterfall, and a steep rocky chute. It looked worse than it was, and we climbed carefully down, handing down packs and guiding feet and hands to safe purchase. But the next section I feared: a sidle round a bluff with footholds under water and bottomless mud if you missed them. I went first, heart in mouth but without problems, then dropped my pack and again guided feet and hands for the others. A few deep, muddy bounds and we were clear! Around the lake through swampy scrubland, then through the bush following the stream down to the sound, and 50 minutes later we were home. There was still work to do, though, before we could change wet clothes: gear to recover, a camp to build. Like zombies, we pitched in for one last effort.

An hour later, under a rigged fly and in dry clothes, I was coaxing wet twigs into a reluctant fire. Finally we passed around mugs of coffee, hot and sweet and laced with rum.

'Cheers Max!' I said, with genuine admiration for the guy who had so doggedly stuck to the unfamiliar task of pack-carrying on a bloody unpleasant day. 'Welcome to Fiordland!'

Three mugs touched in a well-earned salute, as rain drummed noisily on the nylon fly above.

The boat rocked gently in bright sunshine. Marg's rod over one side and mine over the other. A kilometre away across the glass-smooth sound, a thin plume of blue smoke marked our Wet Jacket home. Among the trees near the shore, a colourful line of clothes and sleeping bags was drying. We fished happily; it was an extra tot of rum to whoever caught the first blue cod.

Max was back at camp frantically shoving soaked clothing and tentage into packs for the float plane, due to arrive any minute. The days after our arrival at camp had been stormy, but one—Max's last—had finally cleared to showers. We had been largely campbound, but managed a few excursions in bush and boat, accepting another soaking in exchange for a few hours' look-around. On Max's final morning the day had dawned cool but clear. Leaving Marg drying gear, he and I had raced up to the lake for a few photos, finding it postcard-perfect. Max was beginning to understand our fascination with Fiordland. Finally, out of time, we had returned to camp.

Around the campfire we had talked about the film. To our surprise Max was enthusiastic about it. It wasn't just a hunt for a beast presumed extinct, he said, but the story of a game animal which had never flourished. Why? There were biological and historical reasons to explore.

Set in this wild and little-known place, he especially liked the adventure aspects: even in 1994 an ordinary couple like Marg and I could come here and have a shot at solving a wildlife mystery. If Natural History directors agreed, he said, we would have a documentary. Anyhow, whatever followed wasn't our immediate concern as we lowered 40 fathoms of fishing line into the black depths of Wet Jacket Arm for a cod or two for Max to take home to Dunedin.

'Here we go!'

Marg reeled her line in, rod bent nearly double, and won the rum with a two-kilo cod, flapping and glaring, iridescent green in the bright light. A second later my own rod jerked.

'Here he comes,' said Marg a few minutes later as engine noise suddenly broke the silence. Around the point the float plane lined up for touchdown, bright white against the green bush. We wound in and I pulled the outboard into life.

Ten minutes later we waved off Max together with his bag of fish.

'I'll try and get back in a couple of weeks,' were his last words. 'Keep in touch with Carol on the radio.' He left the Hi-8 with us, and we worked out a coded message so he would know if we had got our photo.

The plane idled out into the sound, then ploughed away with a roar and lifted off. We were alone again. We would miss Max's good cheer and campfire banter, but we had work to do. Four hours' travel away a moose was living at the head of the valley.

11

April-May 1994

'Stay close,' I whispered to Marg. 'He's around here somewhere. And keep the camera handy.'

We could smell him.

We were travelling lower Herrick Creek. A red stag had had a wallow in a small clearing nearby. I had seen him twice before. Close together, we stalked carefully through thick scrub as quietly as the muddy conditions would allow. Sure enough—a touch of red-brown, the line of a back. I motioned to Marg. We crept forward keeping low. She eased slowly upright, the video camera running. The stag swung his antlered head up, staring right at us from only 30 metres away, on the point of bolting. I cupped my hands and gave a cough and a roar in a not particularly good imitation of a rival. He moved, barked, hesitated, barked again, then spun and disappeared into the bush.

'I don't think he'll go far.'

We followed him into the thick cover, but progress was too noisy. I tried another roar. He answered half-heartedly from about 60 metres distant, then again from a hundred or so. We retraced our steps and continued on our way.

An hour later we had a quick lunch of cheese and dates, planning to hunt the big fuchsia faces mid-valley.

'I'm pleased we caught the stag on video,' Marg said. 'I'm going to call him Fred. I can't believe he could trot through that thick bush without making a sound. No breaking twigs, no squelching or antler noise on the scrub. Nothing. We could never be that silent. That's amazing.'

'Unless they're panicking they can be unbelievably quiet,' I said, 'although he was alarmed and travelling fast.'

Then I added, 'People say about moose, "How can you miss seeing a moose for Christ's sake? They're so bloody huge!" But big doesn't mean clumsy. They're more furtive than deer in the bush. And another thing: if we do make contact, keep watching behind you. They've a habit of planting—or freezing—then sneaking out quietly after you've passed. They're similar to sambar or rusa deer in that respect; bush-hunting them is very difficult.'

A glance at Fiordland forest says it all: how easy it would be to bypass an animal which was willing to hold still and risk being seen, rather than flee and ensure it. I thought of earlier moose hunts and how many times that could have happened. Perhaps that's why moose haven't been noticed from helicopters.

There is no group more knowledgeable about game in Fiordland forests than the helicopter pilots and their shooters who spend their working lives hunting there. These people are extraordinarily observant, experienced in the ways of deer, familiar with the terrain and always searching from their airborne platform. It seems unlikely they could overlook anything. But despite great interest, they are usually dismissive about the possibility of moose survival. How is it, they reasonably ask, that they have never seen one, even though they regularly hunt areas where we have found sign? Why hasn't a moose been surprised at a forest edge, when helicopters have roared into countless forest clearings at first light at treetop level, hoping to catch a deer outside the safety of the bush? Or while one was standing or swimming in the water? Or, over the live-capture or intensive-shooting eras, why did no one disturb a moose when helicopters were slowly and systematically beating up the fuchsia faces at low level, forcing hiding deer to flight?

Why indeed? These questions I cannot answer. But I remind those asking them to consider that the forest on the valley floor is thick, the terrain rough, and clear areas small and few. Hunters are cued for red deer behaviour and colouration, and the moose response to helicopters may differ. If, say, 40 deer live in Herrick Creek, and helicopters only occasionally spot one or two, how much less chance do they have of seeing a solitary moose, and when the valley is only sometimes occupied? I am encouraged when helicopter hunters confess that, just occasionally, they will finally shoot some hoary old stag or toothless old hind which has been evading them for nearly a lifetime.

We sat on a mossy log with our lunch, talking about moose senses. Their eyesight is relatively poor, but they are particularly adept at discerning movement. Moose seem at ease in open country in their homeland, probably trusting their vision to pick up predators in terrain where they can either run off or make a stand. A healthy adult moose is more than a match for wolves or bears. Calves are more at risk, although a cow moose will fiercely protect her offspring. In forest, however, moose are open to ambush by predators and may have insufficient room or time to take flight or stand defence. Therefore, it seems, evolution has demanded acute senses of hearing and smell. In contrast, alpine animals such as chamois and tahr live in a noisy environment of avalanche and rockfall. They pay little attention to sounds, but experience has told me their eyesight is truly remarkable.

We split up for the remainder of the afternoon. I hunted high along the interface of slope and valley wall while Marg sidled through thickets of fuchsia and regenerating shrubs lower down. We arranged a meeting time at the lake edge. Sometimes bush-hunting seems futile, given the sensory qualities of our quarry, but it is a pleasant way to develop an awareness of life in the bush, and we always learn something. Skills aside, there is a huge measure of sheer luck involved in finding a moose in New Zealand forest. Maybe moose too had their off days, and we would stumble on one who didn't feel like hiding.

It is a habit of ours at camp to take coffee down to the beach after breakfast, look out over the water, and soak up the mood of the day. Marg was peering intently up the sound when I turned up with the two mugs one morning.

'There's a kayak up there near Oke Island,' she announced.

'Horse poo,' I replied. 'This place is too far away for kayaks.'

'No, you look. Where that band of bush crosses Oke Island. A yellow kayak.'

'Here. Hang onto these.'

I handed over the coffee, went back to camp and returned with binoculars. We took turns propping one another up on a nearby rock for a better view.

'It's a log,' came my verdict.

'It's a kayak.' Marg was adamant.

'Log. A kayak wouldn't be alone.'

'Kayak,' insisted Marg. 'Look, it's pulling away to the right now.'

Sure enough, whatever it was appeared suddenly to make steady progress round the point and vanished from sight. It had seemed the wrong colour for a log. Having argued against a kayak for 15 minutes I was now convinced.

'If he's by himself he could probably do with a yarn, maybe some help. Shall we go and say hello?'

'You mean "she"!' said Marg. 'We should at least go and make sure she's OK.'

'Yeah, let's do that. Give me a hand with the boat.'

'Let's take her a few things.'

We didn't have much in the way of gifts, but there was a freshly baked loaf of bread and some cod fillets.

'Why don't we take a billy and have a brew up with him.' I was warming to the idea. We didn't usually have visitors.

'You can't carry much in those canoes. I'll put a few tins of things together for her. In fact, I'll take some pasta and cheese and we'll have a cook-up on a beach.'

By the time the boat was launched we had each mentally rehearsed conversations with our new friend: sharing news, plans, a tip or two, then relaxing on a remote beach over an unexpected meal. Back-country buddies. Companions in adversity. The Fiordland Club. Need a hand with anything? Spotted you and thought we'd surprise you with a Cup of Tea. No, please take it, we can easily bake another.

We sped up the sound with our packages and turned the point.

'He must be paddling fast.'

'She'll be in the next bay. Can't wait to see her face when we show up!'

But the next bay was empty. Bewildered, we sped round the back of Oke Island. Empty sea.

'Maybe he's pulled ashore for a spell.'

We checked the shores. No sign of life. Fifteen minutes later we gave up, puzzled, and turned for home.

'Hello! Marg, look over here.'

I pointed. A log, quite large, was wallowing in the water, partly submerged, its bark stripped in some recent flood, the newly bared wood yellowish. We looked at each other, then both burst out laughing.

In the evening we tucked in among some low scrubby bushes near the lake, trying to get comfortable. The small tent was well hidden in high fern under a patch of old beeches behind us. It wasn't much of a campsite. Darkness gathered, light rain turned steady. We sat, silent and still, binoculars on hand, trying to ignore the sandflies.

For two mornings running a moose had walked the nearby sandspit and swum the lake, returning late each day. From the prints we guessed it was a cow. We had seen where she had been feeding below the lake, breaking down fuchsia and some small-leaved coprosmas. We had missed her the first day by only a few minutes; her tracks had headed into a rough stand of bush alongside the creek. Marg had had the camera.

'Wait here,' I had whispered to her, heart hammering. 'She'll break out to the right or take to the lake. Either way you'll get a shot of her.'

But we had been too late, or she had hidden up in a place where I was unable to find her, and nothing had come of it. I had tried following tracks but lost them in the heavy cover. Eventually, mystified, we had given it away and continued up the valley. But the next day sign showed she had repeated her movements.

Now we were in position for a third show. Everything was quiet. A few waterfowl bobbed around on the lake: New Zealand scaup, a single blue duck and a pair of paradise duck. Nothing else moved. Light became bleak and grey. Rain continued. Darkness fell. Teeth chattered. Finally, cold, wet and disappointed, we slipped away to the tent to wait for morning.

A short time later rain increased in earnest, thrumming alarmingly on the nylon fly. Strong gusts of wind shook the tent, bringing showers of twigs from above; we became nervous about big overhanging branches. Around midnight came a tremendous sound-and-light show; lightning snapped and the world flashed blue-white. Thunder growled continuously, every few seconds letting rip an earth-vibrating, ear-splitting peal. We stayed awake anxiously on a night too noisy to talk.

Near morning the thunder ceased, but rain still hammered on the tent. We were on the wrong side of the creek; even if it was possible to cross it, I wasn't sure we could get round the bluff alongside the lake en route to camp.

At first light we bundled soaked gear into packs, crossed the waist-high creek, and managed to claw our way round the bluff under a waterfall of run-off. With the tricky parts over we had only a 50-minute, saturated walk back to camp. We moved off, relieved to be safe.

Partway through a tangle of bouldery fuchsia I heard a mushy crack, a slithery thump, a gasp of frustrated anger and a Terrible Word. I was almost afraid to look. A sodden moss-covered log had given way and a sodden moss-covered Marg was face down in the swamp, held there by her pack. I hauled her upright, hardly daring to look at my mud streaked, foul-smelling wife. She caught my eye. There was a twinkle of amusement there.

'Maybe you should have other hobbies, Margie,' I said, 'like needlework or cooking.'

Standing in that lonely place, hair plastered in the pelting rain, hungry, dishevelled, covered in mud, plant debris and moss, we laughed and laughed. It was another round to the moose.

We saw little human sign at our camp in Wet Jacket Arm. Only seldom did a float plane drone high overhead, or the distant rattle of a hunting helicopter waft through the silence. Very occasionally, when storms raged to the west, a fishing boat might steam up for a change of scenery, but there are safer anchorages at more convenient places in the outer sounds, like Luncheon Cove and Beach Harbour, and we had our wilderness more or less to ourselves.

It was therefore a surprise one evening to hear a cheery greeting and see a row of ruddy farmers' faces appear up the short track from the sea, all three dressed in bright-yellow plastic coats and looking round curiously at our camp. It was raining steadily and we had not long come home, peeled off wet clothes for dry ones and lit the fire. We had had a scrub-up and were looking forward to a hot drink and meal before darkness fell, but they insisted we come out to their chartered launch for a drink with them and their wives, who were still aboard, no doubt wondering whether their men were being consumed by cannibals. The

'Tutuko' was cruising the sounds. They had seen our smoke and, beset by curiosity, had tracked us down. We pulled wet parkas back on and filed down the track to their dinghy.

We followed the men into a different world, transported neatly from the wilds of Fiordland into a realistic ship's bar by the closing of the door. Polished wood, bright brass fittings, carpet: we could have been in any imaginatively decorated hotel in inner Christchurch. The atmosphere was hot and thick with cigarette smoke, noisy, crowded and colourful. About eight couples, all neatly dressed and with the women fashionably groomed, exchanged cheerful banter and filled each other with gin. Fiordland, invisible through misted windows, was a million miles away.

There was a brief silence when the door shut behind us, then an inquisitive buzz. We each fielded massive gins and a barrage of questions. Without hats and bulky coats it was revealed, to the astonishment of all, that Marg was Woman. That aroused a lot of interest, especially from the ladies. More questions. We couldn't say anything about moose, but mentioned we were enjoying a holiday in the bush.

It was nearly dark when the skipper called the party to a halt; he had shelter to find. We opened the door, ducking our heads, and were back on deck.

Outside, in the gathering dusk, Wet Jacket Arm was cold and grey. Rain slanted down from leaden clouds. In the mist, subdued charcoal ridges were barely visible. We climbed over the railing with a crew member, back into the dinghy, and clanked ashore, then sloshed up the dark track to camp. We fumbled around in the black, befuddled by gin, trying to find something easy to eat. The fire was out and the ashes cold. Watery mud was running ankle deep through the kitchen area. A precious set of dry clothes was soaked. Our previously inviting camp now looked dreadful. We stumbled off to bed, wet, hungry and unsettled, more than a little dismayed that our simple order had been so easily shattered.

Further up the sound the occupants of the 'Tutuko' were probably shaking their heads over the eccentric couple they had discovered in the bush.

It is impossible not to fall in love with the dolphins of Fiordland. They feature among the moments we cherish from our times there. Although the boat gave us access to the world of these wonderful animals, one of our fondest memories of them came from ashore.

Rain had stopped overnight but the morning was heavy with mist. We took coffee down to the water's edge below camp to watch the sky clear. It was hauntingly beautiful beside the sea, a black-and-white landscape of cloud, bush and still water where black snags were etched like stags' heads. Overhanging trees framed the silent picture. We could see glimpses of forest slopes inside towering, motionless white clouds. The far side of the sound showed under the fog as a fine, dark line. It was so hushed we felt we should whisper.

Then came a rhythmic sighing—an exhalation—and a regular splashing. Through the mist came a group of dolphins, perhaps eight of them, making for an invisible headland. They passed close in front of us, clearing the water with effortless grace, seemingly in slow motion, black and shiny against a backdrop of pure white, then disappeared, their sighs and splashes sounding long out of sight. Like the closing of a curtain, the stillness resumed. Afraid of breaking the spell, we finally glanced at each other, shaking our heads in disbelief. Had it been real? Or just a perfect dream?

12

May 1994

It began as another awful day, then the wind turned southwest and it became very cold, with snow down to midslope. We certainly did not expect Max's return, but the sudden roar of a helicopter brought us to the beach. Bill Black's Squirrel landed with a rush of flailing shrubbery and drops of water, travelling horizontally for a change. Max's cheerful face emerged, with another we knew to be that of Guy Marris. We helped the two of them unload an alarming amount of gear from the rear of the helicopter, then the tail-boom compartment, and finally the side lockers. Anxious about weather and fuel, Blackie took off immediately after the thumbs-up all clear.

We stood in light rain, surveying the mountain of equipment. Two big cameras, two huge tripods, a generator for battery charging and fuel for it, sound equipment, batteries, lights, a tracking rail, seats, even an inflatable canoe for filming and transport on the lake. There were personal belongings, tentage, food, and a heap of unidentifiables. It dawned on us that making a film was not going to be just Max looking over our shoulder with the little Hi-8. How on earth could you hunt the wary moose with all this junk? It was a worry.

It was good to see Max again, though, to meet Guy and to catch up on news. Marg and I helped carry equipment under cover, then put a billy on the fire for tea and read newspapers while Max and Guy set up their tents. Film folk are more generous with food than we allow ourselves to be, so we had already made a hole in a packet of biscuits and some chocolate when they turned up at the campfire.

'OK, you two,' Max began, 'how've things been going?'

'Mostly good,' I said through a mouth full of goodies. 'We've been back to the head of the valley. There's still a moose there. We believe it's a bull. The best news is that there's another, a cow we think, and she's now living below the lake on these northern faces.'

We headed off early next morning in showers and low cloud. Now we were four I was keen to use our numbers to find our local moose. Marg and I, together and alone, had stalked her over the previous few days without success. She had lived above the lake, then commuted twice daily, swimming across it, and had now shifted below. She was unbelievably handy, residing only 40 minutes' travel from camp, living in exactly the same locality as the animal I had chased all over this place on the first survey, 22 years before.

We quickly picked up sign, some of it new, inside the edge of the scrubby forest: small-leaved coprosmas and similar shrubs broken or bent; marble-leaf stripped and freshly barked; broadleaf branches pulled down from high up, some branches as thick as Marg's wrist; a bedding place, the sedges flattened; piles of droppings, too big for even the biggest red stag; footprints, big tapered impressions with their distinctive dewclaw marks. Maybe she had been watching us from somewhere—she would almost certainly have heard us. But I feared things had come too easily for the filmmakers to be impressed with how fortunate they were, surrounded by definitive sign so quickly. They had not yet realised how difficult it would be to hunt, find and photograph an animal with such acute senses. Nonetheless, it was a marvellous start, and we could easily become lucky. Max brought the Hi-8 for the day and was busy recording the sign with it.

I thought if we drove the area we might be able to shift the moose.

Even if she slipped off from close quarters, disturbed by one of us, another might catch sight of her. We split up, trying to remain about 100 metres apart, and quietly worked in one direction for over an hour, then back at another level, further from the forest edge. The bush, shrubs and ground cover were a dozen times denser than 20 years previously, and visibility was very limited. Our quarry could have been sitting tight in cover while we passed nearby—from earlier hunters' accounts, that seemed likely. And with the unavoidable noise of our passage through the bush, both underfoot and from brushing past vegetation, we could be nowhere near quiet enough. Our moose could probably have heard us from a long way off and moved away, far ahead of our swathe. I thought of Ivan Murdoch sneaking around barefoot. It had worked for him.

We drew a blank, perhaps not unexpectedly, and headed back to camp midafternoon, wet, cold, and out of ideas for the moment. We tried the same approach the next day for a couple of hours, then searched alone. The moose was still around—we found feeding sign additional to that of the day before. I hunted high up against the valley wall and surprised a red stag from five metres, my heart stopping for a moment. Later, Marg and Guy told us that shortly after Max and I had left them, while they were still together, they had heard a crack and saw branches shaking only 50 metres away. Our moose grabbing lunch from an overhanging branch? Maybe—there was sign all around. But they saw nothing further and we will never know. Later Guy put up another animal from close range, but after questioning him closely we agreed it was probably a deer. Back at camp, wet, weary and exasperated, we pondered what else we could do. It was a familiar feeling.

Rain poured overnight and all the next day. Marg stayed at camp to catch some fish for the evening meal, while Max, Guy and I went back up the valley for the afternoon and tried variations of our previous moves, but without success. Our moose was not far away, unperturbed by the traffic, or at least not enough to vacate the area. We returned, soaked and frustrated. It helped to come back to Marg's campfire, soup and freshly baked bread and a line-up of freshly caught blue cod.

We brooded over the problem of getting our moose photograph. Clearly, trying to stalk the bloody thing was not working. Perhaps we could fly-camp on the spot, watch the semi-open spots, and catch a glimpse of her. Marg and I had tried a little of that already, but each time had been defeated by weather and the limited outlook. Maybe we would hear her feeding and be able to sneak up close enough?

It was time for some lateral thinking. Marg's suggestion of floating around in helium balloons was eventually rejected, but the third mug of whisky that came with it was not. Max and Guy were keen for a hide to be put up somewhere to house an observer with a camera. That meant a site with an overview. But there seemed no such places. A tree? We had already checked—there was none suitable. A slip or clearing? There was nowhere obvious, but the lake did have a steep face on its northeastern side. Somewhere on the ridge above? Maybe. Guy had noticed a gap in the trees on the ridge line and a small area of ferns, maybe an old slip. We would check that tomorrow.

It was still pouring with rain the next day and we waited until early afternoon, hoping it would ease. It didn't, so we pulled on wet clothing again and went up the valley, this time crossing Herrick Creek and climbing through the steep bush. We worked past a bluff and eventually found ourselves on the ridge crest, and not long afterwards came the slip we had been looking for. With some clearing of shrubs and ferns the outlook was nearly perfect: about 200 metres above the lake, high enough to look into the scrubby forest for some distance behind the swampy flats the moose sometimes used. There was even an upended kamahi to tie a tent fly to. We rigged up a shelter with a couple of pepperwood poles, and after some searching found an acceptable tent site and cleared it of ferns. This would do very nicely. The main drawback was the fairly restricted field of view, but if our moose kept to her movements of the last few days, we would have a sighting. Additionally, it was a perfect spot for one of the big cameras to make a movie of her, with the problem of distance being solved by the powerful lens.

Soaked to the skin, and cold now, we slithered back down the slope, crossed the creek and returned to camp. For the first time in ages I thought we had made a breakthrough. It felt thrilling! A sighting, and a photograph, suddenly seemed inevitable if we were patient enough. I decided I could be very patient indeed.

Betweentimes Max and Guy had been using the big cameras around camp and down at the sound, Max filming while Guy held an umbrella overhead and beat off sandflies. They had filmed a few domestic activities, some scenics, birdlife, and out in the boat one evening while we had caught a few fish. Max had set the camera up several times on a tripod, on a rocky point at the sea's edge, for time-lapse sequences of cloud, mist and rain. It was always beautiful there, whatever the weather. However, the cameras were not enjoying the trip. One was a 16mm film camera, the other was electronic, and together they were worth about $150,000. Neither was coping with the all-pervading dampness of Fiordland, and to Max's despair kept fogging up and generally sulking. There was little he could do while we lived under tentage. Our only source of clean heat was a low-wattage light bulb run from the generator being used to recharge batteries. Max spent hours in his tent each night trying to dry the equipment.

'If the cameras can't handle wet conditions,' I remarked quietly to Marg, 'it's going to be a bloody short film.'

It stopped raining that night for the first time in days. We retraced our tracks of the day before, loaded with gear for Max and Guy's camp at the Lookout. Partway up rain set in again, harder than before, this time with some impressive thunder and lightning. Marg and I helped set up camp. Around late afternoon, with no sign of life on the flats below, it was time for the two of us to leave. There was unlikely to be any animal movement until nearly nightfall. We wished the others luck and set off.

I was more than a little envious. Maybe, despite my own years of effort, our visitors would be the first to see the moose. But the Lookout camp had room for only two, and the camera needed the two film experts. Marg and I would have our chance later. Anyhow, I kept my mouth shut and my jealousies to myself.

If the rain had been hard that afternoon, it surpassed itself during the night, with thunder and lightning ripping the blackness apart. Next morning the downpour persisted, a continuous torrent from above. Our plans had been to revisit the Lookout but the creek, thundering nearby, was advertising that this would be impossible, so we lay low. We wondered if Max and Guy had a picture of our moose.

By early afternoon the rain had eased. I went up the valley to look at the creek, decided I could cross—just—and carried on. Max and Guy had endured a wet time but faithfully kept guard over the clearing, despite losing vision to thick rain and mist much of the time. We had all had rain, but up here they had had a better view of it. They were due out the next day if the helicopter could make it, so we packed up, leaving tent and shelter fly in place. Marg and I would continue the vigil.

Back at camp that night we celebrated progress—the little we had made so far—on the documentary. Never mind, we finished the rum anyway. Constant rain was a problem for equipment, and a photo of the Big One had so far eluded us, but Max would leave us the Hi-8. On full zoom we would still get an acceptable image of the moose from the Lookout. Even with the telephoto lens on our still camera, the colour, size and shape of a moose would show up easily after enlargement.

Anyway, it had been fun, and we were still in with a chance as Marg and I had five more days.

'This would be the time to have a remote camera out there,' said Max that night. Natural History had photographed kakapo using heat-and-movement-triggered cameras without the presence of a clumsy hide or observer. He thought we could borrow a unit or two if they were not being used for other projects. We tried to think of alternatives. Outside the small circle of light from the camp, the night brooded blackly. Rain spattered on the overhead fly. Water dripped brightly, and green ferns bobbed and shone under the drops. It was no place to be hunched under a tree overnight, chancing a glimpse of a moose at first light. Even in a hide a watcher's movement, noise and scent, however slight, could be detected by an alert moose. But a camera out there, keeping station in all conditions? Patiently watching for us, snapping off a photograph when an animal crossed in front? It seemed a great idea.

The rain was lighter the next day. Blackie arrived for the pick-up at 1.00 p.m. Max and Guy, wet, unshaven and covered in mud, leaves and strings of moss, bundled their gear into the helicopter looking like two recently captured desperados. There would be a couple of divorces on the cards if they turned up at home looking like that, Marg suggested. The helicopter lifted off. Their relieved wave through misted-up Perspex was our last view of them.

Silence. Alone again. Marg and I read the newspapers Blackie had thoughtfully brought, already limp with moisture, and tried to dry our sleeping bags using Andy Leigh's body-warmth method. We were waiting for the creek to drop so we could return to the Lookout.

Not long before dark, four days later, we stepped out of the helicopter, marvelling at being on firm ground again. We had spent three days at the Lookout, finally leaving with just enough time to pack up camp and get a late afternoon lift out to Te Anau. Our surveillance had yielded no sign of the moose, or even a deer. In five weeks we had had only four days without rain—an unlucky spell even for Fiordland, Blackie noted.

Moose or not, the trip had been very successful. We knew a lot more now, and there was a film in the making. But we had run out of time and, quite frankly, steam. Our clothes were moulding and our skin crinkling from the never-ending damp. In ten days we would be back in Vientiane, trying to adjust to a life beyond the lower flats of Herrick Creek. For a time, anyway.

13

August 1994

We had looked forward to this day for a long time: the return to Wet Jacket Arm to service the video cameras. Did we have a moose movie?

Natural History's technical whiz for developing remote-camera equipment was Ray Sharp. He had made up two video units for us, and we had sited them more than a month earlier. Now was the time of reckoning.

Dennis Egerton's Hughes 500 settled uneasily onto the swampy ground at the upper clearing. It was a cool, overcast day with the odd rain shower. Herrick Creek looked cold and uninviting. Having walked to this familiar place so many times, it felt surreal and intrusive to arrive suddenly and noisily by helicopter.

Max and Ray were on board, but there was no room for Marg; all floor space was taken up by the 12 car batteries needed to run the two systems we had in place. Dennis switched off the helicopter engine while the rest of us hurried over to the first of the two sites.

Each site had two video cameras, activated by an infrared sensor in the same way as a home-security light system is triggered by movement or heat within short range. A black-and-white video camera recorded for 60 seconds when tripped, then switched itself off. The other camera, a colour one, did the same, but in addition was set to automatic time-lapse mode, exposing a single frame every four seconds without being triggered. Each 'alarm' was recorded and listed alongside a sequential time code. Both cameras recorded onto the same tape, and the system switched itself on at daybreak and off at nightfall.

Everything seemed as we had left it. The deer trail at which the black-and-white camera was pointing had been used, but not recently. The colour camera set on time-lapse covered a small bush clearing to its right. We removed the moss camouflage and layers of waterproof sheeting. The equipment was dry inside—a good sign—but the batteries were dead. The cameras had been in place five weeks and Ray had not been sure how long batteries would last in these conditions.

Without power restored we would learn nothing. For 20 minutes we trudged the swamp between helicopter and camera site, exchanging batteries. Ray hooked the new ones up along with a monitor he had brought, like a small TV screen. The unit sprang to life with a flicker of coloured test lights and the odd beep.

'Well,' Ray murmured, half to himself, 'the tape's pretty well finished, so it's been working OK.'

He rewound it and we crowded over his shoulder waiting for the replay.

'Seventeen alarms,' he announced triumphantly, then pressed 'Play' while we fidgeted expectantly. The small screen flickered into life, reproducing the image of the clearing in colour, with the racing shadows of time-lapse. Ray fast-forwarded the tape to the first alarm point. We chewed our nails. The image switched from time-lapse to real time, and we expected our first animal. Deer? Moose?

Nothing.

'Oh, that's a pity. Must have been tripped by a bird.'

Ray forwarded the tape to the next alarm. We breathed again.

'Another bird maybe. See, it's triggering, but nothing's coming up on the screen.'

Next one was the same again. And again, and again, and again.

'Poop!'

'Maybe the wind's triggering it.'

'Hello! We've got something here. Look!'

Our flagging attention revived in a millisecond. The colour image suddenly flipped off and a black-and-white picture of the trail in front of us appeared on the screen. For a second, nothing; then, sharp and clear, a red deer hind slowly and calmly came from behind the moss-covered buttress of the beech tree, head low, walked forward a few paces, mobile ears on medium-alert, then stepped back and disappeared. The screen continued to show the trail for a time, then switched back to time-lapse of the clearing. Then the flickering shot suddenly cleared to a real-time colour image of the same deer walking across the clearing. She exited right. The tape resumed its time-lapse mode. There was a ragged cheer from us all. It had worked!

The remainder of the tape had only false alarms, like the beginning. The batteries had lasted just nine days. That was disappointing. Nevertheless, the system had proved itself and we were now aware of some of its limitations. We reboarded the helicopter and lifted off for camera number two, at the head of the lake.

I had felt the lake site was a good one—in April our cow moose had walked past many times—but now there was little animal tracking nearby and the videos had recorded only empty scenes. The large number of alarms were almost certainly bird-triggered—two tomtits flitting around the sensor tree seemed to confirm this. To avoid repeating the problem Ray adjusted the sensitivity of the unit.

Large diameter stems of pate (Schefflera digitata) browsed by moose. Herrick Creek, 1972.

Marg examines a fuschia (Fuschia excorticata) bush, broken and stripped by moose. Herrick Creek, 1994.

Bark biting on pate. Note the width of the incisor scrape (compared to fingers). Herrick Creek, 1996.

Typical breakage, barking and stripping by moose on a fuschia. Herrick Creek, 1995.

The trunk of this small totara (above) was freshly stripped by antler rubbings. Because of this and other signs, we suspected a bull moose was resident in upper Herrick Creek in April 1995.

The same totara (left) fifteen months later.

Three-finger (Neopanax simplex) is a clear favourite of moose for its fleshy leaves, bark and soft stems. Herrick Creek, 1972.

Jim Hilton alongside a fuschia typically wrenched down by moose. Note the litter of stripped branches on the ground nearby. Herrick Creek, 1972.

Browse line created by moose on fuschia; Jim Hilton shows how high it is. Red deer, even rearing up on hind legs, can reach only just to beyond head height. Henry Burn, 1972.

A comparison of droppings: suspected moose alongside typical red deer pellets.

We were absent, searching the upper valley, when a moose took the top out of this three-finger on the beach near main camp at Herrick Creek, 1996.

This wineberry (Aristotelia serrata) branch was broken down and stripped of leaves only 60 metres from a remote camera site. Herrick Creek, 1996.

Red stag and bull moose forefeet, compared. Note the difference in position of the dew claws.

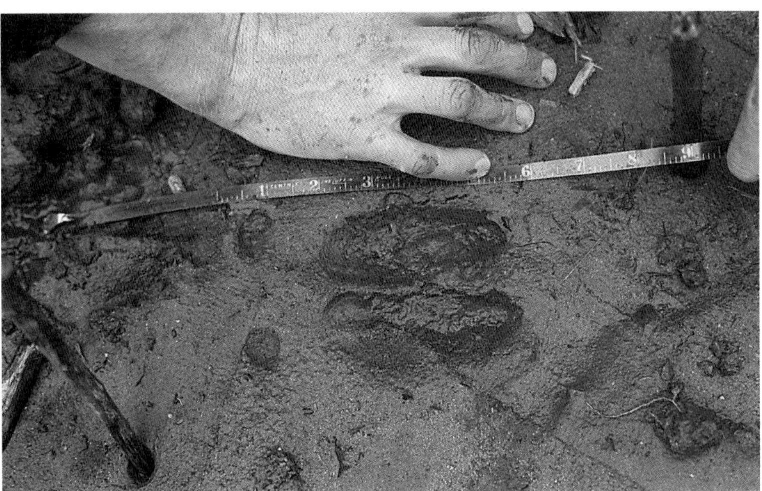

Suspected moose hoofprints, bigger than red deer and with the dew claw imprints showing even in firm underfoot conditions.

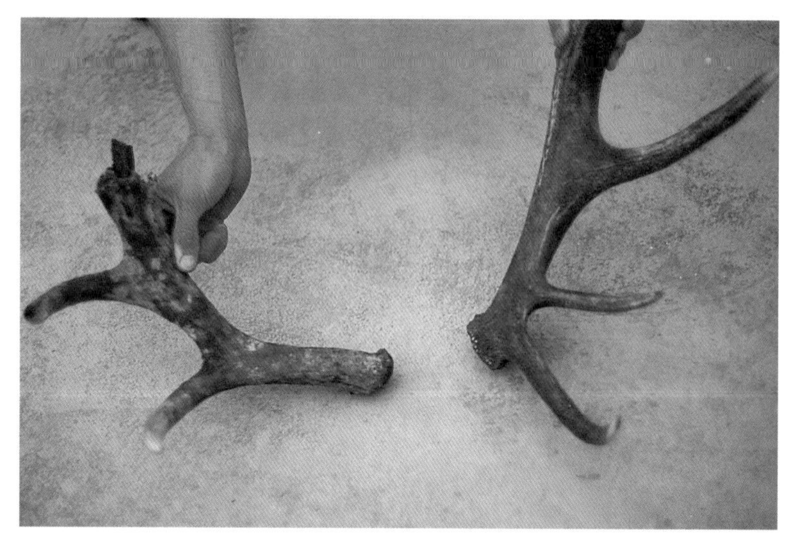

The cast moose antler (left) picked up opposite Oke Island, Wet Jacket Arm, 1972, compared to to a red deer antler.

Seaforth Valley above Loch Maree, home for New Zealand moose in the 1930s.On the '72 survey we first found moose sign at the top of Bessie Burn, to the right of Tripod Hill, in the centre of the photograph.

The lake forms a true obstruction in the valley, channelling animal traffic along only a few routes, and we decided to retain the camera at the site. There are not many places in Herrick Creek where a helicopter can land, and fewer options for a camera system requiring such heavy batteries. Tapes were replaced, equipment waterproofed and hidden under moss, and we prepared to leave. Maybe as winter gave way to spring the route would get more use.

Dennis started the helicopter and we lifted off as rain began to fall. Wrapped in our own thoughts, there wasn't much to say. Remote photography seemed a great idea, but it was not going to be easy.

14

March-April 1995

Red deer and moose rut during late March and early April. It is a good time to hunt, for the males of both species are active and, in their own ways, vocal. Marg and I, just back from Asia, were intent on another month's moose search during the 1995 season. Natural History wanted to be involved for ten days' filming, some with just Max, focusing on the hunt, but mostly with more crew, looking at background life in the bush. We had a ten-day head start on the circus.

With few exceptions, we told no one about our moose searches. It seemed a bit corny and we didn't want people to think of us as a New Zealand version of yeti or sasquatch freaks. Friends knew we enjoyed tramping and camping, and our frequent absences in Laos made us only occasional additions to the Wanaka landscape anyway. Closer friends knew we had a passion for Fiordland, and a few guessed about moose, but almost no one knew anything about the film. That was the way we wanted things.

Once the documentary was released there would be a flurry of interest, hopefully focused on the animal itself. My ambition to photograph a moose face to face remained undiminished; a shot by a remote camera would also be wonderful, if rather like winning a game of rugby by kicking penalties. Either would greatly help the film. In the broader picture, I hoped this would help prompt debate about some of the lesser game animals which I felt no longer deserved their status as pests.

'Isn't it great,' Marg said one day as we carried the inflatable ashore, 'that each time we take the boat out something really special happens.'

We had been returning to camp from searching another valley, boating past a small headland we called Seal Point as there were usually a couple of friendly fur seals there. As we had drawn alongside, we had noticed a flipper extended vertically above the water, and against the rocky wall a cascade of flashing silver, repeated every minute or so. We had changed course, shut down the outboard and let the boat glide close by. It had been a remarkable display of cooperative fishing by two seals.

Underwater was a dense shoal, about twice the size of our boat, of herring-like fish. One seal patrolled the edge of this flexible cloud, head beneath the surface and both flippers extended, one below and the other above. The other seal shepherded the shoal until it was compact and in position, then charged into the centre, scattering the small fish in panic. Some of the fish pelted towards an increasingly steep rock incline which began underwater and extended above. Fleeing up the slope, some of these became airborne and slithered back down the rock, and the hunting seal would snap them up before gently back-stroking into position with a full mouth. A brief pause, and the action would resume: herding, a chase, a flurry, and more fish.

We took the boat to only a few metres away.

'Drop me off,' Marg whispered, picking up Max's video camera. She worked her way around the rocky point until the entire sequence was being played out at her feet, and began filming. I joined her.

'Let me know when he's making his run,' she called quietly, 'and I'll try for an underwater shot.'

I was above and could see deeper into the water. 'OK, wait a minute. Ready? Coming...now!'

Marg was kneeling by the water's edge. Around her ankles swept a wave of fish. A split second later the seal surged out behind them. For a shocked second the two were eyeball to eyeball, half an arm's length apart. Both started backwards, Marg laughing, the seal with a look of stunned astonishment. Then, safely back in the water, the seal back-paddled off, head high and looking back, indignation written all over its furry face. Marg looked up, eyes alight.

'How was that?'

'Brilliant,' I said, laughing behind my own camera.

'Probably not good enough for the film,' she said, 'but what a lovely thing to be part of.'

We dropped back into the boat and left our two friends to it. They had already regained their composure and were back to fishing.

It was Marg's 37th birthday. We had been campbound during days of storm, were tired of eating rice and were aching for a stretch. Then the wind dropped and the sound was calm. We donned wet-weather gear and carried the boat to the water. Nothing struck us as being better than fresh fish for a special day.

We drifted quietly on an incoming tide close to a mossy, dripping rock wall, rods out each side of the boat, waiting. Suddenly, without warning, rod tips nodded simultaneously and for a moment we thought we had hooked each other's line. We reeled in. A two- and a three-kilo groper flapped in the bottom of the boat. No problems now! That was a relief. Macaroni was no dish for a birthday.

'I bet the main reason you bring me to Fiordland for my birthday is to save buying me a present,' she challenged, with a twinkle in her eye.

Marg was being unfair; it was only her second birthday in Wet Jacket Arm. I tried to evade her interrogation.

'Margie, the god of the sea has just delivered you the gift of a beautiful hapuka.'

'Not her, silly. You. Where's your present?'

Time for some quick thinking.

'Of course, sweetheart. Sorry. I didn't have time to wrap it.'

I handed her my groper, tongue firmly in cheek.

'Thank you darling,' she responded with a wink. 'It's everything I've ever dreamed of.'

It was a perfect night, cold and clear. Three of us were at the dry rock near the Henry Burn–Herrick Creek saddle. The last of the campfire cast a flickering light on the rock wall above; stars showed through the forest canopy. We lay in sleeping bags listening to a morepork. It was too peaceful to break the silence by talking, too pleasant to contemplate sleep. Then, not far below, a red stag roared. Among such tranquillity the primeval bellow made my scalp prickle. I glanced at Marg, who was wide-eyed. I could imagine the stag picking his way along the trail just below, head cocked for a response, ivory-tipped antlers held high. He roared again. Silence. Then another answered, far below in the Henry Burn. Silence. Long, long silence. Somewhere faintly was the rush of a distant waterfall. The morepork resumed its haunting cry.

One day we discovered that the bulge in Max's pack was a megaphone. A megaphone? He pulled out another small package: a tape recorder.

'Here's a way to attract a bull moose,' he told us. 'Put in a tape of a cow's call, and stand back.'

It had been sent from a contact in Canada. We envisaged clambering up trees as the ground shook with the thundering hooves of lovesick moose.

We slipped quietly through the forest near the edge of the top clearing at Herrick Creek. There was a moose close by. Everywhere we looked there was fresh sign: fuchsia pulled down here, lacebark there; a heavy kamahi branch crushed to splinters and bent at fingertip height; big footprints. Percy Lyes had shot his bull very close to this place. We moved together, tense and alert. No hurry. Stop. Wait. Look. A few more steps. Easing through pepperwood, then, immediately ahead, the trunk of a medium-sized totara glared brightly in the dull bush, stripped of bark for most of its circumference from knee to head height, and moss knocked off the trunk for another half-metre. Fresh antler rubbing! Red deer stags thrash shrubbery and smallish saplings in the frenzy of rutting, but I had never seen a tree this size taken on. Moose? I thought so. Had the big animal stood here only a few days before and leaned his antlers hard into this tree, pushing and swiping at an imaginary rival? Whatever it was, the tines had left heavy scores in the hard totara. We took a photograph. Robin Francis Smith had taken one near here in 1952 that was almost identical. We resumed our stalk with expectation rising.

A stag roared in the bush on the far side of the biggest clearing. It took us 45 minutes to manoeuvre opposite, hoping to see him, but he kept inside the forest edge. We quietly crossed the creek under cover and stopped, hidden by dense scrub. We waited 15 minutes. Silence. The stag roared again. This time he was answered by another far up the face. Somewhere, quiet and not far away, was a bull moose.

It seemed a good time to try Max's toy, although we risked blowing our contact. He quietly took out the megaphone and recorder, waited a few seconds, then flipped the tiny switch. A peal of noise burst across the clearing, an undulating bellow, something like a heifer bawling. We waited tensely in the shocked silence which followed. Nothing. No sound from the stag. Nothing from his rival. Twenty minutes.

No moose.

October 1995

Max wanted some aerial shots which required using a helicopter on a day of reasonable weather. Among them were to be general overviews of the sounds to show landscape and scale, tracking shots of Marg and me in the boat, and some footage of Supper Cove and the Seaforth Valley, the starting point for the Fiordland moose story. At Herrick Creek a southwesterly cleared the sky, and by late afternoon the weather was brilliant. We radioed in the evening to ensure Blackie was available, then sat round the campfire with a large rum, discussing the next few days.

Midmorning on a cool but perfect day. Marg and I were thrumming up Wet Jacket Arm in the boat on obsidian-black water. Our wake curved behind us. Only the breeze from our travel flapped the nylon spray cover. With just two people on board, plus lightweight packs and emergency gear, the little inflatable seemed on the point of soaring. Supper Cove was 50 kilometres away; making 15 knots we would be there in two hours.

There had been few fine days over the previous three weeks, so it was great to be out on the water away from dripping bush. Wonderful, exhilarating freedom in a breathtakingly beautiful landscape. Thirty dolphins joined us for a few kilometres, their effortless leaps only enhancing the feeling of joy and abandon. It was the stuff of dreams.

We turned into Acheron Passage, the long narrow gap between Resolution Island and the mainland. I am nervous about this stretch of water—it has given us some anxious moments in the past. But that day even the Acheron was magic.

A short time later Marg suddenly pulled off her woollen hat and ran her fingers through her hair. A puzzled expression quickly turned to horror.

'What's up?' I asked.

'Ewwww, *yuk!* Maggots!'

On the back of her hand and in writhing clusters on her hat were maggots—tens, no, dozens and dozens of them. Earlier I had noticed a few bluebottles around camp; they have a habit of blowing woollen gear, especially wet wool, which has a musty smell as it dries.

'Yuk! Look at them all. Horrible filthy things. I'm throwing this hat overboard.'

'You can't throw away a perfectly good hat,' I said reasonably, hoping there were no maggots on my own. 'They're only little grubs. It's the flies that are dirty, not the wee grubs.'

'Well swap me then. I'll take your hat.'

'Your hat'd look stupid on me.'

'Who cares? There's only the two of us.'

'Here, take the outboard. I'll get rid of them. There, look. Gone. Don't be silly.'

The hat was suspiciously retrieved and inspected minutely.

'Ha! You missed some.'

More aggravated handwork.

Silence.

'What? What! What are you laughing at, you great ape?'

'Hi there maggot head,' I chuckled, dodging the mock baleful glare.

Silence. I couldn't resist twisting the knife further, and giggled.

'Now what?'

'I'll tell Max. It'd make a nice little sequence: mama chimpanzee looking for nits.'

'Don't you dare!'

I was trespassing on the grounds of feminine pride, more dangerous than any Fiordland bog. I wisely shut my mouth.

'Around here somewhere,' I offered a little later, changing the subject to safer ground, 'Charlie West and his mates tried to lasso a bull moose they found swimming. In the early 1930s.'

Charlie West's name crops up in some of the more colourful moose stories from that era. Ray Tinsley had later written of this incident in his book 'The Call of the Moose'.

'What happened?'

'They finally killed it with an axe and hauled the carcass on board with the boat's winch.'

'Poor thing.'

It wasn't too hard to picture the uneven contest between fishing boat and beast. Thoughtful now, we turned into the main arm of Dusky Sound.

Dusky was idyllic: tiny islets and bush-clad, rocky headlands; the forest a mosaic of textures, every hue of green, in the bright sunlight.

In Supper Cove I switched the outboard off and lifted the prop; we scrunched onto the pebble beach in front of the boatshed. The helicopter had just arrived. We held a quick conference while Blackie took the Squirrel's passenger-side door off and rigged a harness to enable Max to film from the air. We pushed the boat back to the water, climbed in, and pulled the outboard into life. Over the next hour Marg and I buzzed around the lower sound while the helicopter positioned itself above us at various levels. From the corner of my eye I could see Max's long legs dangling out of the open doorway, at times only a few metres away. We headed up the Seaforth estuary. I had to stand to find the channel, but still maintain the boat's speed to prevent coming off the plane. Half-submerged logs flashed alongside; just touching one of them would have had me cartwheeling over the front, legs and arms flailing on film which would no doubt be played later at the staff Christmas party, along with other cock-ups. It was difficult to keep a straight face.

Soon after, the helicopter took off back to Te Anau. We hitched the national park dinghy to our inflatable and towed Max and Julian Grimmond around for more filming, ship to ship. Finally, Max happily nodded his satisfaction and we turned back towards Supper Cove. It was evening, and—luxury time—we were to spend the night in a hut!

Supper Cove is attractive to visitors. It is the only point in Dusky Sound serviced by a walking track, and its simple shelter is a rare presence in those parts. For company that night we had four hunters who had flown in a few days before and a tramper who had walked down the Seaforth. They were entertaining enough; the hunters were farmers from South Otago, the tramper an eccentric Yorkshireman. But there was little space for another five of us. The hut was festooned inside with drying clothes and littered with packs and boots, while everyone was trying to cook on separate primuses. We piled our gear on the verandah, waiting for some room, and watched the moon come up over the placid water. There was plenty to talk about—Supper Cove, the Seaforth mouth, the Henry Burn. Much of the history of New Zealand moose had taken place here. Eventually activity inside the hut lulled and we cleared a spot for our cooker.

The morning was not too inviting for sea voyages, with slightly grey weather and a ruffle of wind, but one night in a hut full of people snoring, blowing off and crashing around for a midnight pee had been too much.

Max, Marg and I dodged breakfast and the chaos of another round of cooking, loaded ourselves into the inflatable, and headed thankfully back towards our Wet Jacket home. We were carrying enough personal gear to camp out safely if need be, and Max sat up front with the camera to record any visual treats on the way. The extra load meant that however we rearranged our weight it was impossible for the boat to plane, so we were obliged to sledge along with the engine labouring at full throttle.

The inflatable felt unresponsive, surly and vulnerable.

Opposite Cooper Island we caught a brisk southwesterly breeze and had to endure an uncomfortable chop and flying spray. Conditions became alarming closer to Passage Point, and we pounded our way along anxiously. There was nowhere to land, but we knew the boat was not about to sink—that is, unless we were unlucky enough to run into submerged branches invisible in the tousled water.

We eventually turned into the Acheron. The wind was behind us now and the chop eased, and not long after we headed into Wet Jacket Arm. Away from the southwesterly, the sea was calm and the sun warm. It became hard to remember the earlier discomfort. We stopped on a stony beach to empty the boat of water, boiled the billy, then continued the journey. The remainder of the trip down the sound was a delight. Finally, we ploughed into the beach at Herrick Creek, nearly four hours after leaving Supper Cove and almost out of fuel. We upended the boat and hung clothes to dry in the sun, feeling like country yokels just back from a hassled trip to the city.

'Let's hope they never put a hut in here,' said Max.

15

Moose hunts 1930s and 1950s

The low bush saddle linking Dusky Sound and Wet Jacket Arm is not too difficult by Fiordland standards. Passes like it are not common; this one was first noticed by Jim Muir and Eddie Herrick in 1929 when they were exploring the Henry Burn. In March 1930 the two men returned and searched the valley more thoroughly after they found the Seaforth unrewarding and in flood. They discovered no trophies there, but 'I beg to report having shot a cow moose with three legs,' Herrick wrote afterwards,'the fourth leg being off below the stifle joint. It was obvious it had met with some injury, gangarine [sic] had set in and she had lost her leg. She was consequently in very low condition, and judging by her teeth, not young and had never bred.' It seems likely this cow was the female reported as breaking a leg at the time of liberation, 20 years earlier.

The herd's potential had been struck a double blow: one young female had already been shot while another, injured, had evidently failed to breed. Capital females numbered only four. Difficulties also remained for the others, for Herrick continued: 'I also found a dead moose calf that had apparently aborted, as it was without any hair.'

Herrick and Muir returned again to hunt the 1934 season, once more trying the Seaforth unsuccessfully before turning to the Henry Burn, where they were hot on the tracks of a bull moose they never saw. After a gruelling month they returned to Supper Cove for their prearranged pick-up, but they remained intrigued by the pass through to Wet Jacket Arm, and Herrick persuaded Mr Thomson, the owner of the 'Pegasus', to extend their trip just two more days so they could explore the unknown and unnamed valley. He agreed, and the 'Pegasus' made her way to Wet Jacket Arm.

There are not many New Zealanders who have heard the grunts of a bull moose coming at them through heavy cover, at the height of the rut. Eddie Herrick, Jim Muir and Thomson did, and I'll bet their hair stood on end.

Herrick's diary relates the events of that day in April 1934:

> Left Schooner 8am with Jim & Thomson. Went up [Herrick Creek] to left of...lake very bad going, bad bush, rocky & very steep, arrived at head about 10am hunted all around head of lake found very fresh tracks. Decided to explore further inland. While going up through very bad area of high rocks and ferns heard noise in bush coming towards us, we all crouched down & decided it was a moose, after waiting a bit grunting getting closer we indistinctly made him out through the trees, rocks, ferns. After waiting we saw he was a good bull, getting a view of his shoulder I fired and he went down but rose again... I fired again & hit him in the neck, he then fell... We found we had shot a 13 pointer with very good palmation at the prime of his life about 8 or 9 years old—although in poor condition. We photographed him...

Thomson looked for a better way back round the lake while the others were taking the head and skin from the moose. The western side looked possible with the use of a rope, but they had a very difficult time climbing that way with the trophy and the rest of their gear, and they reached the boat well after nightfall.

Eddie Herrick had won his second moose trophy, and the valley was later named in his honour. This was only the second bull moose to be shot under licence, but it was also the last. The dream that had inspired the liberations—the orderly and licensed hunting of big game animals—had ended.

Seventeen years later the solid bang of a .303 rolled round the upper Henry Burn. Robin Francis Smith stood doubtfully alongside a dead cow moose. Minutes later Percy Lyes turned up, camera still in hand. He had disturbed the animal on the faces above and had been chasing it through the bush trying to get a photograph.

They had struck fresh hoofprints on the river terrace earlier and had split up, hoping for a shot at a bull. The commotion of Percy's chase had had Robin scrambling through thick scrub, swamp and mud. He had caught a brief glimpse of the animal: 'it was HUGE and I knew it was a moose. I thought it was a bull.'

A snap shot and it was dead. Francis Smith's regret at shooting a cow still lingers after 45 years. In his letter to me of June 1996, he wrote: 'as if life was not difficult enough for them, hanging on by a thread down there in that country that is so inhospitable and for which they are so unsuited'.

It was Francis Smith's second moose hunt. The year before he had walked into the Seaforth from Lake Manapouri and the Spey River with Max Curtis—a tough trip with no sign of moose. In April 1951 they had returned with Curtis's deer-culling mate, Percy Lyes, flying into Supper Cove on the new amphibian service. They had found old moose sign in the Seaforth and picked up three moose skeletons, one a young bull, dead only about two years. Like Herrick and Muir before them, they had been enticed by the pass through to Wet Jacket Arm. Now they were already planning a trip for the following year. But on that trip the prize would go to Percy Lyes.

It was not a hunt for moose that brought Jim Mackintosh to Herrick Creek in August 1951, but a quest to find axis deer. Axis, or cheetal, are small, spotted deer. They are attractive and shy, native to India. The three females and two males released at Supper Cove in 1908 were the fourth liberation of the species in New Zealand, the intention being, as with other releases, to form a trophy herd. Mackintosh was an acclimatisation society officer based near Invercargill. His interest in the wildlife and history of the sounds often found him taking his month's annual leave there, exploring in his small boat. But this time, with Allan Harrison, he flew by amphibian to Herrick Creek.

The two men discovered big tracks not far short of the lake the day after they arrived. As they slipped through the scrub and sedges near the outlet, Mackintosh happened to turn. At the far side of a small clearing a cow moose was circling behind them (a habit they had, he later told me). One shot from his .303 and it was dead.

Damage to vegetation, barking and tracking indicated the cow had been in the area for some time. Red deer in the area were seemingly in poor condition, but the moose, a mature cow, was 'a perfect specimen', although—significantly—not pregnant.

Mackintosh, a naturalist, was unmoved his kill was female; Allan Harrison, a dedicated trophy hunter, still apologises he could not persuade Jim not to shoot it.

Moose had been out of the news since the mid-1930s, presumed by most people to be extinct. When the two cows were shot within a few months of each other in 1951, the press picked up the story again. A storm of controversy broke out among hunters as arguments raged about ethics and whether the loss of two females would spell the end for moose.

The deer-culler trio of Robin Francis Smith, Max Curtis and Percy Lyes flew into Wet Jacket for another busman's holiday in April 1952. Amphibian Airways' Widgeon dropped them at the head of Wet Jacket Arm. They based themselves at the big rock shelter for a few days of hunting and more of bad weather before concluding there were no moose in the upper sound. Herrick Creek, pinpointed the year before, was a long seven kilometres away. The only water transport they had was Curtis's one-person inflatable dinghy, so they spent two days building a raft of logs for the others, and another rowing the contraption up the sound.

Once at Herrick Creek the men set up camp. The next day they spent exploring, reaching the upper valley by midafternoon. Near the top of the upper clearings they found fresh moose tracks and droppings. The three drew straws for a beat downstream, and split up. Fifteen minutes and a couple of hundred metres later, Francis Smith and Curtis heard the boom of a .303, followed by a wild yell from Lyes, and they hurried over to find him sitting on a dead bull moose.

Lyes had been moving quietly through a patch of pepperwood when the animal had stood up, its head hidden behind a broadleaf, only six metres away. Rifle ready, he waited to be sure it was a bull. It moved its head, and he caught the flash of an antler and fired through the scrub from the hip. The bull staggered forward and fell dead. Lyes recalled a pepperwood sapling gracefully folding over, its stem cut by the bullet.

It was getting late in the day and the three returned to camp, intending to return the next day for the trophy and some photographs. At the lake Curtis decided to try the bluff on the western side rather than repeat the difficult route of that morning. Eventually he succeeded, and was making his way through high fern when he disturbed a resting moose. In the half-light it looked like a young bull. It walked into the bush and was lost from sight.

Next morning Lyes and Francis Smith returned to the dead bull. Francis Smith took some photographs and helped with the headskin until Lyes had loaded up for the trip back, then went hunting. He later wrote he was 'travelling fast through the heavy bush [when] I almost walked on a sleeping moose. As soon as it jumped up I saw it was a young bull with two points on either side'. He managed a couple of quick photographs of it.

In the meantime Curtis was determined to refind his moose of the day before with his camera. He hunted in a profusion of sign until, below the outlet of the lake, he came upon a cow lying back-on to him. He took one photo in the bush as she moved off, then followed her tracks to the lake edge, where she was staring back at him. She ran into the lake and swam to the upper side, but Curtis had his photographs.

Francis Smith found her later in the day. 'I was almost in view of the lake, walking down the stream's bank, when I saw four long black legs beneath the overhanging vegetation. I could see it was a cow moose, so I set about getting a series [of photos] as she plucked at a fuchsia bush. Soon she detected something was amiss, became uneasy, and ambled off.' Francis Smith, waist-deep in icy water, had taken 14 shots.

That night campfire talk must have been jubilant. It had been quite a day.

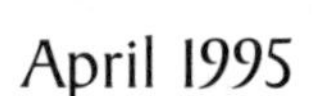

April 1995

The remote video cameras had been surrendered to other projects, but we had two still cameras in their place. Ray had made up a third, and Max wanted to film us putting the camera in place. We landed in the helicopter and made our way to the spot I had in mind.

The bluff, midway round the lake, would make a good camera site. The progress of animals intending to travel up the valley was blocked at this point and they had to walk a small sandspit and take to the water.

From sign on other trips, we knew moose had used this route before.

We set the camera and sensor in a handy wineberry. Later we would find the sun had struck the sensor at a critical angle, heating the unit, triggering the camera and exhausting the film on the first fine day. It took three months to identify the fault, and we ended up with 108 identical photographs of the lake.

August 1995

'How about you and I going in for a short trip on the next film and battery change?' Max had said. 'We'll get dropped off near the dry rock and work our way down to the sea, take a few days, then get picked up. We'll travel light. I'll take just the Hi-8 and a few batteries.'

It could only be a few days. Max and I were already booked on flights to Napier and Nelson to talk with old moose-hunters Percy Lyes and Max Curtis, then Marg and I were due in Laos, and Max required for film work in Chile. But the trip would give us a glimpse of Fiordland in the cold and help us learn how animals used the area in winter.

Herrick Creek was like a deepfreeze. There was more snow in the sounds than Blackie could remember in his 30 years of flying there. With Ray Sharp on board, we left a small cache of supplies at the mouth of Herrick Creek, then flew on to the two still-camera sites. Neither device had taken more than a few shots in the previous six weeks. That was disappointing, but the valley floor is not too attractive over winter. Above the top of the lake, we installed a video camera Ray had borrowed. It was cumbersome but the battery system was longer-lasting than those in the units we had used previously. I felt sure that video units were the answer to remote photography. There were too many problems with still cameras; even when operating perfectly they could exhaust an entire film on one loitering deer, thereafter becoming useless. Video units, however, had three-hour tapes.

Battery changes completed, Max and I scrambled out of the helicopter at the largest of the top clearings with our packs. Our original drop-off point was out of the question as snow was waist-deep there, although it was not much better where we were. Blackie and Ray flew off, and we sat on our packs in the fading light, snow up to our calves, wondering where we would find anywhere to camp.

It was an uncomfortable night on the frozen ground. Waking up wasn't any problem. We positioned ourselves before daylight for a clearing watch. With so much snow underfoot there was no point in stalking, but animals had been using the open areas, and we would hear any that were inbound. A couple of unrewarding hours later we returned to the tent fly for a breakfast of rice and an attempt at a warm-up. The rest of the morning we spent trudging around in the snow, disregarding noise. The reason for the plentiful sign became clear: many branches and even some trees had been felled by the snow and animals had been feeding on them. Mostly deer, but any moose? The snow cover was too deep; it was impossible to tell. Any breakage caused by moose was lost among the massive destruction caused by snowfall.

There was nothing more we could do in the upper valley. We rolled up the fly, packed our gear and headed off, glad to be moving again and getting warm. The day was dull, the bush wet, but at least it wasn't raining.

The lower valley was snow-free. Once through the gorge we pushed through the rough forest and dense scrub, getting wet but making reasonable time. At the top of the lake we surprised three hinds in the clearing where we had set the video the day before. They were in front of Ray's new unit, which was busy making movies of them. They took off as we approached, but it was interesting to note they had been unworried by any scent lingering from our activity there.

We worked our way past the bluff and round the lake without much drama as cloudy drizzle turned to light rain, and then began through the scrub-covered swampy clearings. Almost immediately I noticed some bushes bent, barked and broken. We stopped and checked. Moose sign! And very fresh! More and more evidence showed up as we travelled; the moose had spent some time here.

'How old do you think it is?' asked Max.

'It's hard to tell when everything's so cold. Not more than a week I'd guess.'

When the lake is low, muddy deltas emerge where small creeks drain into it. The mud and sand there is a good place to review traffic. We made our way onto the first of them. Deer tracks pitted the frozen ground. Then:

'Whoa! Hey, Max, have a look at this.'

There was another set of hoofprints impressed in the wet mud, larger, more tapered, and with prominent dewclaw imprints behind—and only a day or so old.

'Moose?'

'Sure is!'

'If we'd been up at the Lookout, we'd have been looking right down on it.'

'Don't tell me!'

It was tempting to head there immediately, but there was not enough time for the climb in daylight. Rain was steady now, we had only a tent fly, and food would be short if we were trapped up there.

The light was failing. It was still 30 minutes to the sound, and once there we still had to organise ourselves before dark. It was hard to leave with so many signposts pointing moosewards. We shouldered our packs again—feeling lighter this time—through sodden thickets of scrub where the moose had been standing, maybe yesterday. Could she hear us? Probably. It didn't bear thinking about.

We were only 50 metres from camp, the place where Guy and Julian had pitched tent a few months before, when the white underside of fuchsia leaves showed up in the dusk. A large branch had been torn down. A few metres further on a couple of pate saplings had been snapped. Around the camp site every pate bush was broken off at chest level. The saplings we had hung wet socks on had been demolished.

'Hell's bloody teeth Max!'

There wasn't much else to say.

The sign was so fresh that every break in the stems, each barking incisor scrape, shone bright white in the near dark. A moose had been making itself at home here, too.

'D'you think it's the same one?'

'I don't know. I doubt it. Both lots are so recent, and it can't have been in two places at once.'

'Christ!'

It was raining harder now, and so near dark there was no time to explore. We set up camp hastily and got the billy on. We had a lot to think about. Two moose out there in the dark? Very close by? And only the next day to find them.

It poured with rain overnight and the next morning. We were up early, wincing at pulling on wet clothing—the penalty for travelling light. We spent the day hunting, at first round the camp end of the valley, then on the fuchsia faces nearby, and finally up towards the lake. By midafternoon it seemed we had exhausted any easy chances of finding the animals. We returned to camp wet, cold, weary and disappointed. No moose. Bugger! Well, it wasn't an easy area to hunt.

Nonetheless we had had a fascinating day. The moose near camp had spent a long time there, weeks maybe, for feeding sign was everywhere. We had learned a lot about feeding behaviour and food preferences.

'What's this tree again?' Max asked.'There's barking on it everywhere you look.'

'Pate, Schefflera digitata,' I explained. 'Its leaves look like five-finger but the bark is woodier.'

Pate had made a big comeback since deer numbers had dropped. Its leaves and bark are an important food source for New Zealand moose.

The Indian name for moose translates as 'eater of twigs', and I am sure that bark and small stems are a significant food source. Their ability to eat them is probably a major reason for their survival in earlier years when food was short.

Moose love the bark of five- and three-finger too. These are the closest local approximation to willow, which is a major food item in the northern hemisphere, that I have seen here.

'Have a look at these young kamahi,' I suggested to Max. The moose had bent them over, some to the left, some to the right. It takes a lot of strength to break upright stems; some were five centimetres thick. In other places, pate saplings had been walked down and left leaning in all directions, with their tops eaten off and their bark methodically stripped.

Next morning the weather was better. We made another search but quickly ran out of time. We sat on packs at the water's edge, listening for Blackie's helicopter, killing time and sandflies and reflecting on our all-too-short trip.

Once again we had been outfoxed, or maybe outmoosed, at Herrick Creek. The animal had left some clear messages. A perfect hoofprint on the site where Max usually pitched his tent said,'Fingers to you, Natural History.' And there is only one small area where it is possible to land a helicopter at high tide; on this was a large pile of droppings. I interpreted this sporting gesture as a moosey way of insisting Blackie gave me my dozen back.

The big bull moose stared fixedly ahead, seemingly unconcerned. I had never been so close to one before; it looked enormous.

'It's just so immense,' I said to Percy Lyes. 'I can't think how we keep missing them.'

'Six foot one at the shoulder,' Percy recalled, indicating with his hand above head level, 'and over a thousand pounds.'

He should remember; 43 years earlier he had struggled the length of Herrick Creek with its 40-kilogram head and cape across his shoulders.

Max Quinn, John Patrick and I were at Percy and Melva Lyes' immaculate Taradale home to film Percy's trophy and hear his story. I had met Percy 25 years before, and was enjoying our reunion. Besides, it was a chance to share a few snippets of information about moose behaviour.

'I was lucky,' Percy told us, 'but it's interesting that when the three of us travelled up that top clearing, we must have passed within a chain of that bull, sitting there in the pepperwood, and he didn't move.'

I could not help wondering how many moose had sat on their big black backsides watching me out of the corner of an eye as I sneaked past only 20 metres away.

Percy's photo albums took us through the familiar country and he patiently recalled those days of the 1950s. As we were leaving I turned for a last look at the trophy head. This animal had been a resident of upper Herrick Creek. We had found sign of another bull there a few months previously. We still had a camera in place there. That we could catch a shot—a camera shot—of him in this same place was an exciting possibility. And another thought: the two moose were almost certainly related. Was I looking at his great-great-granddaddy?

The song of tui from a nearby flowering eucalyptus rang around Max and Necia Curtis's comfortable home in Nelson. It seemed a fitting audio-background for the old hunter. The affable Max led us past a row of hunting trophies on the outside wall of the house, and we spent an entertaining few hours chatting over the old days and filming the cow moose photographs from his album while he told the story of stalking her alongside the lake at Herrick Creek. I asked him if he had any tips for a beginner. Find fresh sign and follow up the tracks he said. You'll come across one eventually.

16

October, November 1995

Marg and I had a final six weeks in Laos, arriving home at the end of September 1995 after nearly three years, on and off, of living and working there. Back in Wanaka I rang Ray Sharp to check if any moose had shown up on the remotes he had been servicing while we had been away. I still felt the frustration of leaving Herrick Creek after our short winter trip when the trail was so hot. I can't recall how many times, sweltering under a mosquito net in some crummy bamboo shack on the Ho Chi Minh Trail, I had dreamt of Fiordland and moose.

Max rang in the evening and we quickly worked out a plan. It had to be quick, as we both had commitments for the coming summer.

'We'll go to Herrick Creek for a short trip,' he suggested, 'and get the bulk of the filming involving other people done, and some air-to-air helicopter stuff out of the way. Then early next year we'll go back with only the three of us.'

We had footage of one of the three known New Zealand trophy moose heads. I thought we should include the other two, and weave their story into our film.

'Where are they?' asked Max.

'There's one with the Herrick family in Hawke's Bay,' I said. Eddie Herrick had died in 1971; his son Jasper had generously let me look through his father's diaries and photo albums 20 years before.'The other's on the wall of the Deerstalkers' Lodge in Te Anau.'

'OK. I'll try to organise filming the Te Anau one. There's another thing I'd like to do,' added Max. 'I think it would spice up the film. It's to re-enact Percy Lyes' shooting of his moose. It'd come out in the main film as black-and-white with Percy's own voice telling us the story. We wouldn't need to show a face; Julian can be Percy. Can you dig up a .303 rifle from somewhere?'

There were two helicopters at Bill Black's hangar the next morning. Max went over the game plan with Blackie and Dennis Egerton. We loaded up, joined by Ray, who was hitchhiking in to service the remote cameras. Both aircraft took off, Max sitting with the camera in the open doorway of Dennis's Hughes 500, dressed like an Antarctic explorer. By the time we arrived at Herrick Creek the air-to-air filming was complete. Dennis left for Queenstown, Ray and I getting a drop-off at the first remote-camera site. Blackie returned to Te Anau for another load of equipment, leaving Max, Julian and Marg to put up camp.

After the rush of the last few days the silence of Fiordland was bliss. Ray and I trudged across the swampy ground to the camera.

'We haven't had much luck,' Ray said apologetically. While Marg and I had been overseas, he had faithfully serviced the cameras, and we had a growing collection of red deer portraits, but no moose.

'There may be none in the valley,' I told him.'They seem to come and go for quite long periods. About all we can do is find a good trail in a valley bottleneck and keep monitoring it.'

The helicopter returned, and we finished our work with the other cameras. A discouragingly small amount of film had been used. If a still camera had caught a moose, Ray would be first to know. Blackie dropped me at camp, then left with Ray for Te Anau.

It was late evening. Rain was falling but camp was a cheerful sight. A camp oven full of sausages was bubbling over the fire. The bar was open: Marg, Max and Julian were sampling cask wine. Some big tarpaulins we had brought weren't too elegant but gave dry standing room around the blaze. It had been a productive day, and there was something to celebrate: we were back in Wet Jacket Arm, in moose country.

Heavy rain prevented serious outdoor filming for the first few days. We explored the places in which Max and I had seen fresh moose sign only seven weeks before. It was almost as if our arrival in August had scared the moose away; there was no sign more recent than we had already seen. We could now age the browsing, bark-biting and stem-crunching—that would be useful information for the future—but both moose had gone.

The next day dawned dull and showery, ideal for the re-enactment. Julian wore clothing similar to that worn by Percy Lyes: baggy shorts, checked shirt, leather boots and woollen socks. I gave him a pikau, a day-pack made from a sack everyone carried in those days for parka, ammunition, lunch and deer-tails. Finally, I handed him Marg's brother's cut-down .303, but hung onto the ammo.

Poor Julian, he was an easy target.

'Julian, they're not deer-culler's legs. I've seen better one's on a weta.'

We replayed the hands of the three hunters drawing straws for their place in the beat down valley, after they had discovered the big bull's tracks.

'Julian, those hands've never seen a blister from an axe or a burn from a billy-handle.'

We filmed Julian's boots and legs sneaking through the fernery, trailing moose tracks.

'Julian, only Mary Poppins walks like that for God's sake.'

Percy and Max Curtis had told us of the exuberant 'Yahoo!' when Percy had shot the moose. Julian yahooed as instructed.

'Julian, that bloody yahoo's grey warbler stuff. Give us a decent one.'

Max wanted a shot of a pepperwood, cut in half by the bullet, slowly folding over. Damn film directors! It would be hard to get it right. There wasn't any pepperwood, but a handy pate sapling on the beach front would do. I lined it up in the sights of the .303 while Max, camera on tripod set on high speed, zoomed in. I fired, and the sapling slowly bent in half.

We had everything on film and retired to camp, where Marg had the billy on for us. It had been hilarious. Max was satisfied with the footage, and Julian was finally released from his tormentors. I hoped he would be merciful when seeking revenge.

There were a few hours of daylight left. We had been 'pretend' moose-hunting most of the day. I left camp to spend the remainder of it looking for a real one.

One afternoon it was pouring with rain as usual, but for once it suited Max.

'It's always raining here,' he observed, as if we hadn't noticed. 'How about we do an interview with you down by the sound?'

It was to be one of those bloody 'Here I am at–' things which I was dreading, but the way Max had described it made it seem easy. I worked out a script and memorised it word for word: a simple introduction to Wet Jacket Arm, delivered in the rain with me looking suitably bedraggled.

'Here I am at Wet Jacket Arm, named by Captain Cook's men after they became stranded and spent an uncomfortable night under their longboat here—'

I ran out of words—something about Fiordland's rainfall being over eight metres a year. Bugger.

'Sorry.'

'Don't worry. We'll try it again.'

An hour later we all trudged back to camp. By then it wasn't only me who was bedraggled.

Max telephoned the day after we had all returned home. He had received the letter for which we had been waiting for over a year, from Environmental Science and Research, along with a bill for $500.

'You'll be disappointed,' he said. 'It's the first batch of hair. It says, more or less, that most of the samples look more like red deer. There's one they're not sure about. Too bad, eh? It could be they're playing safe. I'll photocopy it and send it up.'

I had been collecting hair samples from moose browse sites, tufts of hair that had got caught on the jagged breaks of branches. We had sent away eight small envelopes with suspected moose hair for analysis. For comparison we had retrieved real moose hair from Percy Lyes' trophy and some red deer hair from a skin I had had tanned. We guessed it would not be hard to see if the Dusky Sound samples matched either of the known ones. Moose hair definitively identified from Fiordland would be a handy back-up if we failed to get a photograph.

A day later Max's copy of the letter arrived. The hair had been examined microscopically. Since the lab was usually dealing with material from criminal proceedings, the report was couched in very cautious terms. For most samples the hair 'conformed in size, shape, and medullar characteristics to red deer'.

It wasn't what we had expected.

'What about the Oke Creek sample?' Marg asked.'That was a good one.'

'Oke Creek. It says here that they're from extremities—face and ears—which "are not diagnostic at the species level".'

'I'll keep the rest of them for the meantime,' I told Marg. I had another dozen samples but doubted whether Max had another $500.

'Bugger the hair,' I grumbled. 'We'll stick to trying for a photograph.'

November 1995

A few years earlier I would never have guessed it possible we would have an aircraft fitted with sophisticated state-of-the-art technology overflying our moose area, searching for animals invisible beneath the forest canopy. But here it was: Neil Harraway's dream of a high-tech moose hunt was about to take place.

In November 1995 New Zealand hosted the Commonwealth Heads of State Conference. The proceedings took place mainly in Auckland but ended in Queenstown. As part of the security for dignitaries, the Auckland police 'Eagle' helicopter and its crew were on standby in Queenstown for the final meetings. When the last delegates left, the Eagle team was to return to Auckland, but Natural History somehow gained approval for them to stay one further day. As a 'training exercise', they agreed their specially equipped helicopter and its skilled crew could search for a moose for us.

There was only a short search time available. Max and I privately shared doubts that it would be enough, but Neil was enthusiastic and optimistic. It was, anyhow, a rare opportunity. The helicopter was handy and the crew seemed willing. It would be a pity not to give it a shot.

The device which makes the Eagle team so effective against night crime and errant traffic is its thermal-imaging equipment. The sensor, like a big soccer ball with a lens, is mounted below the nose of their Squirrel helicopter and operated from the front passenger seat. In simple terms, the device intensifies infrared-spectrum heat radiated by objects and transmits the images to a screen in front of the operator. Thus a burglar fleeing through someone's back yard clutching Granny's TV on his shoulder can be tracked on the screen as a bright, man-shaped target with no head. Or a stolen car speeding through city streets can be followed, and when the neighbour's kids abandon it for the bushes in the park, their whereabouts can be radioed to teams on the ground.

The Eagle lads were confident they could get an identifiable picture on their screen; they had told Max they could pick up rabbits in open terrain with their gear, and had helped locate deer in scrubland when a farmer's herd once escaped through a broken fence. A moose, the size of a horse, would not be a problem.

Perfect conditions for the Fiordland search would have been during winter. The deciduous component of the forest is without leaves then, and low ambient temperatures maximise the contrast of warm-bodied animals. However, we would have to make do with spring. To get the best results the plan was to leave early in the morning, before any sun warmed up bush and rock.

To my disappointment both Max and I would be away. Max was filming another documentary in the fiords of Chile, and I was spending the summer flying a helicopter in Antarctica. We had been in Herrick Creek the month before, and I had been sure there wasn't a moose below the lake. Marg knew the situation, and I left her with a sketch map for the others. It outlined my idea of the best places to search, focusing on upper Herrick Creek and the Henry Burn, and along particular forest types.

Our team consisted of Marg, to advise on moose whereabouts; Guy Marris and Julian Grimmond, who would record the events on video and audio tape respectively; and Ray Sharp, who would use the occasion to change batteries and films at the remotes. The three men would travel with Dennis Egerton in the Hughes 500. Dennis would position Ray and, betweentimes, take Guy for air-to-air shots of the Eagle searching.

At daybreak in Queenstown there was no sign of the Eagle team. They turned up a few hours later, having celebrated the end of the conference the night before. They had probably missed breakfast, because their first question was about arrangements for lunch. Marg and Guy exchanged glances. The pilots swapped notes, and shortly afterwards both helicopters lifted off for Te Anau, refuelled at Bill Black's hangar en route, and pressed on through doubtful weather to rendezvous finally on a sand bar at the lakeside in Herrick Creek.

There was a brief stop and some rearrangment of personnel, then the Eagle became airborne again, this time to begin the hunt. Ray set off on foot to service a nearby remote camera. Dennis took the door off his helicopter for Guy's filming, then followed the Eagle.

It soon became clear that searching and filming with the two aircraft in combination was not compatible or safe. Dennis and Guy returned to the lake, where Guy could film the Eagle at work from ground level. Marg sat inside the Eagle helicopter with the crew, helping direct the hunt.

The helicopter began sweeps of the valley. There were a few alarms when bright images appeared on the screen, but these turned out to be rotting logs and, on one occasion, Ray, who was walking back from the remote. At least the thermal-imaging gear was working. The sun came out briefly, adding another dimension to the problems of identifying heat sources.

The Eagle continued until all areas in the valley seemed to have been covered, but made no deerlike contacts. Marg urged some runs along the steeper midslopes, but fuel was low. The valley was declared animal-free.

It became showery, and cloud, always threatening, thickened. Passengers were gathered hurriedly and the return trip began. But cloud now filled the Seaforth and the way home was blocked. After some searching for a way out, both aircraft, now very short of gas, put down on a gravel riverbank near Loch Maree to wait for a clearance and more fuel. Dennis called up Bill Black on his radio for a drum or two.

While they were waiting Guy set up a film interview between Brian, the Eagle team operator, and Marg. Brian described the thermal-imaging equipment and how it worked.

'I can understand not finding a moose,' Marg said, 'but what about deer? We know there're quite a few in Herrick Creek.'

'If there'd been any there, we'd have seen them,' Brian said confidently, now that he was going home.

Shortly afterwards Blackie's Squirrel appeared through the mist with a couple of drums of Jet AI underslung in a net. The helicopters refuelled and some breaks appeared in the murk. All three aircraft lifted off for the return to Te Anau. The exercise was over.

So we had had a crack at the high tech. What had we learned? We had found no moose. It was possible there were one or two in the search area, but we also knew the valley was often vacant of moose. We had found no deer, but knew for certain that at least 25 lived there at the time, possibly up to 40. Thermal-imaging systems had limitations above a forest canopy and, certainly, time had been much too short and the equipment never truly tested. Also, as we well knew, combining a search with a film sometimes does justice to neither.

There was another thing. Our team was disappointed that somehow the effort from the Eagle had lacked the intensity we had hoped for. But after I had thought about this I was sympathetic: flying helicopters around Fiordland can be spooky at the best of times; low cloud and showery conditions among such steep and unforgiving terrain can be very unsettling. This can easily translate into apparent offhandedness. If the Eagle lads had seemed a little casual, we had only to look to the intimidating nature of the environment. A Fiordland pilot would be equally uncomfortable flying over Auckland city at night; he might totally disguise his apprehension, and simply 'not care' if the bad guys got away.

17
March 1996

There is something special about dry-rock camps in Fiordland. I have great affection for the one at the saddle above Herrick Creek. I reflected on earlier times there as I unrolled my sleeping bag on the crusty, dry surface. It is more a cliff than a cave. Without the claustrophobic cocoon of tent or fly, it overlooks a wide-angle panorama of forest trees with glimpses of the far side of the valley. In recent times a medium-size silver beech growing alongside has snapped off and now lies through the middle of the space, giving it a feeling of cosiness in firelight, somewhere to hang wet clothes, and a grand supply of dry firewood.

I had been careful to refrain from making wood smoke during the ten days of fly-camping in the valleys below, but here it didn't matter. Smoke drifted up the rockface, and the fire's cheerful flicker transformed a sombre grey wall into a living thing. A billy heated water for tea. A kaka gave a last whistle, a morepork called regularly near by. I was tired, warm, comfortable, and very happy here in this peaceful place.

I was not long back from three months in Antarctica: a great place in every respect, but as with most people my time there had reinforced a passion for greenery. And things don't come much greener than the inside of Fiordland forest. Back at Wet Jacket Arm I had gone solo, hoping that being alone might break our string of near misses. There was no one to consider but myself: discomfort, exhaustion, motivation were now personal. So far, ten days of walking, searching, boating and camping out had yielded no moose sign. That night, somehow, it didn't matter. It was great just to be there.

Over the next few days I hunted the Henry Burn, running south to Dusky Sound from below the saddle. Like Herrick Creek, it has a generous dollop of our moose herd's short history. There are probably a few stories still to tell.

One incident, which has remained a well-kept secret, took place there in February 1955. A young bull moose was shot, and not far away two others were seen together, a cow and yearling. The hunter was Max Kershaw, then senior field officer in charge of the Department of Internal Affairs' southern-area deer-control operations. Kershaw and Keith Purdon, another field officer, had hunters operating under their control in the Lake Hauroko and Lake Monowai regions. Knowing the density and dispersal of deer in southern areas was their responsibility.

With two Department of Lands and Survey staff, the pair boated to Supper Cove with gear to repair the old hut at the lower Seaforth, which had been neglected since being built for track-cutters in 1900. However, no chance was missed to survey nearby country for deer, and Kershaw and Purdon were busy over the next 12 days. They described deer numbers in the area as 'not plentiful', seeing 67, mostly in the swampy clearings of the Seaforth, and shooting 57 of these. Forest in the area had 'suffered severely', and they mentioned the poor condition of deer and the absence of fawns. Purdon found the dried-up carcass of a cow moose in Waterfall Creek, running west from Supper Cove, which he thought might have died of starvation about six months earlier. He brought the shells from a hoof back to the hut.

Kershaw had seen moose before. Sometime in the 1946–47 season he had spotted two females together in a clearing in the upper Roa Stream, with binoculars from the tops high above.

Kershaw shot the bull in the upper Henry Burn. He wrote in an internal report that it was 'a very poor specimen and in poor condition... Practically no palmation of antlers and carrying six points.' Apart from the other pair seen, he added there was evidence of another moose present, but they had seen no sign in the Seaforth. It says something of the secrecy that accompanied this incident that neither of the Lands and Survey staff sharing the hut with Kershaw and Purdon were aware of anything other than Purdon's discovery of the dead cow.

Max Kerhaw's sparse report is revealing: overgrazed forest, deer in miserable condition, hinds without calves; a dead cow moose, possibly starved, a now-dead bull in poor condition, a cow moose accompanied by a yearling. Had the cow bred that year she would have had a two-month calf at foot; that she tolerated the presence of her previous year's calf is clear evidence she hadn't. All indications pointed to animal populations on the verge of collapse.

Max Kershaw was a likeable, tough, blustery character. For years he dominated official deer-control efforts in Southland. He had a wealth of information at his fingertips but was cagey about passing it onto anyone who hadn't earned it the hard way, as he had. It was his impression, he told me, that moose had peaked in numbers around 1940, and declined suddenly thereafter. He eventually elaborated on his moose kill at my urging, but not until I had spent 15 weeks searching for moose in 1972 and 1975, and his reluctance was clear. My guess is he was aware the news would not make his job any easier. Anyone who knew had been sworn to silence.

Stags had been roaring for a week when we pulled out at the end of March. I had hoped for a moose contact by then. I had been in for a month, with Marg joining me for the last fortnight. We had travelled by foot and boat throughout Wet Jacket and lower Dusky Sound, searching and camping out, finding nothing. During the 1972 survey, sign had suddenly materialised after a long period without luck; this time it did not. We hitched back to Te Anau by helicopter with Ray and Blackie, who came in on a film-and-battery change, burnt out, disappointed and puzzled. Where do the moose go? It seemed we were back to zero, a long way from a photograph of one.

June 1996

Helicopter pilots are bad passengers in other helicopters, but they are worse in float planes. There was a dull southeasterly blowing over Te Anau, but the coast would be OK if a pass was clear. Pilot Marty Davies was steering the Cessna 206 among the cloud-shrouded granite cliffs of the main divide. Wind-flattened tussock and patches of snow slid by the wing tips only metres away. We glanced at one another nervously. At least helicopters have reverse.

We knew moose had occupied parts of Herrick Creek over the winters of 1991, 1994 and 1995. It seemed a good idea to try a search during the cold periods in 1996. In winter the valley floor remains in frozen shadow for several months, but three north-facing slopes in the valley get varying periods of sunlight. I reasoned that any animal activity, deer or moose, should be focused in these relatively attractive sites. The largest and best was in the lower valley, extending from the lake to the coast.

Netball had nearly kept Marg in Wanaka, but after a few hours of hesitation I had found her sorting out warm clothing. I would be grateful for her company on the long winter nights.

It was low tide and raining lightly at Herrick Creek. We unloaded the float plane thankfully, and Marty took off quickly before the weather worsened.

'Home sweet home,' said Marg happily as we carried gear up through familiar bush in the silence following his departure.

We put up camp together, then I spent the last few hours of daylight searching the fuchsia faces behind. The only moose sign was that Max and I had already seen the winter before, ten months previously.

At camp the forest was hushed except for the noise of the creek. A misty moon penetrated the drizzle, making ghostly light in the bush. A kiwi called, quite close. It was great to be back.

Marg weatherproofed the camp the next morning while I made a recce towards the lake. Before concentrating our hunt on the warm faces, we would check to see if moose were resident within sight of the Lookout. Any moose sign near the lake would be enough; we would take our small tent to the Lookout and camp out the entire trip if necessary until we saw the animal.

Not far short of the lake I was hunting quietly through the scrub when I caught a flicker of movement ahead. I kept behind cover, moving cautiously in the frosted mushy ground, Max's Hi-8 held ready, heart in mouth. A breath of wind came from behind—I could feel it on the back of my legs. From ten metres a stag threw his head up and our eyes met. He stood rigid for a few seconds, then wheeled, splashed through the creek and bounded into the bush. It was Fred. I lowered the camera, unused, and let my breathing relax.

Near the lakeside my heart leapt. Some shrubs had been shredded. It looked like moose browse. Closer inspection revealed it was only red-stag antler-thrashing. The area was active; there were plenty of tracks, unreadable in the mud, but almost certainly made by deer. The wind was wrong; I didn't want to disturb the area so turned back for camp.

It is an hour's trip under load up the steep bush ridge to the Lookout. We cleared some fern at the camp site and set up tent and fly, then at the point 50 metres below we tied up another fly for shelter and glassed the scrubby flats below with binoculars. A few grey duck and a black swan on the lake were the only sign of life. The wind had swung round to the west, and cold squalls of rain now sliced across our vision. We wished for a few extra clothes. The Primus buzzed under a billy.

'It would be a chance in a million if a moose walked past down there,' said Marg, looking at the empty scene below. The surrounding forested landscape looked enormous in contrast with the small patches of clearing, semi-open scrubland and ragged short forest where animals would be visible.

'It's better than that,' I told Marg, remembering my trip with Max. 'If we'd been here this time last year we'd have seen one.'

We worked it out: on about ten of the 100-odd days we had spent in the area so far since 1992, there had been a moose living in sight of where we sat on our mossy kamahi log.

'That's ten per cent. You'd take a raffle with odds like that.'

'What if they move around only after dark?' Marg added, spoiling my arithmetic. The remotes had photographed a lot of night movement by deer.

'Yeah. That would alter the odds,' I had to admit, 'but it's worth a shot, and a better bet than stalking that thick stuff.'

The problem was knowing when to be in place.

Just before dark a hind materialised below. For about 20 minutes she remained in sight, sometimes feeding, frequently craning her head as if expecting something, always alert. For much of the time only her back was visible in the tall swampy tussock. When a grey duck swept over her head and landed in the lake, she sprung to rigid attention.

'Can you imagine how hard it would be to get close to her?' Marg asked.

'Hopeless!'

We thought of all the times we had tried stalking through there, or in similar places, trying to keep silent. The resident animals had everything in their favour: superbly acute senses; familiarity with their range; alertness to any factor which differed from normal.

We stumbled back through wet ferns after dark, cooked a meal in torchlight under the fly and ate in our sleeping bags.

By early morning light rain had set in. Layers of mist kept forming, disappearing and reforming. We were back on site, wrapped up in all our clothing, as a bleak grey dawn grew into daylight.

Suddenly Marg hissed: 'Hey! There's something! No. Yes! Hang on. Damn the rain. There it is again.'

We had a clockface reference system: two o'clock from a solitary beech, 50 metres from a tiny gap in the fuchsia. Too late—the animal disappeared. Mist spread across the landscape again.

'A big grey body,' she said. 'It had antlers.'

I quizzed her on the rear end.

'I'm sure it had a lighter rump patch,' she recalled.

OK. A red stag. The mist cleared and we both resumed watching.

It was a bitter day. We took spells, one warming up in a sleeping bag, the other on guard duty. A highlight was when Marg went for a warm-up walk and discovered a pair of parakeets living in a dead tree. Meanwhile light rain turned steady, then steady rain became hard. Visibility changed from sometimes to only occasional. Thinking of the creek rising below, we pulled on wet clothes and headed down through sodden bush back to camp, leaving our tentage in place.

For the next three days the rain became a deluge. It drummed on the fly and the ground ran with water. Wind gusts flapped and billowed our flimsy home. The creek roared alarmingly. Rain turned to sleet. Bitter cold penetrated every article of damp clothing and bedding. A heavy snow line appeared 300 metres above camp.

We are used to Fiordland rain; we expect to get wet. And we want to see a moose. When conditions are unpleasant, we coax each another on. We'll never find a moose in Wanaka, we tell each other, but we'll never see one from inside the tent at Dusky Sound either. So we grit teeth, pull on wet clothes and head out, even for just an hour or two. But not this time. We didn't even consider it. We huddled into sleeping bags, dragged the Primus under the fly for brews and soup, read limp books, yarned, snoozed, and got damper.

Midmorning on the seventh day the storm stopped abruptly. Apart from the thundering of the creek the silence was palpable. Then the bellbirds started.

'After all this rain,' I told Marg, 'the animals will be out in the open at first chance, trying to keep out of the dripping bush.'

We gave the creek a few hours to go down and sloshed off to the Lookout again.

The creek crossing was waist-deep. We worked our way over in tandem, me taking the upstream side, getting a foothold, and Marg swinging below in my wake. The rest of the trip was saturating but normal. At the Lookout the tent floor was full of water. We emptied it out, then quickly settled back to watching. Nothing moved. We stayed until it was too dark to see.

Back in the tent we slid into damp sleeping bags. It was very cold but the sky was clear. We looked forward to daylight.

Morning found ice everywhere and the area below white with hoarfrost. There was no animal movement. The sun came out on the opposite face and edged its way down, stopping short of the valley floor, which remained bright with frost. Shortly after, it began retreating back up the slope. Unable to stop shivering we packed everything at midday, fumbling iced-up knots with numb fingers, hoisted on packs and headed back to camp, tents and all. Our visit to the Lookout hadn't been a good idea.

We radioed Carol Brown as soon as we reached camp. She would be wondering how we were faring. Her voice boomed in. Yes, a message from Ray Sharp: 'Arriving Tuesday for camera servicing, not Friday as expected.' We looked up the diary to see what day it was. Tomorrow! Bugger! Much too soon. I picked up the camera and took off to hunt the sunny faces. It was already afternoon.

I returned near dark. There had been red deer sign around, as expected, but nothing moosey. Marg searched an area closer to camp: a deer had walked along the shoreline between tides while we had been away, she reported. We steamed a bucket of mussels she had collected in the camp oven.

'Next time,' she told me, 'we mustn't forget the garlic butter.'

Leaving Marg the task of packing, I left at daylight for one last effort—a long traverse high up through the fuchsia. That, after all, was the purpose of the trip. After a stiff climb and long sidle, I put up one deer and got close to another, enough to smell it and find its bedding place, but caught sight of neither animal in the thick bush. Deer were using these slopes, though; compared to lower areas the air was warm and the bush dry. I saw a stoat; I watched two kaka feeding. But there was only old moose sign. I turned back for camp. It seemed clear there were no moose living in the lower valley; we had been wasting our time at the Lookout. We were going home and we had achieved nothing.

The helicopter arrived early afternoon and we loaded the gear. Blackie lifted off for the camera sites. Ray was on board and through the headsets we caught up on news.

The first camera was above the lake. We hadn't even got there this trip, despite being nine days in place. At the site I searched around for sign while Ray and Marg attended the video unit. The ground was frosted and there was no clear tracking. Then I found some larger prints; a big stag lived here and I suspected it was him. Scouting around for other sign near the clearing fringe, a flash of white caught my eye.

Only 60 metres behind the camera two stems on a wineberry had been snapped off at upstretched-fingertip height, and the lower branches stripped of leaves. That was a moose. Maybe a week before a moose had been this close to our camera! I hurried over towards Ray and Marg, bursting with the news. Did we have it? A picture of a moose? Had it walked the spit? Swum the lake?

The expressions of both stopped me in my tracks. Ray held up the sensor with a shrug. It had been torn apart by kea.

On the drive home we discussed the trip. It had been too short and we had been in the wrong place, with not enough time for correction. The solution was simple: we would go back before the end of winter and try again. Meanwhile there were plenty of other things to think about: I had some heliskiing flying, and Marg was beginning local-competition netball, for which carrying a pack through jungle is not bad training. The moose project could wait until the weather warmed up, even a little, and the days lengthened. Meantime the cameras would keep their patient watch, kea permitting.

We arrived home well after dark. Sodden piles of tentage and mud-stained clothing could wait for next day. Marg was first to the bath. I heard a wail.

Something serious was wrong. A spider in the water? I hurried into the bathroom.

'What's up?'

'Oh God. What on earth will the other players think?'

Marg was sitting up in the bath, aghast at the sight of her legs. Both were crisscrossed with cuts, scratches and a colourful display of bright purple bruises, while one thigh had a livid blue-and-yellow welt—the legacy of scrub-bashing with a pack.

'What can I tell them? The netball team. They'll think you're a wife-basher.'

'You could say you've been run over by a truck and trailer,' I offered helpfully.

July 1996

Blackie's helicopter touched down in an alarming flurry of blowing snow. It wasn't easy to recognise landmarks. I opened the door to check the skid on my side. He shut down the engine and the rotors finally swung to a halt.

Snow was calf-deep on the Herrick Creek–Henry Burn saddle. Trees were bowed down under its weight, smaller shrubs mere humps. Hard frosts had dried the snow, and the surface had a layer of delicate crystals; every branch, twig and leaf had become a feathery flower. It was breathtakingly beautiful to look at, but tough to walk around in. The slightest brush against any bush would bring down cascades of snow. This didn't matter right now—it would brush off—but once the thaw started it would be dreadful up here. Max had brought the camera and tripod for some winter shots of Fiordland, and, boy, did he have them; it was a filmmaker's dream.

The tree holding our camera was upright, but its foliage had collapsed in a frozen umbrella. Sensor and camera lens were opaque with ice crystals. Max set up and filmed us shaking the tree free of snow and Ray taking out film and replacing batteries. Fifteen photographs had been taken. Ray was sure the storm had triggered the system; I was hopeful we had captured a shot or two of animals travelling between the two catchments before snowfall rendered it useless.

I scouted around for tracks. Something big had travelled through on a purposeful journey, but the snow was too deep to know whether it was a large red stag or a moose. Anyway, the whatever-it-was would not be on film this time. This was no place for animals, us included, but the camera was serviceable again. We returned to the helicopter, where Blackie had wisely remained, warm and dry, with the 'Southland Times'. He started up and we lifted off in another whirling cloud of snow.

The camera inside the bush at the top flat was also iced up, only five shots taken. There wasn't much choice for camera sites, but more than once we had had a close brush with moose near this location, and the forest above the valley floor was sunny and attractive. This camera would remain in place. Max busied himself shooting winter scenes while Ray and I replaced batteries and film, cleaned the lens and hoped for better luck over the month to follow. We lifted off for the final site.

The lake in Herrick Creek was completely frozen over except for a small triangle at the inlet. Half a dozen New Zealand scaup paddled about nervously, more worried about their disappearing lake than our helicopter. The landscape was white with ice and frost; normally swampy ground was rock hard. The video camera waited here for animals to swim the lake, but there would be no swimming right now. It had been triggered only once. Ray played the tape back through the camera while we watched over his shoulder.

The image of a red deer hind walked gingerly down the frozen spit to the lake, stood for a short time, and returned past the camera. Beautiful, but not a moose, and little reward for five weeks' waiting. This was no site for the camera in midwinter. We took the unit and its battery pack down from the tree.

Bill cranked up the Squirrel again and we shifted to 'Fred's clearing', the favourite place of the stag Marg and I had come to know over numerous trips. It was presently on the frost line at the base of a large, sunny, seral-forest slope—a perfect place for animals to catch the sun. From sign it seemed the area was popular with deer. With moose? We wouldn't know for another five weeks, but moose had wintered around here before. We studied the network of tracks and possible routes before finally agreeing on a camera site, then mounted the video unit on a sturdy kamahi, the sensor above it with a kea-proof guard. Job complete, we headed back to the helicopter. Blackie folded up the 'Times', we thanked him for his patience, and the helicopter lifted off for Te Anau. A perfect winter's day in Fiordland fell behind us.

I looked back. There were moose down there somewhere. It would take only one to walk in front of a working camera for the documentary to have some punch. So far two years of effort had come to little. The film rolls in Ray's pocket would be processed the next day, but it was clear animal activity was low and keeping cameras workable was a problem. Natural history film-makers have to be patient, but funds are always limited. How long could Natural History wait? Surely at one of these sites, sometime, it would happen. At the very least we had a ticket in the moose lottery.

Below us, Wet Jacket Arm was dark and sombre, frozen across for its first nine kilometres. Fiordland's valleys were black with shadow, white with frost, washed in misty blue-grey with cold. They looked starkly cheerless. For once I was glad not to be camping.

'I'm really nervous Marg. I think I'll have another Scotch. It'll help get me started.'

'If you have too many more,' she warned, 'they won't be able to stop you.'

We were sitting in a small restaurant in the Octagon in Dunedin, counting down the time to 8.00 p.m., when I was to give my talk.

I had reason to be anxious: the event was a double-banger. The talk was to be filmed. The prospect of either the talk or the filming by itself was enough to white out the brain and jelly the legs; both of which always worked OK out in the bush.

It had begun a couple of weeks earlier. One night the phone had rung. It was Max.

'I've been thinking about this film,' he began, 'and I can see there's a problem of giving your moose-hunting story the appropriate feeling of time. It may come across that you're doing just one trip of a few weeks and not searching over a period of years. So we need to know something of you and Marg between trips to Fiordland.

'Also,' he added, 'I'd like to expand it to involve other people, especially those who know what hunting is all about and might be sceptical about there being any moose. I've got a few contacts with Otago Deerstalkers' Association guys. How do you feel about giving a talk to them at their clubrooms in Dunedin? We'll get it on film, and that should help carry the story.'

He said it all so nicely I had to agree.

It was a shocking winter's night in Dunedin. Heavy rain had turned to snow, and big flakes were falling thickly. There was a promise of roads closing. But any hopes I harboured of a cosy fewsome turning out evaporated as the hall filled to standing room only. It was an indication of the level of interest among local sportspeople in New Zealand moose. Finally the President, Kevin Weir, explained what was going on. Max added a little and pleaded members take no notice of the camera. I got the nod to go ahead. With shaking hands and dry throat, I checked the tiny microphone attached inside my collar and switched on the small sound-control box in my back pocket, getting a green light. Craig Watson checked his array of sound equipment and gave a thumbs-up.

Brightly lit, on camera, in front of a packed hall of expectant faces, surrounded by stuffed trophies belonging to generations of grandfathers and wishing I had had a few more whiskies, I stammered out the first few words.

Marg and I turned up at Natural History's studios the next morning. The evening before had gone off OK, but it was a relief to have it over and finished with. Despite my faltering start it had turned out to be an enjoyable occasion with an enthusiastic audience.

We had nearly three days to help with other aspects of the project. We spent a morning cataloguing two years of still photographs from the remotes. The majority of shots were misfires or bird triggers, but among them were some beautiful prints of deer taken in day and night, rain and sun, snow and storm. We ranked them for quality; some would be used in the film.

Then Ray showed us to the edit room, sat us down in front of panels of dials, knobs and switches and two screens, and gave us some instruction. We would make a start of reviewing time-lapse tapes. He inserted the first, pushed 'Play' and left us alone. The image lit up on both screens. We played the tape through slowly, in some places frame-by-frame, so nothing would be missed. Everything of interest we noted, along with its time code, for future retrieval. These sequences were, in film-industry jargon, user bits. On the first tape the only loggable shot was a sequence of a hind strolling past. It was slow, deliberate work: a moose might appear in only a single frame. Three hours later we staggered into the lunch room, heads reeling, eyes falling out, only two short tapes completed.

In the afternoon Mike Muir called. We had met at the meeting the night before. His grandfather, Jim Muir, had been Eddie Herrick's guide and companion. Mike left us a wad of photographs from Jim's hunting days and the mounted forefoot from the first moose trophy, the bull shot in 1929. We measured the hoof, and from my field notebook compared sizes with the recent residents of Herrick Creek. It was similar to most records, larger than some. But the tracks from our suspected bull in the upper clearings a year before we judged to be slightly bigger. Bigger? It was an exciting thought.

18

Fiordland living

Fiordland can be an intimidating monster which, like some eccentric pet, sometimes bails you up, glowering. Occasionally it allows itself to be cautiously petted; it may even purr. Just when you think it loves you, fangs sink deep into your leg. Then while you wait to be eaten, it will sit on your lap and lick your face. It is easy to love, easy to hate. The difference is attitude.

Marg and I like our trips to the sounds to last a month. Time passes so quickly it is seldom long enough, and long trips are appealing because we feel like residents rather than visitors. More time means less urgency, a healthy constraint in an environment which is always imposing its will. Fly-camping is usually arduous and spartan, but the main camp we treat as home. We never stockpile jobs because we're in the bush. Instead of keeping soiled clothes, we wash them in the creek. Instead of taking bread, we make it. We stay away from huts, keep camp life uncomplicated by too much gadgetry, and use only small, portable tentage for simple living. Keeping ourselves clean, the camp tidy, and eating well is only the discipline of normal life. I have seen so many people turn into barbarians when they are in the bush.

An indispensable part of our Fiordland lifestyle is the boat. It is our single release from the closeness of the forest, all too often dripping, dank, and cloying. It gives freedom of travel, access, food, and a glimpse into the life of our neighbours, the seals and dolphins. Sometimes they seem to enjoy us as much as we enjoy them.

Our boat is a three-and-a-half metre Lancer inflatable with a hinged wooden floor. It is made of PVC—vulnerable to puncturing but at least portable and light. It bundles not much bigger than a large suitcase and weighs 45 kilograms. Two of us manage it fairly easily when inflated—and have to, for we are always pulling it into the safety of the bush, or dragging it to deeper water after big Fiordland tides. We swapped the eight-horsepower outboard for a 15-horsepower Yamaha after our first trip; the boat now planes with both of us, our two packs, and emergency gear onboard. Speed is safety around the sounds. The engine weighs another 45 kilograms, which doesn't sound much, but when staggering up a beach of slippery stones it is quite enough, and leaves no hands free to wipe away a thousand sandflies.

You cannot talk Fiordland without talking sandflies, for the two words come out with the same breath. Always present, sandflies vary in number and nuisance value with weather and from one place to another. At best, the small bloodsucking insects are mildly annoying, and you develop a rhythm of stroking exposed skin to squash those that are settling before they bite. At worst they form an airborne haze, cluster in their hundreds on dark clothing, and crawl through scalp, into eyes and ears and up trouser legs, finding the tiniest holes and gaps in clothing and biting through stretched fabric. Bites are not painful or long-lasting, just a sudden fierce itch, pinprick-hot and very difficult to ignore.

The key to tolerating sandflies is not to focus on them. Sometimes that can be hard. It helps to change your body smell by secretion, the story goes. We have tried dosing ourselves with vitamin B1 before trips but noticed no difference. The old bushman's method was to drink a shot of kerosene with a slug of whisky each day for a couple of weeks beforehand, and what the hell if you smelt like a Primus when you sweated. I am partial to a wee dram but can't bring myself to add kero to it, and have never suggested Marg tamper with her favourite white wine either. Eating garlic is a supposed remedy, but we always forget to take it with us. Anyhow, there are repellents, which we often use around camp. I loathe applying them elsewhere; it's difficult enough bush-hunting for a moose without smelling like a cross between a rose garden and the Wellington railway station dunny.

Taking a can of aerosol fly spray is a good idea if you intend living around the Fiordland coast for any time. Despite zip-up netting screens on tents, sandflies always find their way inside, where they blacken the roof in their hundreds, waiting for you in ambush. They stop biting at nightfall, but if you cannot clear the tent of them somehow, you can be sure of an early start next day, and they'll spoil the peace of a wet day inside. We can recognise books from our shelves at home that have travelled to camp: not only are the volumes slightly corrugated from the damp, but flattened black flakes like tea-leaves dot the text, each a kamikaze sandfly, neatly pressed.

Sandflies are never a problem walking, and the further from the coast or higher in altitude you get, the less they are bothersome. However, at camp on a still, sunny day they can be a torment. The same days are perfect for boating, so, if sandflies are bad, we simply pack up and go fishing for a few hours, cheat them of a meal and get one for ourselves.

Fishing is the ideal antidote to days of tough tramping, hunting and camping in the mud, rain and gloom of the forest. We have many happy fishing memories: gently rocking in the sun on still, black water, behind us a landscape of almost surreal perfection; suddenly awakening from a sun-sleepy daydream to boisterous tugging; reeling in 100 fathoms of nylon, wondering what's on the end this time.

There are many good eating fish in the deep water of the inner sounds, but our favourite is blue cod. There is always rivalry to catch the first, the biggest or the most. We fillet larger cod for frying in the camp oven, but Marg wraps smaller ones whole in tin foil and puts them in the embers of the fire, and they are always the best. I cannot remember how many times in Laos, as we wrestled with a scrawny spring-steel chicken in some grubby bamboo restaurant among the dogs, pigs and surviving chickens, we would dream of cod and kumara back home in Wet Jacket Arm.

Marg was up pottering around camp making bread one day when I launched the boat by myself for a quick spot of fishing, rowing just 40 metres offshore to try my luck. A few seconds later a very large something grabbed my line, and I found myself being towed briskly up the sound towards Resolution Island, making about four knots. When Marg came down 30 minutes later I was dragging a two-metre shark onto the beach.

Mussels are common on rocks and snags along the beach at Herrick Creek. We often collect a bucket of them at low tide, steaming them quickly over a hot fire in the camp oven for a treat while the rest of the meal is cooking.

Dolphins are the highlight of boat trips. They—pods of bottlenose dolphins of up to 100 or more individuals—are never far away in Dusky Sound or Wet Jacket. Each time we meet them they are different, sometimes busy, following the boat only for a short time, other times seeming to relish the opportunity to play. We will probably never know how dolphins think, but their teasing playfulness, their acrobatics underwater and their exhibitionist choreography above it express elements of power, freedom and joy. Dolphins remain a very special part of the appeal of the sounds for us.

If dolphins have a sense of speed, purpose and organisation about them, fur seals seem the opposite, although their lolling casualness can be deceptive. Onshore they heave themselves awkwardly around on rocky headlands and nervously crane short necks, keeping the boat in sight, seeming to recognise that they are out of their element. But in the water they have a graceful mastery and are almost unafraid. We have spent many fascinating hours in the boat alongside seals, silently keeping station with the occasional touch of a paddle while they fish or play. Twice we have watched a seal thrash a big fish it has caught into manageable pieces by head-shaking while we sat only metres away. And our morning and evening strolls along the beach are frequently accompanied by a solitary seal rolling gently past, one flipper raised in an off-hand salute.

Cooking over an open fire may sound like a chore, but the fire is the focus of camp life; without a fire, a camp is only shelter. For all their efficiency, a Primus or gas burner warms neither heart nor soul, although it is ideal for fly-camping and useful at base during prolonged wet weather. Sitting around the fire with a mug of tea in hand, chatting over the day's activities, is a special part of outdoor living. It would not be quite the same sitting over a Primus.

To make and sustain a fire in Fiordland is often hard work. A first task after arrival is to collect firewood and store it under cover. Driftwood is a good start. Dead wood, still standing, is often dry enough to burn, even if you first have to peel off a cocoon of moss then split it into fragments. Learning which tree species burn well is a worthwhile investment. Beeches have a good litter of dry branchlets underneath, but they burn quickly with only moderate heat and leave no embers. Manuka and kanuka are not plentiful around the sounds, but they burn beautifully and we always keep a lookout for them if we are boating. The best of all is rata. At the mouth of Herrick Creek one medium sized flood victim has lain for as long as I can remember, submerged twice daily by the tide. We have taken a bowsaw and recovered pieces of it, black and slimy with marine growth, and split it carefully. The wood, pink and heavy and seemingly saturated, burned like household kindling, but with enduring heat and good embers.

Fire-lighting with wet wood is a survival skill in Fiordland. Lighting the first fire can be difficult, but is helped by carefully grading the size of the sticks, from slivers up. The old bushman's trick of using a candle to start and dripping wax to follow is useful, then fanning it gently with a tin plate. If camp supplies permit, a little kerosene for this purpose is sensible, where pride is not at stake or desperation rules. Just a touch in a shallow shell or sardine tin with a moss wick will suffice. If you pour it onto the sticks, it will just burn off with a flourish; your drying polyprop underwear will shrivel and smoulder, companions will laugh and you will soon have no kerosene for the Primus when you really need it.

With the first fire going, a good idea is to prepare for the next by keeping some kindling to one side, drying in the heat. Once, after film-making had begun and we realised we would be cooking for six people for a week, we added a couple of small bags of coal to the equipment list. That small addition was all that was needed to make the task enjoyable.

'We may not be able to find a moose,' Max said one night, sitting on a rock, his head lamp focused on a brimming plate nestled between his knees while rain streamed down outside the fly only an arm's length away, 'but we sure eat well!'

You can cook almost anything over a fire that you can at home, provided you have a camp oven. The main difference with a fire is the need to anticipate the heat you will require, and this means keeping an eye on the quantity and quality of wood, then controlling the heat by shifting the billy or camp oven. For longer, slower cooking of, say, roasts, pies or something like bread, you simply adjust the heat source accordingly with fire, hook or branch. A pie may need to be placed on an upside-down plate to centre it inside the camp oven and prevent it burning from below. Browning a crust is done with a shovel-full of embers on the lid.

I came back to camp one evening to find a delicious-looking meal simmering over the fire, but Marg busy scooping peas from the top of one small billy into another. A few minutes later she repeated the process, and now three billies of peas were bubbling away enticingly.

'There didn't seem that many in the packet,' she explained sheepishly as I hooked the remains of the empty package out of the fire with a stick and read the blackening label.

'It says here "32 generous servings",' I relayed.

Coming up with the unexpected is always fun. One night it was my turn as chef.

'The potatoes,' Marg said. 'They're great. Mint! That's what it is! Where on earth did you find mint?'

'The bush is a wonderful garden,' I answered solemnly, 'of foods, remedies and herbs, and it takes only a good eye and a little knowledge.'

I hoped she wouldn't notice the big kink in our toothpaste tube.

When we plan a month in Fiordland, we must assume long periods of foul weather. In small tents and simple living conditions, that can be testing, so we come well prepared with thick books that never get a chance at home. Day-to-day living in bad weather gives lots of small jobs. Even under an overhead tent fly, keeping a fire going is just one of them. It is a good time to cook bread or some tantalising dish you are unwilling to experiment with when you are busy.

One concession we make is 'present day', an exchange of gifts about two-thirds of the way through a trip, the date singled out well in advance. It is better than Christmas. Each of us will have packed a parcel of goodies for the other and kept it hidden, only hinting at the contents. The day is looked forward to all trip. When it comes, it is with mock fanfare and real fun. Then the unwrapping begins.

'How did you know that was exactly what I wanted?'

'Do you take a broadcast radio?' people sometimes ask.

'Eh? You're joking!'

Advertising jingles, junk music and national politics seem out of place there. We are content with the sound of bellbirds, kaka and waterfalls.

'How about news and weather forecasts?'

We are often curious about news, but there is nothing that cannot wait a month. That is one of the treats about coming home. For weather, we simply do what early Maori, Captain Cook and Richard Henry did: note wind direction and look westward up the sound.

Max, who we regard as a bit of an insomniac, always brings his

Walkman.

'There's nothing like a bit of Beethoven to mix with the noise of rain on the tent.'

Misadventure is different. I have taken part in too many helicopter rescues in much more benign places to take it lightly. We take a portable high-frequency radio, courtesy of my old employer, The Helicopter Line, tuned to the same frequency Bill Black and Trevor Green use in their helicopters, and keep in periodic contact with Carol Brown at Te Anau.

We have never used the radio in an emergency role, but came close one time. Marg and I were back from a few days at Lookout Point, saturated and muddy, and Marg was heating water in the camp oven for a hot wash. While she was hooking the heavy container off the fire, the wire handle, which had a kink in it, caught momentarily. She lost balance for a second, enough for a surge of boiling water to pour down one boot. We instantly doused her clothed foot in cold water, then pulled off the boot and woollen sock. She sat beside the creek with her foot underwater until she could no longer stand the cold, the rain and the sandflies, then we bandaged it up. It blistered badly and she rested up for a few days, but was soon able to walk on it. It was a near thing, and she still carries the scars.

The one time I have used the radio in conditions of genuine urgency was when the All Blacks were touring South Africa. Unable to wait until my return, I called Carol for the score in the second test.

It takes some skill, patience, and more than a little self-discipline to learn to cope with Fiordland's sullen moods without rancour. But at any time, mostly unexpectedly, it will gift a glimpse of magic that will live with you forever. Hardships and discomfort are forgiven in a second. Our most enduring memories remain simple flashes: a kaka feeding acrobatically in an overhanging fuchsia; locking eyes at five metres' distance with a startled stag; the caring thrust of a mug of hot soup into numbed hands; grey mist ghosting over still water; the soaring jump of a playful dolphin; a wink shared over the campfire at the end of a tough day. Oh yes, and fresh hoofprints in the sand.

19
August 1996

First light on day six, a wet fly camp in Herrick Creek, winter trip number two. Dragging on wet clothes at the beginning of a day. The thought is worse than the event; it's all a matter of attitude. Well, that's what you tell yourself.

What was I doing here? Maybe I was a slow learner. I knelt inside the tent, naked, pushing everything into the pack, leaving travelling clothes until last, then leapt out into the rain. Icy drops on bare shoulders. The slap and shock of sodden cloth on warm skin. Ahhhh! Shirts are the worst. I have never minded wet boots. I pulled down tent and fly and screwed them into a wringing-wet ball. Pack done up, parka on, hat on, I hoisted the lot onto my shoulders and got moving.

Five minutes later, wetter but warmed by the tramping, it didn't seem so bad. The security of knowing you are carrying dry clothes for the day's end gives you the ability to disregard other discomforts—and there would be plenty of those during another day's hunting in dripping bush. Fiordland can be mean enough without making things harder for yourself.

There had been few highlights on the bleak, wet trip so far, and no moose sign in the lower valley. The trip was shaping up to be another fizzer. I decided to try to ignore the rain, fly-camp, and hunt the upper reaches. The evening before I had got video of the big red stag which lived above the lake, and was feeling very pleased with myself. He had been in a small clearing; I had wormed close to him under cover in the half dark and photographed him from ten metres. Not long afterwards, taut with excitement and with pulse racing, I had stalked a moose standing 80 metres away, half-hidden in the trees, on the opposite side of the creek. I could make out the dark body and lighter underside, but the head, no doubt watching me, was hidden from view. Ten minutes later it was still there, unmoving, and I wondered whether to risk taking the housing off the Hi-8 to erase the tape; Max would wonder about nine minutes' footage of a fallen log.

It was still early morning in the mid-valley. Rain tumbled from the dark, overcast sky. I pushed carefully through scrubby thickets towards a small clearing, water streaming down my face, trying to remain alert.

'Woof!'

The deep, guttural bark of a red deer hind echoed in the still air. I jumped at the unexpected sound, then froze, which wasn't too hard in the circumstances.

'Woof!'

Only 40 metres away three hinds were standing in the open swamp. I was still in cover, only partly visible to them.

'Woof!'

The lead hind barked again. The other two, waiting for Mummy to decide where to go, milled around uncertainly. I inched the pack from my shoulders and quietly pulled out the Hi-8 from the top. Keeping movements slow, I carefully brought it up to eye level. She was staring right at me. Shit! I couldn't see through the fogged-up eyepiece. I slowly reached in my parka pocket for the tissue I kept wrapped in a plastic bag for cleaning lenses. Bugger! The paper was a soggy ball. I rubbed the lens with my thumb.

'Woof!'

I triggered the camera. Great! I had her! She watched me, moved away, wheeled, came back, stamped her foot.

'Woof!'

I stepped forward through the scrub for a better shot. All three deer lunged across the flooded creek, stopping on the other side for a long look. I kept filming for a time, then swung my pack back on and walked into the open, still carrying the camera. The deer moved away, but without panic. They were probably out in the open to get away from the dripping bush. I didn't blame them; it was bloody miserable.

In the early afternoon I repitched the little tent inside the bush edge near the swampy clearings of upper Herrick Creek. It was difficult finding space enough on ground that was not awash. Rain had stopped midmorning but the sky remained overcast and it was very cold. I crawled into my sleeping bag to warm up and cooked soup inside the tent on the Primus, waiting for late evening, when animals are on the move. It was bloody tempting to zip the tent shut and remain there, but moose don't go around peering into tents.

Ouch! In the cold, grey evening it is even harder to shake out muddy, sodden clothes and force them over dry, warm skin.

Back on the hunt again, I drifted as quietly as I could round the forest edges. Under the forest canopy a litter of fallen branches of all sizes, from two seasons of heavy snowfall, made silent stalking impossible. Keeping to the clearing edges was not ideal but it was the best I could do.

Based on sign, there had not been much animal movement on the valley floor. We had a remote-camera site not far away. I made my way over to it, reached round the tree and checked the unit. The lens was misted over with condensation. I triggered it and it flash-clicked. It was working. I cleaned the lens, ducked round it, and kept hunting.

Two hours later I had nearly completed the circuit and was only 100 metres from camp, but on the far side of the clearing. I was soaked from the dripping bush and very cold from the refrigerator atmosphere of the valley floor. I was looking forward to dry clothes again, and hot tea, and turned for home, following the edge of the stream to avoid the swamp. A hind and calf had left marks there earlier in the day. Then, right alongside the creek on the raised sandbank, I found myself staring at other hoofprints. Big ones. And very recent. I traced them up and down in the failing light until I was sure. Moose tracks! The cold was forgotten. Wet clothes could wait. It had been a long time, but I was back in contact.

The footprints told a story. That morning a moose had walked up the valley alongside the creek, then returned later. One track was from before—the other after—the rain had stopped. That, I remembered well, had been at 10.00 a.m. I had arrived at 2.30 p.m., and so had missed the show.

But there was another thing: this animal was different from others. These hoofprints were splayed, and the dewclaw impressions very slotted. I took off my day pack and found my notebook. The animal we had called a bull here two years before had had a rounded hoofprint, and the dewclaw marks had also been rounded. The prints I was looking at now were smaller, the dewclaw marks very different. From notebook drawings, it was clearly a different moose from the one Max and I had tracked alongside the lake the winter before. That had left quite disc-shaped dewclaw impressions. All were different from the first cow we had chased with Marg, Max and Guy. She had had narrow, quite tapered hooves. I was starting to build up a fingerprint collection, and it was showing me that we were dealing with more individuals than we had guessed. I returned to my tent with my mind whirling. Tomorrow was another chance for the Big One.

Something else was different too; it took a few moments to pinpoint it. Silence. It wasn't raining!

I was jolted out of sleep by a string of piecing shrieks—a kiwi calling only 20 metres from the tent. It was a great way to wake up, and I had too much to think about for more sleep. It was 5.30 a.m., still two hours off daylight. I listened to the forest gradually awaken: the harsh call of a kaka in the forest faces above; a last solo from a morepork; a duet by a pair of paradise ducks.

At 6.30 came the familiar prickle of light rain on the tent, and a few minutes later heavier splots off the beeches. Bugger! At 7.30 I swapped clothes again, crept through grey morning light into drizzle, and began the hunt.

I searched all day without even seeing a deer, returning to camp weary, wet and dejected. It was a very difficult place to hunt. I had found moose sign sufficient to tell me the animal had spent only a short time around the area and had arrived only recently. The rain had stopped midafternoon and the weather cleared, but the bush had remained dripping. There seemed no relief from cold and wet. I did an evening shift, hunting locally and watching the clearing. Nothing.

There was a hard frost overnight, and the morning torture stepped up a notch: wet clothes were now frozen cardboard-stiff. I did another morning shift around the clearings. Still no life. The ground crackled underfoot with ice as well as squelched, although I couldn't hear it above my teeth clacking.

Shivering nearly uncontrollably I packed up and left for the saddle and the dry rock. I desperately wanted some space, dry surroundings and a fire for release from the cold.

I stumbled into main camp at the sound two days later. I had spent most of the time exploring parts of the Henry Burn, but without result. Like Herrick Creek, most of it was in winter shadow and bitterly cold. I had come from the dry rock after a few hours' hunt that morning around the pass area; it was another five hours from the saddle to the sea. Above the trees it was a perfect winter's day, sunny and clear; inside the forest it was the opposite: dark, gloomy and dripping. Every nudge against shrub or tree brought a cascade of icy drops. Winter was not a kind time to be here.

I arrived at the sound exhausted, bedraggled, clumsy with cold and quite despondent. I walked straight through camp to the shoreline without taking my pack off—and immediately stepped into another world.

Bright, warm, tranquil. Water sparkled in sunshine. Perfect reflections were mirrored in the still sound. Bellbirds filled the air with song. The transition was moving and spectacular.

All the wet clothes came off. All the pack contents were strewn, steaming, over shrubbery. Fiordland's sodden winter bush was temporarily forgotten. Even the sandflies were forgiven; had no one told them it was off-season? I gathered driftwood, humming songs. I lit a fire and heated water for a bush shower. I collected mussels for a treat meal. I basked in the delicious sun, whistled to the bellbirds, watched a friendly pair of oystercatchers, waved to a passing seal. For once I forgot about moose.

The helicopter would come tomorrow. The trip had been a worthwhile shot: I had re-established contact with a moose. Perhaps it would lead to a photograph. But now I looked forward to standing on firm ground in a landscape that didn't drip, a hot bath, a meal (not rice), and a wine by the fire with Margie. And pulling on dry clothes in the mornings.

20

August 1996

The phone rang Saturday evening. Max usually telephoned when he had picked up the photographs from the remotes, or when we had got back from Dusky Sound and he hadn't been there. Not normally on a Saturday though. He asked about my trip. He didn't sound quite our usual Max. The flu?

'What about the photos?' I asked.

Nothing there, he said. A red deer bum, a paradise duck.

'Then what about my video?' I asked again, proud of my efforts with the stag and the group of hinds.

He could see a stag in one shot, he said, but the autofocus had focused on a foreground shrub, so it was blurry. There was another long sequence with other deer in, not bad, but very shaky. I remembered the cold and wet. Bugger! He kindly didn't mention my moose–tree.

'That's not why I rang,' he finally confessed, the catch still in his voice. He explained he had been putting together a 'promo' of our moose documentary, a promotional film made up of segments of the film-to-be, enough to give potential buyers an impression of the finished production. Michael Stedman, the Natural History unit's managing director, was taking it to a wildlife film festival in England. (This is one way film-makers in the industry presell their films and secure both buyers and funding.)

'Hey, I don't want to get you too excited,' he finally blurted out. 'I've just got back from the office. I've been searching out footage from the remote videos for the promo, later than the stuff you and Marg logged, and there was this thing on one. We had only scanned the alarms on those tapes. We missed this one because the camera hadn't properly triggered. It's from the top flat, sometime last winter.'

All this information came a bit quickly.

'Eh? Last winter? What? What! A moose? Max? Max!'

'I'm not sure. I'd like you two to see it. It's, well, very different. Could be an old stag. But there were other deer on the same tape. They looked red, this one was dark. It's a very poor picture though, only a few frames on time-lapse.'

He wouldn't tell me any more, and I was left dangling.

I told him Marg and I would be in Dunedin on Monday.

We talked about it all weekend.

On Monday, Max and Ray were in the edit room expecting us, Max with a camera set up. He wanted to film our reaction to the tape. The equipment in the room, as we recalled, resembled the controls in a Boeing 727 cockpit.

The two had been watching other tapes from the remotes before we arrived. A group of red deer hinds on time-lapse jerked over the two screens until one came close enough to trigger the sensor and became a real-time subject, feeding and at play. Then heads up, fully alert, the hinds looked to their left before running off. Max and I came into picture with packs, dripping wet, watching after them. I remembered the day.

But we had come for The Thing. Ray changed tapes and we stood at his shoulder. The screens flickered. We watched, spellbound, as daylight grew in the small bush clearing. On time-lapse each day is compressed into about six minutes. It had been snowing and trees and shrubs were drooping under its weight. Gradually the day progressed, light fluttering under changing cloud cover, until it faded into nightfall. The screens went black. Day one.

When day two lit up, snow was blanketing the ground and a broadleaf branch had lowered itself in front of the lens. As it snowed more during the day the branch lowered further, jerking up now and then as snow overloaded and released. Daylight faded, the screens blacked out.

Day three.

'Coming up soon,' murmured Ray.

Tension increased. It was raining on the snow now; branches flicked all over the clearing as it melted, the broadleaf branch lifted partly, and our vision of the clearing improved. Suddenly a number of reddish shapes flickered across the screen for a few seconds and disappeared. Three red hinds.

'Now watch this,' said Ray.

I had almost forgotten to breathe.

We locked onto the shimmering image of the clearing. Without warning, a dark shape sprung into the picture, bounded across the screen in lightning leaps and strolled out of the right-hand corner.

We both exclaimed at once. ('Max may have to edit that word out,' I remembered afterwards.) Ray rewound the tape and replayed it. There it was again, bolting across the screen, then walking quickly out of frame.

'You can see how we missed it,' said Ray. 'What's happened is the sensor was on a small tree bent down by snow, so it was pointing at the ground, only triggering when the animal was really close.'

He replayed it again, this time frame by frame. Then again. A problem was when he froze on a single frame, the image, already indistinct, became worse. He replayed it. Again. And again.

The animal came from the bush at the clearing's far-left corner. The first frame had it, head low and swung right, behind a low bush. The next was front-on, head down and out of sight. Then it moved towards the right, and for three frames stood side-on, its hindquarters visible but partly obscured by the broadleaf, head still invisible. The next frame found it to the right of our picture, more side-on, closer, but among scrub. Close to the creature exiting, the sensor triggered, and there was less than two seconds of real-time footage, just enough to see a dark-brown body rearwards from the neck walk quickly from our screen, partly hidden by scrub.

'There's no view of its head, dammit. Every frame it's hidden by bushes.'

That seemed unbelievably bad luck.

'Look at the colour though—brown.'

'Yeah, those deer were quite reddish.'

'Could that be different light?'

'No, I doubt it. The shots of the deer and this are only about half an hour apart.'

'It's much bigger, too. And look at the shape and bulk of it. It's thick.

Deer are more lightly built, more elegant.'

'It could be a hoary old stag.'

'No way. It's July remember. You'd see antlers.'

'Well, that's something. It's a female.'

'Maybe it's an old hind that's been wallowing in the mud?'

'No, look at the coat. There's no mud there. It's uniform grey-brown. Moose colour.'

'On a red deer you'd definitely see the fringe of a rump patch in that last shot, while it's walking. See?'

'There's no rump patch there.'

'And no tail. It must be a moose. Eh?'

'Well, it's not a bloody possum and it's not a red deer, so why are we even bothering to argue? That leaves moose.'

'I'm trying to think what a sceptic might say.'

'Significant that it's alone? All the deer we've seen have been in groups.'

'Yes, very definitely. And look at the shape. The thickness through the chest. Humped shoulders. And the walk, that rolling gait. See how it swings that right forefoot? That's not a red deer stepping, that's a big-animal walk.'

'Hey Ray,' I suddenly asked, 'is there any way we can improve on these pictures? I mean with better gear?'

'Yes. We can go downstairs. Hang on, I'll give Gerry a call.'

If the upstairs edit room was a 727 cockpit, Gerry Browne's domain was a spaceship. He loaded the tape and we spent the next hour examining it frame by frame, dividing images, placing the deer beside what was rapidly becoming our moose, rolling it through in slow motion to capture the gait. We leaned into the screens, taut with concentration, straining to identify anything we might have missed ears—shoulder hump, dewlap, rump patch, tail, leg length, colour.

Finally Max, long forgotten, made a noise from behind his camera.

'Well, what do you think?'

I thought for a long moment, suddenly aware I was on film and needed to be cautious.

'We've got our moose,' I said. 'It's not eye-to-eye, which I would have preferred. But we have an image, not a perfect image, the colour, the shape, the size, the lack of a rump patch, the gait... We have our moose alright, and that's very satisfying.'

And it was. But it felt strangely flat. The pictures of her were heartbreakingly disappointing.

'Those pictures. I can't believe our bad luck,' I lamented again as we packed up Max's film gear. We'd come so close to getting it right.

'It's bloody exasperating. If the sensor tree had stayed upright, we'd have a 40-second movie of the old girl.'

'Or even if she'd had her head up, just for one frame,' added Max, sharing the frustration.

'What do you think, Max? Is it good enough for the film?'

He thought for a moment.

'Hmmmm. I think we had better try for another.'

There were too many friends around to scream, swear or weep.

I caught Marg's eye.

'Let's go for a drink somewhere,' I croaked.

On our way out, still excited but more composed, a thought crossed my mind.

'That's interesting,' I said to Marg. 'We knew a bull lived near the top flat in Herrick Creek. Remember the big prints and the antler rubbing on that totara? Now we know he had a girlfriend.'

It was well past office hours when Max let us onto the Dunedin streets in the gathering twilight. We had arranged to meet him and his wife, Carol, later for a celebratory dinner out. A traffic officer was standing alongside our Subaru, completing the paperwork on a parking ticket, about to put it under the windscreen wiper. I thought about explaining how we had been delayed watching a New Zealand moose on telly, but somehow it didn't seem worth the trouble.

At Lookout Point we had a good overview of terrain near the lake in Herrick Creek which was sometimes used by moose.

Travel around the lake edge at Herrick Creek was always good for a wetting — water from above, mud from below.

Fresh camp oven bread at Herrick Creek camp.

Marg with regenerating plants on a slip site at Herrick Creek in 1994. There has been spectacular vegetation recovery after the massive removal of red deer from these areas in the 1970s–1980s, but travelling and hunting difficulties are increased.

Taking a bath at camp for the brave (above)...
and the not-so-brave (below).

One of my favourite places: Marg and I at the dry rock at the Henry Burn-Herrick Creek saddle. Courtesy of Max Quinn.

Filming around the lake at Herrick Creek. Julian Grimmond on the umbrella and Max Quinn with the camera. Courtesy of Guy Marris.

Filming domestic scenes at main camp. With Marg are Max Quinn and Merv Aitchison.

Examining red deer antler-thrashing at the top clearing in Herrick Creek. Max Quinn with the camera and Errol Samuelson on sound.

Still camera and sensor unit wait patiently in ambush for passing animal traffic.

Herrick Creek, mid-winter 1996, filming with Max Quinn.

Remote video camera equipment. Ray Sharp prepares the tape. Lakeside at Herrick Creek, 1994.

Bill Black's Squirrel helicopter at one of the remote still camera sites, on a deer trail at upper Herrick Creek in 1995. Ray Sharp changes the film and batteries.

Red deer captured by remote cameras over the years 1995–1997.

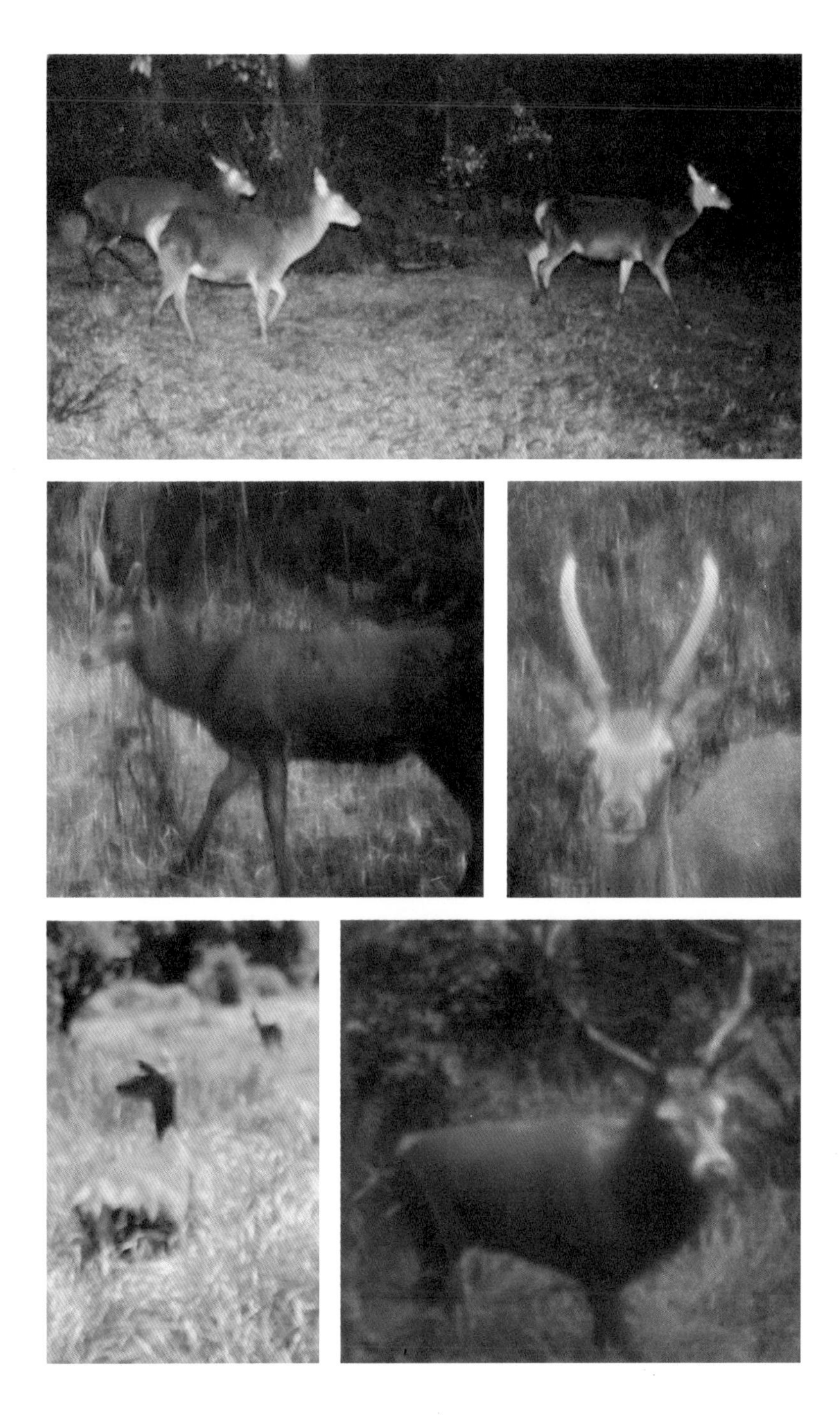

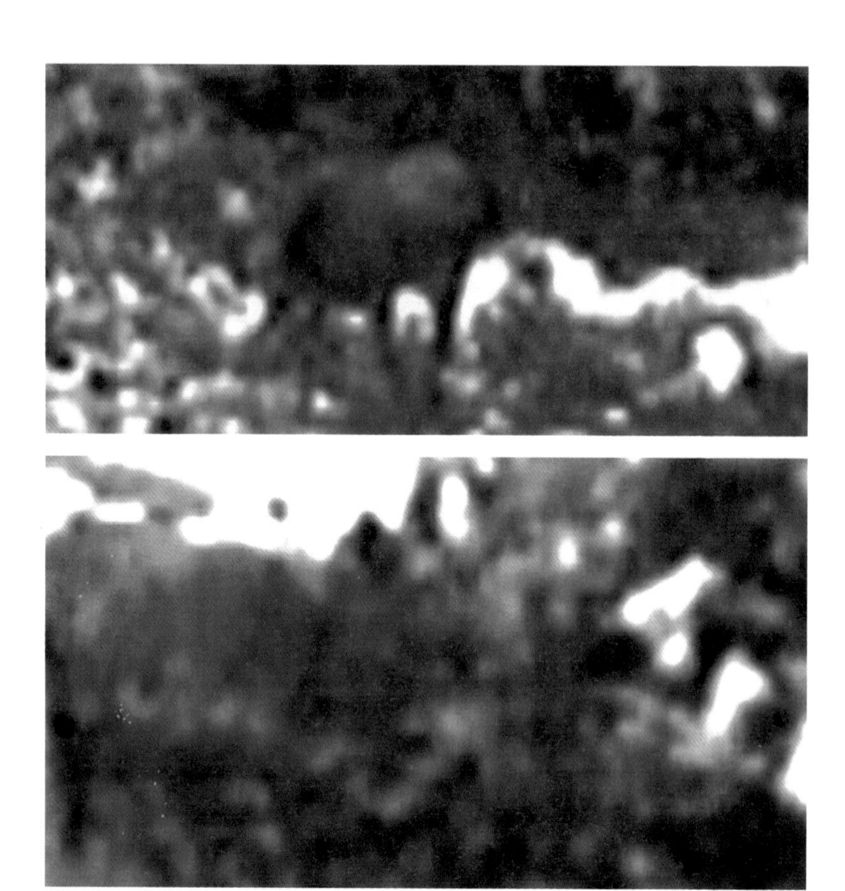

Two frames from time-lapse video footage from upper Herrick Creek, winter 1995. We believe this animal is a moose. Note the big ears and suggestion of a long muzzle in the lower photograph.

*Red deer shot on video at the same site only 30 minutes earlier.
Note differences in coloration, body size and bulk, and stance from that of the suspected moose in the upper photograph.*

21

September, October 1996

For weeks we agonised over our moose movie. Marg and I took a copy of the tape home and played it about 40 times every day. We had managed the almost unbelievable—footage of a New Zealand moose—but any elation was dampened by the quality of the images. What would it look like on TV? Was it enough to get Blackie to repay my beer? Would our image satisfy a sceptic? Max was doubtful: ours was a 'moose by deduction', he thought, and we needed a clear 'moose by observation'. We were conscious we had already been lucky. Could we do it again?

For the moment it was essential no one should know what we had. A news leak would rob the documentary of any element of surprise. It would be easy for Marg and I to keep the secret, harder for Max, who had to work with the footage towards the final documentary. He locked the tape away, and the few people who knew of it were sworn to silence. Sworn to silence? Hadn't we heard that before?

It wasn't easy to keep our knowledge to ourselves. Sometimes doubts would have us replaying the footage, but that was enough to be reconvinced. Finally, for another opinion, we cautiously showed the tape to Gary Cruickshank, who knew moose from his time in Alaska. We were further reassured by his reaction, and swore him to silence too.

Deadlines were now in sight for the film. There was only one thing to do: pretend we had no image, return to Fiordland and keep hunting.

November–December 1996

Springtime transformed the view from the Lookout. The air was warm and still. An evening sun slanted across the scrubby clearings, bright and green with new growth. On the lake a raft of New Zealand scaup and two pairs of paradise duck left weird double images with shadows on the shallow bottom. We nursed binoculars, full of expectation at seeing at least a deer or two. It was great to be back. The scene had never looked so inviting.

The afternoon before we had found Fred—alas, shot a few months earlier by a trophy hunter, his head and antlers removed; a forlorn mound of hair, skin and whitening bones.

'I'll miss him,' Marg had said sadly, remembering the times we had swapped stares across his clearing.

'You can't get too sentimental about these things,' I had told her, but without conviction. Antlers look better on stags than on walls.

'Hello, we're in business!' I said not long afterwards.

'Where?'

'Coming out above the first delta, two o'clock.'

A single hind stepped cautiously into sight, head up and alert in the semi-open scrubland, and began grazing on short grasses, pausing frequently to listen and gaze about her. We watched her for 20 minutes as she moved and fed among the scrub and high tussock. Then, with startling suddenness, she burst into a wild gallop, zig-zagging wildly among the high tussock, slid to a halt, kicked up her legs, changed direction, reared up, lashed out with her forelegs, then bolted through scrub, disappearing from sight. A few seconds later she reappeared in a mad dash to the lakeside, where she skidded to a halt, kicking and whirling in a couple of circles, then stopped to feed. We couldn't contain our laughter at her mad antics.

'She'd be embarrassed if she knew we were watching,' giggled Marg. Then, after a couple of moments' thought, added 'I used to wonder about all the tracks we find in some places, expecially along sandbars and clearings, making it look like there's lots of deer, when we know there's only a few. Now I can see it can be made by one or two animals just playing and goofing around.'

Half an hour before dark another two deer came into sight, a hind and a yearling. Right on dark, just when it was almost impossible to see, another hind and yearling joined them. It was an entertaining evening; a privileged insight into animal life only the Lookout could have provided.

We had been watching a yearling red stag—a 'spiker'—at first light, but he had slipped back into the scrub 30 minutes before. Everything was still. Only the waterfalls across the valley challenged the quiet. Engine noise suddenly broke the silence and quickly grew louder, then with a roar a helicopter swept past below us on a low run over the flats. I recognised Mark Hollows' black-and-yellow Soloy Hiller, a hunting aircraft from Te Anau.

The pressure was back on deer. The price of venison had peaked briefly at $8.10 a kilogram, and a hind was worth around $325, a medium-sized stag with antlers in velvet returned twice that. A helicopter like Mark's needed about $1000 an hour—two or three deer for every hour of airborne time—to be profitable, and spring is the most rewarding time to hunt. His was one of half a dozen or more helicopters hunting Fiordland. Mark's efforts were helping moose generally but not our chances for the moment, although we had already decided to leave Lookout Point.

Six days later we returned to the sound, looking forward to the better standard of living at base camp. The weather had been reasonably kind and we had worked hard. We had covered a lot of country, camping together in a different place most nights and often searching alone during the days. We were satisfied there were no resident moose in Herrick Creek, nor in the upper Henry Burn. That was not to say there were no moose at all; a transient animal leaves little sign. The plan was for a day's break, then to turn our efforts to other places in Wet Jacket, and onto Supper Cove by boat to search lower Dusky Sound. The sky was dark and a mild northerly gusted on the sea—not a good sign for next day.

We scrubbed up, caught a cod, and collected some driftwood and a few mussels. Then we went for a walk along the beach while the tide was low, before rain started.

The beach at Herrick Creek is only walkable at low tide, when it's about 500 metres long. During the winter of 1995 a moose had browsed its way along there, breaking and stripping the most easily reached favourites, as Max and I had noted at the time. There had been considerable regrowth on these plants since. I called them my marker plants and could recognise them individually. Monitoring them each trip would show if a moose had fed there betweentimes.

We scrunched along the stony shoreline chatting, coffee in hand. I glanced up now and then to check my plants, expecting nothing.

'Jesus Christ!'

I almost dropped my coffee.

'What?'

'Have a look at this!'

Towards the far end of the beach a single three-finger stem had been growing above some boulders. It had been wrenched down from beach level, the tip stripped and one lateral branch cropped. The remnants of the other lateral lay at our feet, still to be taken by the tide. A moose had announced its presence as surely as a signature on a factory time sheet.

We spent the remainder of the evening and all the next morning on detective work. By then we had traced the animal 500 metres back into the bush, picking up odd bits of browse sign, indicating the moose had walked through grabbing a bite now and then. Lack of sign near the waterfront suggested it had not lingered there. An arrival or departure? The impression was it had travelled from up the valley and swum off somewhere.

Bad weather prevented any early follow-up to seaward, but we used the boat extensively later in the week, attempting to determine where the moose had made landfall or come from—without success. The weather frustrated our plans and the trip to Dusky Sound was cut short. By the time the helicopter was due, a few days before Christmas, we had found no further moose sign. We were becoming weary, but I thought another week or two might change our luck. I tentatively mentioned it to Marg.

'You mean Christmas in here, as well as birthdays? No way!'

It wasn't that Santa wouldn't be able to find Wet Jacket Arm, she explained, but because all the rellies were coming to Wanaka on Boxing Day.

Ray had a new video unit in place, improved in portability and battery longevity. Its one drawback was requiring a seven-second delay to switch from 'Standby' to 'Record'. We had it aimed along a trail close to where we had photographed our 'moose without a head', and had so often struck moose sign at other times. With only one sensor for the unit, the target animal needed to walk from right to left to trigger the camera, when, providing it was travelling at normal speed, it would register on tape. Anything moving the other way, from left to right, would cross in front of the camera before crossing the sensor, so would probably be out of frame before the camera engaged 'Record'.

The helicopter picked us up with our gear. We picked up the film from the two still cameras, both with 36 exposures taken, before stopping at the upper clearing for the video. Marg and I scouted around for sign close to the unit. I crossed in front of the camera towards the sensor.

My blood ran cold. Directly in front of it was a hoofprint from the day before. Big, clear dewclaw marks. Moose! Right in front of the sensor! But I had an awful premonition. The animal had headed from left to right. The tracking looked purposeful and we could see where it had scrambled up the bank. Unless the animal had loitered it would have been away before the camera had triggered. I glanced at Marg. We looked back at Ray. He had taken the cover off the camera.

'Fifty minutes!' he exclaimed. 'Fifty minutes of tape. We've never had that before!'

'Could you play back the last few minutes?' I asked, heart thumping.

'Sure.'

He wasn't aware of our find.

'Hello, there's something here. Have a look at this.'

The tension had us rigid. We peered past his shoulder into the camera's tiny viewfinder. A hind came into shot and walked casually past, new calf at foot. The image flicked off, then on again. A spiker walked the same path, stopped, then slowly walked from shot. Both nice pictures, both from up valley and down the trail. Another image sprang up, this time the scene of an empty trail, played for a minute, then switched off.

'That one must have come from the other direction,' Ray said brightly.

The next shot was of ourselves triggering the camera a few minutes earlier.

I shook my head in disbelief, almost sick with disappointment.

'If it lives here,' Marg said quietly, 'sometime it'll come back down the track.'

Unable to say anything, I only nodded.

We spoke with Max a day later. He sympathised with our near miss. Ray was making a second sensor for that unit, he assured us. In the meantime, the increased deer activity we had seen from the Lookout had been reflected in the camera shots recently collected.

'We've got some great shots from the stills,' he said. Many were at night, but the best were from the video unit.

'There's some wonderful stuff; we can use some in the film. One, especially, with a hind standing on her back legs reaching for fuschia and grabbing mouthfuls of leaves. She does it several times, centre-frame and in good light. Beautiful shots; you couldn't wish for better.'

That would be useful to show how high red deer reach, I thought.

There was also several minutes of tape showing hinds with calves, he told me, and one amazing sequence with seven deer in frame at one time. What did I think of that, after so many months with near nothing on record!

'That'll be yearlings, probably mostly spikers,' I told him. 'They gang up after the hinds boot them out prior to calving; they're the deer equivalent of car loads of teenagers. They are without their Mums' experience; the helicopter tallies are full of them for a few months after December.'

There was another thing: the moose project had run on for much longer than expected, and had now exhausted its field-work funds. Max needed to finish editing a film he had shot betweentimes, then turn his full attention to the moose film.

'We'll have only one more trip,' he said, 'then we'll have to pull out.'

'Can you delay that until April?' I begged. 'I want to be there for the rut.'

Financing the documentary had never been easy. Natural History was obliged to provide for it from its own budget. New Zealand On Air had been set up to support locally made programmes, yet two applications had failed to gain even a token amount. Someone suggested this was because the promo sent with the applications had shots of trophy heads, and hunting was a sensitive and politically incorrect topic.

It would take only a few thousand dollars to retain cameras in place until winter. It was then, especially, when moose occupied areas we monitored. I called a good friend involved with the New Zealand chapter of Safari Club International, a hunting organisation which has a reputation for helping wildlife management, conservation and research causes. He was enthusiastic and arranged a committee meeting to hear my case.

I drove all afternoon to meet with them. In the evening I gave the five executive members a presentation, showed them our promo and photographs of moose sign, promised them acknowledgement in the film credits, and asked them for a few thousand bucks and, politely, to keep their mouths shut about the project. They listened, but kept their purse shut too. Some members were impressed, but others were obviously unmoved by my evidence and voting ran against us. One suggested that SCI might end up 'with egg on their face'; several hinted I was more boffin than hunter and they could do better searching themselves. I was briefly tempted to mention our prized 'moose with no head' footage, but bit my tongue. I drove back to Wanaka next morning, discouraged, hoping the final film would be more convincing than my show to SCI.

Twice over the next month came something I had hoped for: a talk with people who knew moose from North America. The first was Dick Gunlogson, a guest of Gary Cruickshank's. Dick was from the old school of bush pilots/hunting guides/safari outfitters, well known and respected on the Alaskan peninsula, where his company had operated successfully for 20 years. Dick and Gary dropped in. I spread out a few maps and photos and explained our story. The amiable Dick listened attentively. With a giant reputation preceding him, the slightly built, silver-haired and softly spoken man was different from the one I had imagined. Would he mind if I handed him some photos of what we were finding, for his assessment?

'Be happy to,' he replied.

I passed him the small portfolio of prints, the same I had shown to the SCI executive, of suspected moose sign. He paged through them thoughtfully, without comment, reached the end and passed it back.

'What do you reckon, Dick?'

'You got somethin' pretty big down there,' he said with a twinkle in his eye. 'Some of that stuff looks pretty damn familiar to me.'

'Which photos?' I asked.

He pointed out one of barking, those of stripping and droppings, and some of breakage, which he likened to that he had seen on birch one winter when a deep snow surface had hardened enough to enable moose a higher reach.

There was another question I had been waiting to ask. I had been given a Canadian 'moose caller' and a tape of instructions. The rut was approaching in Fiordland.

'What about calling during the rut? Have you used that to attract bulls?'

'Works well in some situations,' Dick responded, and went on to explain the best time for him had been when he had had a client round the wrong side of a patch of brush. He had called in a big bull moose and the animal had come for him at a brisk walk, head down and ears flattened.

'I had a rifle but only three rounds. I gave him the first between his forefeet at twenty-five yards and the second at twenty. The next was reserved for between his eyes. But the second shot turned him. Then I went for my client. By this time the moose was two hundred yards off and moving away. I called him right back in again and the client took him.'

'What I didn't know till after,' he added, 'was that moose had just been fighting a smaller bull, and he was pretty fired up!'

And moose senses?

'It's not often you see one when you're just moving around,' he said, 'but the times when you do, from, say, two hundred yards, it'll be craning its neck tryin' to pick you up, big ears pointing forward like two funnels. Then they'll turn and trot off. The hearing is very astute.'

The afternoon passed too quickly. I saw my visitors to the door.

'You keep lookin', and Good Luck! Let me know how you get on,' were Dick's departing words.

'Thanks, Dick. I will,' I promised.

I had a set of photographs spread out on the table one Saturday morning not long afterwards, when Marg arrived back from netball.

'What's this?' she asked.

I explained they had been sent by Dick. They were prints of winter moose barking on birch, taken 'just 200 yards' from his home in Willow, near Anchorage, Alaska. She ran her eyes over them.

'That looks pretty familiar,' she said.

Max arranged the next meeting in Dunedin. His university contacts had revealed that Corey Bradshaw, a young Canadian ecologist, was now on staff at the University of Otago. Corey was teaching while completing a PhD there. Max told him of our project and the two became friendly. Corey was a graduate of the University of Alberta, had done extensive field work with caribou in Alberta, and was very familiar with moose in the same habitat. Marg and I travelled to Natural History's office for the rendezvous, where Max had set up the video clip of the mystery animal, my photographs of suspected moose sign, and droppings we had picked up and kept in his deepfreeze at home. Corey had seen only a few photographs beforehand.

Corey arrived and we introduced ourselves, immediately on the same wavelength. We started with the video. Corey pointed out some features of the animal which we hadn't considered. Turning to the other items, he was sure some of the droppings were identical to those 'at home'. Unlike Dick, he hadn't seen barking like our photos showed, but on the other hand the breakage of deciduous trees was commonplace.

'Well Corey, you've seen what we've been finding,' I said at the end. 'What do you think? Are we on the right track?'

'We won't know a hundred per cent until you see one or get a complete photo,' he replied with scientist's caution, 'but I'll stake my reputation you've got a moose down there.'

'Yeah,' I laughed. 'That makes two of us.'

April 1997

Wet Jacket Arm. Rain poured past the tarpaulin only an arm's length away. It was dry by the fire and the smoke kept sandflies at bay. I pressed 'Play' on the tiny tape recorder.

'Oooh-ahh, oooh-ahh, oooh-ahh,' came the tinny sound. I raised the caller to my mouth and cupped my hand over the end. It had a wooden mouthpiece with a reed and a corrugated plastic tube.

'OOOH-AHH! OOOH-AHH! OOOH-AHH!'

The tent unzipped and Marg's head came out with a puzzled expression.

'What's that noise?' she asked.

'I'm practising with the moose caller.'

I could make a much more accurate grunt without it, but the sound wouldn't carry.

'They say you can call a bull moose in from 500 metres with it.'

'Pity it's not Opening Morning. You'd be getting a heap of ducks.'

She disappeared back to her book.

It was comforting to know it worked on human females.

We had found no moose sign by the time Max flew in with Errol Samuelson. The weather had been bad. We had camped at the Lookout but hunted only lower Herrick Creek and a few places close around the sound. With the arrival of Max and Errol, priorities changed to filming.

It is impossible to film a real moose hunt in Fiordland rain with sophisticated camera and sound gear, so over the next week we simulated the bits that had not already been caught on film: solo stalking, camping out, some domestics, repeats of scenes that had not worked, link shots to be used between sequences, a few short interviews. On a rare fine day we travelled to the top clearing video site and inspected the fuchsia where the hind had stood to feed. It showed she had reached fractionally over two metres. The shoulder height of an adult moose was only slightly lower and their reach an order above that of deer. It was satisfying to be able to demonstrate that so effectively on film. Next day we returned to the lake area for a sequence using the moose call. I was embarrassed that I could not use it skilfully and hoped the shot would edit up better than it had felt. If the documentary was ever broadcast in Canada and Alaska, the locals would get a good laugh.

Max and Errol departed in a hurry during a small window of fine weather the following day, and Marg and I were alone again. The weather was still bad but it was time to get serious again. We had only a couple of weeks to find a moose.

The weather did not improve—the 'Southland Times' later described April as 'the wettest since 1958'. That autumn was also a surprisingly quiet rut for red deer. We heard only three stags roar, and each only once. With just a week to go we decided I should head up valley by myself for a five-day camp-out while Marg worked the country closer to camp. If I wasn't back by the 26th, she would come looking, Marg said. Then we split.

I was in the Henry Burn on the last day, at the edge of my range, when I picked up fresh moose sign. The more I looked, the more I found. It showed that a moose was resident in a small but very rough patch of seral forest which had been badly storm damaged. Freshly stripped branches, especially fuchsia and lacebark, were everywhere. Droppings were so fresh they had a warm animal smell despite the rain. The moose was probably only 100 metres away, but might as well have been 20 kilometres distant because the place was a nightmare to hunt. I tried as best I could for half a day, then retreated, knowing there was nothing further I could do. For once I wasn't exasperated by my inability. I had answered the question 'Where do they go?' Well, here was one. Maybe over winter it would leave the shadows of the Henry Burn for kinder country in Herrick Creek. Perhaps then, if the cameras were still in place, we would catch it? That was for the future. Meanwhile it was a long, hard haul back to camp. I set off before Marg's alarm bells rang.

Blackie came with Ray a few days later. We moved a camera closer to the moose. At my request we spent five minutes in the helicopter on an overview search for it, hovering over the area where I had found the fresh sign. I held the door open with one hand, peering below, fully expecting the animal to break any minute, but the moose sat tight or had already gone. Finally, we flew on to camp, where Marg was loading gear into a net. She hooked it up and climbed aboard, and we underslung the load back to Te Anau. We would have one more helicopter trip to recover the cameras in another month. Then it would all be over.

I thought of my last interview for the documentary a fortnight before, crammed in only minutes before Max and Errol's final pick-up time.

'We had better get something from you,' Max had said, 'because it looks like we won't get a better shot.'

I had sat by the campfire, composed myself, and let rip. It had sort of summed things up.

'We know we've got moose; maybe just a few, alive and well in Fiordland. We've even managed footage of one, we're sure, on a remote camera. But for me the story doesn't end here. We'll be back, searching, until we see one face-to-face.'

Then the float plane had roared overhead, and Max and Errol had scrambled to pack their gear.

22
Conclusion

And in the morning came the sound of the axe

Sings Harry.

Or the bush-buried shot at mountain deer;

The river talked to the stones and the swamp-smothered flax,

And the hut smoke rose clear.

That was a good place to be camping in

Sings Harry.

'Sings Harry'
Denis Glover

In Laos I would sometimes feel officebound. When it became a bit much I would often slip away from our airport premises early on the motorbike. I would guide it carefully through the dusty, potholed streets of Vientiane among the carts, monks, bicycles, jeeps, geese and pedestrians, to arrive just before lunch at the simple wooden building where Marg had her preschool class. I would sit with the children for the best part of their day: story time.

There was a favourite tale. Fourteen little faces watched Marg intently as she turned the first pages of the book. Like perfect dolls, two tiny Japanese sisters would usually sit on one knee and a flaxen-haired Swedish tot snuggle up on the other. White, brown, black and in-between, there were nine nationalities here, the children of diplomats. Trembling with suppressed excitement, they waited for Marg to begin. Then at page one they all let loose, chanting with unbridled enthusiasm, some in a language they did not understand. It didn't matter; the pictures were enough:

'We're going on a Bear Hunt,

We're going to catch a Big One,

Oh, what a beautiful day,

We're not scared—'

With a lump in my throat, more frequently than I would care to admit, I would wink at Margie. There is a little bit of hunter in all of us.

It strikes me that we are not too far removed from our hunter–gatherer past, despite pretensions otherwise. Whether it is picking our own strawberries or buying pieces of animal from a supermarket, any advances made beyond sneaking through the trees with your mates, armed with wooden clubs, have really only been about guaranteeing supply.

After the turn of the century young New Zealand began tugging impatiently at the apron strings of Mother England. A separate identity emerged from the battlefields of the First World War. In the years that followed, New Zealanders recognised their growing uniqueness. The things that set New Zealand apart from the rest of the world were born of a pioneer's wrestle with landscape, oceans of distance from other nations, freedom from tradition, the fusion of unlikely races, and growing confidence as new generations found solutions for themselves.

Some images which symbolise our development and growth as a nation are comfortably familiar, and sometimes spark quiet pride. For me they include the touch of orange sun on snow; a black singlet breasting the tape; driftwood on an empty beach; a last-minute try from around the scrum; the curl of water under a streamlined bow; ice tinkling on the summit ridge; the whistle to a faraway dog; a rush of water among ferns; dusty antlers in the woolshed.

Deerstalking rests easily among the forces which helped shape the New Zealand pysche. Removing protection for deer and endowing them with the status of pests ended any ideas of exclusivity or privilege that the government had originally held for hunting them. No longer the sport of kings, hunting was now for everybody. Most New Zealand males who grew up in the 30-year period that extended to the 1960s went deerstalking at some time in their lives, even those from the cities. For many it was their first—for some their only—introduction to the bush and mountains. Those taking to the sport regularly did so with the respect of the other users of the outdoors: the high-country musterers who mustered, the trampers who tramped, and the mountaineers who mountaineered. The hunters hunted: for the pot; for sport; for skins or trophies; for the bounties that were being offered; or professionally, as government deer-cullers.

The Forest Service inherited the deer problem from the Department of Internal Affairs, and campaigned vigorously for deer destruction. Deer were Public Enemy Number One. No one disputed that forests and tussock land suffered under heavy deer populations, or that other mountain areas were damaged by Himalayan tahr and European chamois. But the animals were also blamed for monstrous geological processes that had existed for millennia, and that was ridiculous. But the public believed such tales. Christchurch folk trembled at the possibility of great floods originating at the source of the Waimakariri River, the result of too many deer. The blame for the aggradation of river gravels, the formation of slips and screes, and soil loss, was laid at the cloven feet of wild animals. Unfairly, sheep were not similarly portrayed, despite the fact that they coexisted in many places with deer, and that it was for sheep that mountain land had been burned.

War was declared on deer, and small battles raged on a hundred fronts. Professional deer-cullers shot catchment areas considered flood-prone, or where deer competed with stock. Private deerstalkers operated everywhere, restrained only by the length of their weekend or shortness of breath or ammunition.

If the liberation-and-licensed hunting era was the first chapter in the history of our introduced game animals, then the kill-'em-all period that followed was the second. There were two more. Chapter three began with massive exploitation and ended with deer farming. It encompasses the two decades after 1965, when the venison industry transported deer to the marketplace, dead or alive, on the strong backs of hunters, or using wheelbarrows, tractor tubes, horses, jet-boats, Piper Super cubs, ships and, especially, helicopters, helicopters and helicopters.

Although prices fluctuated wildly, deer became valuable again—at times too valuable for comfort—for there were jealousies, brutal competition and sometimes tragedy when physical, financial and emotional boundaries were crossed and recrossed in the scramble for possession. By and large, government agencies were trampled underfoot, although they regrouped and counterattacked with hasty legislation. The deer-farming industry grew from small beginnings over this period. Populations of deer, tahr and chamois were decimated, but their pest status remained unchanged. The deerstalker, the one constant ingredient in the equation up until the helicopter era, was ignored. Hunting became so unrewarding that most hung up their rifles and spent Saturdays watching rugby on television. As for the deer problem, one helicopter operator spoke for all when he muttered darkly: 'The only bloody deer problem now is bloody finding one.'

Chapter four, as yet untitled, deals with the present time. It can be drafted but not completed.

Wild animals are now under the administration of the Department of Conservation. On deer and other game-animal issues, DoC muddles along, pleasing nobody. Policies continue to assume that anything with hair and not feathers is a pest, and that there is no place for sport. It juggles hunting rights between contesting applicants: the commercial helicopter hunters, deerstalkers, and the occasional hunting guide with his more adventurous clients. Schemes purporting to benefit hunters with game resources or access are usually ways of further diminishing animal numbers. Where they are forced to be hunter-friendly, 'management' equates to balloting for blocks or restricting access to limit yield. DoC is spurred on in its efforts by large, well-organised conservation groups, like the Royal Forest and Bird Protection Society, which urge no compromise with animal-control policies.

DoC has a vast empire of other responsibilities; game animals are small cheese. Few staff have experience in wild-animal matters, money is inadequate and professional advice nearly extinct.

Landcare Research, based at Lincoln University, researches wild animals. It is not its fault that research efforts continue to reflect the philosophy that wild ungulates will soon be absent, so any efforts to understand them will prove a waste of time. At present kakapo researchers number one scientist for every 15 birds in existence, which is commendable. But there are just a handful of scientists studying the 70 million troublesome possums, and fewer than that the ungulates.

Deer farming is now a flourishing, stable and profitable industry in New Zealand. Elegant and graceful as ever, deer now peer through netting fences and chase tractors across paddocks for nuts and hay.

The familiar presence of deer on the farm produces side effects of consequence for the sport of deerstalking. How do you tell your son of the thrill and sense of privilege at the sight of a wild deer when there are so many at home, nearby, grazing pasture? Will he ever understand that the glimpse of a grey hind in a forest clearing at first light may be his reward for cold July water filling his boots, an uncomfortable camp and a patient stalk? Or the spine-tingling bellow of an unseen stag in the manuka? My generation was content with that and whatever excitement followed. Will he be?

Antlers, once a tangible tribute to the patience, athleticism or luck of sportsmen, are now grown, cropped and traded for dollars to enhance the nightlife of old men in Korea. But commerce is commerce, and deer farmers deserve applause for their innovation and hard-earned success. It may please our ancestors to know that guided trophy hunting for overseas sportspeople is a small but vigorous industry, for in this way at least the purpose of the early liberations is being realised. But the guides, however skilful, have no privileges of tenure with respect to wild-game hunts, and clients have either to match the hardy Kiwis for the rare game or pay for an advantage. New Zealand is the only place in the world where free-range tahr-hunting is available. Trophies are highly regarded and handsomely paid for by overseas hunters, who invariably require guides with helicopter support. Some high-country run-holders will be looking at their blisters and their wool cheque, and realising that the traditional roles of sheep and wild animals on their property have been reversed. The shearers' quarters would make a good guesthouse, but whatever will we do with the woolshed? Unfortunately, all too often, deer are farm-traded for their antlers and shot in large enclosures that only pretend fair chase—a practice akin to a mountaineer stepping from a helicopter to claim a peak. Such trophy collecting makes a mockery of sporting ethics and simple animal dignity. The animal, and the spirit of the hunt, have both been slaughtered.

The buzz of a helicopter searching for wild game is still a familiar sound in the mountains, but is heard far less frequently now, and net guns for live-capture gather dust at the back of the hangar. Helicopter numbers expanded into areas of high deer density like some newly liberated predator, then dropped, starved off by falling deer numbers. The intensity of hunting now depends on prices for wild-shot meat, but deer, tahr and chamois populations are presently being maintained at low numbers throughout the country, albeit at levels a little above those of a decade ago.

Here is a list of a number of creatures living happily in New Zealand: hedgehogs, kiwi, kiore, cats, kakapo, rabbits, stoats, ostriches, parakeets, moose, mice, mallard duck, whitetail deer, wapiti, pheasant, spur-winged plovers, wallabies, possums, Rangi, Soo Li, you and me. A few have lived here for thousands of years. Most of us have trickled in over recent centuries, products of the never-ending forces of population dispersal. Some arrivals came on cross-Tasman winds, others on bits of wood shaped as canoes or ships, along with various hitchhikers. The pulse of human arrivals quickened, and some strains became numerous. Those of European origin began to dominate. They modified the landscape, and the better habitat attracted more of them. As with human invasions in other places, they brought implements and animals with them for survival, commerce, sport and comfort.

I am pleased and proud to be a New Zealander. I do not feel less of one than Rangi, whose ancestors have been here longer. Kakapo came before both of us, spur-winged plovers found their own way here long after. Sheep, chaffinches, dogs, deer and trout are all now permanent residents—New Zealanders, like us. We have to live with one another.

Think of it this way: these neighbours either add something to, delete something from, or make no change to our personal lives. Perhaps unconsciously we give each of them a mark or score, a kind of personal evaluation. For example, I dislike stoats, don't mind a cat, am scared of horses close up, and rather like moose. You may love horses but not care for cats—that is, until your wife or husband gets you one. Values are rather like fashions or currency: they change with people, time, circumstance. Once there was a trade in dried Maori heads and fur-seal skins. Only a century ago it was quite acceptable to turn your dog loose in the bush to catch kiwi, kakapo and weka for the pot. You could burn forests and mountain slopes. My—white—miner ancestors made Soo Li's feel unwelcome here. How quickly attitudes change. What triumphs and what regrets will we have to explain to our grandchildren?

Chaffinches are inconspicuous little birds; you probably give them no score at all. But what if it was discovered that, in some subtle way, they change a piece of critical habitat so as to preclude some bird we all prefer because it has lived here longer? Or carry a virus found to prove fatal to bellbirds? Then our feelings towards chaffinches would change. So they would if, tomorrow, someone started buying them for $250 each.

Prevailing attitudes among officialdom seem to be stuck in the groove of treating wild-game animals as temporary and unsavoury guests, soon to be vacating and about time too. Not so. They are here for ever. We cannot eliminate them. We've tried that. It follows that we must tolerate them at some level of density. When that fact sinks in, a host of queries are raised. What density? Who decides that? Why? Who researches the matter? If they must be controlled, who will pay, who will do the job, and who decides that? What will be the effects on parts of the environment we value? Values, values, values. This makes me very uneasy. Things I enjoy in our bush will differ from your pleasures. Neither of us is Right or Wrong, but someone in Wellington is making policy which will affect us both. The terrifying thing is, these days, it is likely to be an accountant.

It will never be easy to administer wild-game animals in this country because of the division of opinion about them. Many people insist that our forests should look like New-Zealand-before-we-found-it, despite living here themselves and presumably making their own contribution to the messiness of civilisation and the changes it has wrought on the land. For them, one introduced wild animal is one too many. At the other end of the scale are people who cannot see beyond the animal itself, and are unmoved by any concern about habitat. There are many examples of well-funded animal rights groups overseas wrenching sensible animal management off its tracks. We are not immune to these pressures here, as disputes over the fate of the Kaimanawa horses have shown.

If we left populations of deer, chamois and tahr to themselves, they would eventually establish an equilibrium with their habitats, but those habitats might be different from those first colonised. Human New Zealanders have decided that the time period involved, the changes to the habitats, and the displacement of other species make this unacceptable. Fortuitously, numbers of these animals have been lowered to a fraction of their former levels by game-meat-industry helicopters. The side effect of their efforts, affecting all New Zealanders, human and otherwise, is the gift of a universal recovery of vegetation in mountainlands and forest. But wait a minute: populations that are being artificially held at these low densities are composed of well-conditioned individuals in increasingly good habitat. They will have all the expansionist attributes of first colonists. It is a situation that is inherently unstable, like holding a spring down against its tension.

The hand holding the spring is the force of hunting. Continuation of the viability of helicopter hunting is essential, for in the foreseeable future there are no alternatives. If commercial hunting dies out, populations, which can double every three years, will soon bounce back. Deer are not rabbits; there is no equivalent of calicivirus or myxomatosis. Poisoning is difficult, inaccurate when it comes to targeting particular species and increasingly unacceptable. If we wish to retain the present comfortable situation, wild-game animals will have to be shot: from helicopters, by sportspeople or by the government, or a varying mix of all three. The first two would cost the taxpayer little and have enormous side benefits; the third would be very costly, and the costs would last forever.

The paranoia over high numbers of wild-game animals should be behind us. We are now awake to unfair propaganda and aware of relevant research. With an attitude change, professional input from researchers and a new generation of enlightened managers, we can use this constantly renewing animal resource to great benefit by considering it as an asset. We have made the investment, our accountant will remind us; now we can live off the interest. It would no longer be 'animal control', but 'game-animal management'.

Game management does not necessarily mean more animals. In many cases it means fewer, or close to none at all. It does mean that each of the various species is considered as a resource; that goals are set for harvesting where appropriate; that population levels are deliberated and maintained by reason, not by default; and that the annual increment is harvested, sometimes by more than one user. Given that everyone can shoot selectively and be spaced in time, helicopter and deerstalker can complement each other, and both achieve their aims.

It is possible to manage for countless objectives, but these need to be clearly identified as a first step. They may include maximum yield for meat; maximum numbers for sport; maximum (or minimum) size for trophies; habitat protection for birds or plants; shelter from disturbance for photography or aesthetics. The varying objectives will depend, once again, on that most elusive of criteria, current values.

The structure for administering game animal management is already in place with the Department of Conservation. Expertise will need beefing up and staff will have to be innovative, but New Zealanders are good at that. The need for input would have hunting clubs and organisations flourishing. That will have attendant benefits for youth, the community and the economy. Accountants should be pleased, for it may even prove self-funding.

In any event, managing the hunters will be probably be more difficult than managing the animals. In accessible areas where hunters are numerous, they may have to accept new practices: zoning, blocks, licences, seasons, limits, ballots and—horrors—even fees. Not all New Zealanders are used to this, but trout anglers and game-bird sportspeople put money into their sport. The pest era is over, and that is not unfair. Users must take part with goodwill and self-discipline, and be mature enough not to cheat. The prize is that their sport will be secure.

But I am dreaming: that is for the future. At present the deerstalker has little to hunt. Any animals he chances across are likely to be lucky survivors of a control campaign or overlooked by the last meat-hunting helicopter. It concerns me that this sport has been shunted into the background. Already a generation of sports hunters has been lost. If accessible wild-game populations remain decimated, the sport will wither and die. There are many reasons why it should be nurtured rather than ignored: tradition, culture, conservation awareness, self-esteem, the sensible use of firearms, health and fitness, and alternatives to computer games or glue-sniffing are among them. But the most important—even vital—reason, is that deerstalkers are potentially the most potent force in the management of wild game in this country. They will remain long after helicopters are unavailable or unwelcome.

There are many wilderness users who enjoy seeing wild animals without wanting to hunt, and Marg and I are two of them. Birds and animals bring life to a place that, without them, is only scenery. In many countries folk like us are in the majority. New Zealanders treat some 'native' birds with respect, but the 'pest' legacy of wild-game animals will take time to change. I know that if a carload of Wanaka locals see deer alongside the Haast road, there is a scramble for rifles and not cameras. But under deliberate management there may be some areas where we could enjoy watching a shy chamois with our binoculars after a careful stalk, or a bull tahr in full winter pelage swaggering and posturing during his courtship dance. It is the security of being out there with a chance, rather than being ensured of encountering animals, which is the draw card. Sometimes, knowing there are very few enriches the lure of finding one. If you doubt that, just look at our efforts to find a moose.

And just where do New Zealand moose fit into the big picture? You could be forgiven for saying 'Not at all'. At first glance it might seem that the few individuals living in one of the remotest parts of Fiordland are not really of any significance. They're extremely rare here perhaps, I hear you say, but not threatened in their homeland. And immune to any direct management on account of their sparse numbers and their wariness.

Not so, I will answer you, but not because they are moose and they are few. Rather, because they are there, a tiny population, of historic and biological interest to some of us; living contentedly in a national park where they are, officially, not allowed; having no significant effect on vegetation or other park values, except perhaps to enhance them. So, out there in the jungles of officialdom, their existence must now be acknowledged. Someone must make a judgment on their worth, because someone else has to generate policy with their name on it. And that policy will be the litmus test for other wild-game animals living elsewhere in greater numbers and comfort. It all begins with how we feel about moose.

Now can you see what I am getting at?

And here's another question: what do you think?

Epilogue
July 1997

'The thrill of a hunt isn't in the kill, it's in the chase,' I announced unexpectedly one day.

'What on earth made you say that?' asked Marg.

'Because I've just had a tally-up of all the time you and I have been in Dusky looking for moose, and there's been a helluva lot of chasin' and not many bulls-eyes! I've done forty-six weeks, counting my time in the 1970s and the solos. That's nearly a year. And still never laid eyes on one. I guess I pictured myself as being a better hunter than that! We've done twenty-nine weeks together, over seven months. And Ray's made twenty-six trips for the remote cameras.'

'We may not have seen a moose,' Marg said, 'but neither has anyone else.'

She looked up with a grin.

'Besides, if I know you, you haven't finished yet. And didn't Eddie Herrick and Percy both say it was mostly a matter of luck? We've been a bit short of that! Anyway, the next few months should be really interesting.'

Max and film editor Marilyn McArthur had begun the long and painstaking process of editing over 40 hours of footage, from 70 tapes, into a 52-minute documentary. There would be plenty of gems left on the cutting-room floor. We would be involved after the film was roughed out. We looked forward to that. It would mean trips to Dunedin, new experiences, another language to learn: pulling shots, digitising, voice-over—

'We're aiming to finish it by the end of November,' Max had told us. 'Then we'll hold a premiere at the office or in a hall somewhere. Have a think about who you'd like to invite.'

'Remind me just beforehand,' I asked Marg. 'There's a couple of phone calls I'd like to make.'

'Who to?'

'One is to Dennis Egerton. Remember how mad we were with him after he spilled the beans to Natural History? Well, it's been a lot of fun. I think he should know we're not still crusty.'

'Yes, I agree. The other?'

'To Bill Black. There's still the dozen beer he owes me from our bet twenty-five years ago. He may like to bring it.'

'You mean we've made a three-hundred-and-fifty-thousand-dollar film just so you can win a twelve-dollar bet?'

'It's not the beer, it's the principle. Understand?'

And she did.

Author's note on sources

Many of the references and quotes throughout the book come from personal interviews, letters and diaries (including the author's own), while some factual information arises from the author's original research.

Letters to and reports for the Internal Affairs Department, the Minister of Internal Affairs and Acclimatisation Societies were usually published in newspapers of the time and, after 1928, in the 'New Zealand Fishing & Shooting Gazette'. Internal Affairs Department and New Zealand Forest Service files held newspaper clippings of the day as well as external and internal reports and correspondence; these records are now held at the National Archives.

Bibliography

Books

Banwell, D. Bruce. 'Wapiti in New Zealand: A History of the Fiordland Herd', A H & A W Reed, Auckland, 1966.

Caughley, Graeme. 'The Deer Wars', Heinemann, Auckland, 1983.

Curtis, Max. 'Beyond the River's Bend', Halcyon Press, Auckland, 1991.

Donne, T. E. 'The Game Animals of New Zealand', John Murray, London, 1924.

Forbes, J. 'New Zealand Deer Heads', Country Life, London, 1924.

Francis Smith, R. V. 'Rifle Sport in the South Island' (Second edition), Pegasus Press, Christchurch, 1955.

King, Carolyn M. 'The Handbook of New Zealand Mammals', Oxford University Press, 1990.

Peterson, Randolph L. 'North American Moose', University of Toronto Press, 1955.

Tinsley, Ray. 'Call of the Moose', Reed, Auckland, 1983.

Articles

Caughley, G. 1963, Dispersal rates of several ungulates introduced into New Zealand, 'Nature', no. 200, pp. 280–281.

Caughley, G. 1971, An investigation of hybridisation between free-ranging wapiti and red deer in New Zealand, 'New Zealand Journal of

Science', no. 14, pp. 993–1008.

Challies, C. N. 1990, Red deer, in 'The Handbook of New Zealand Mammals', ed. C. M. King, Oxford University Press, Auckland.

Clarke, C. M. H. 1971, Liberations and dispersal of red deer in northern South Island districts, 'New Zealand Journal of Forestry Science', no. 1, pp. 194–207.

Clarke, C. M. H. 1976, Eruption, deterioration and decline of the Nelson red deer herd, 'New Zealand Journal of Forest Science', No. 5, pp. 235–249.

Davidson, M. M. and Tustin, K. G, 1990, Moose, in 'The Handbook of New Zealand Mammals', ed. C. M. King, Oxford University Press, Auckland.

Francis Smith, R. V. 1954, The Lost Herd, 'Outdoor Life', no. 114, pp 29–31, 60–63.

Geist, V. 1963, On the behaviour of the North American moose in British Columbia, 'Behaviour', vol. XX, pp. 377–416.

King, C. M. 1990, Axis Deer, in 'The Handbook of New Zealand Mammals', ed. C. M. King, Oxford University Press, Auckland.

Logan, P. C. and Harris, L. H. 1967, Introduction and establishment of red deer in New Zealand, New Zealand Forest Service Information Service, no. 55.

McKinnon, A.D. and Coughlan, L. 1962, Data on the establishment of some introduced animals in New Zealand forests, 'Extracts from Annual Reports of Southland Acclimatisation Society 1896–1940', vol VI.

Nugent, G., Parkes, J. P. and Tustin, K. G. 1987, Changes in the density and distribution of red deer and wapiti in northern Fiordland, 'New Zealand Journal of Ecology', no. 10, pp. 11–21.

Parkes, J. Tustin, K. G. and Stanley, L. 1978, The history and control of red deer in the Takahe area, Murchison Mountains, Fiordland National

Park, 'New Zealand Journal of Ecology', no. 1, pp. 145–152.

Tustin, K. G. 1970, Distribution and density of introduced animals in the northern portion of Fiordland National Park, Protection Forestry Branch Report, no. 88 (unpublished).

Tustin, K. G. 1972, Moose in Fiordland, Protection Forestry Branch Report, no. 113 (unpublished).

Tustin, K. G. 1973, Moose in Fiordland, 'New Zealand Wildlife', no. 41, pp. 5–15.

Tustin, K. G. 1974, Status of Moose in New Zealand, 'New Zealand Journal of Mammalogy', no. 55, pp. 199–200.

Tustin, K. G. 1975, Introduced animals: red deer (1), 'New Zealand Nature Heritage 6', pp. 2147–2156.

Tustin, K. G. 1980, Recent changes in Himalayan tahr populations and their effect on recreational hunting, 'New Zealand Wildlife', no. 61, pp. 40–48.

Tustin, K. G. and Parkes, J. P. 1988, Daily movement and activity of female and juvenile Himalayan thar in the eastern Southern Alps, New Zealand, 'New Zealand Journal of Ecology', no. 11, pp, 51–59.

Tustin, K. G. 1990, Himalayan tahr, in 'The Handbook of New Zealand Mammals', ed. C. M. King, Oxford University Press, Auckland.

Wandle, J. A., Evans, G. R., Tustin, K. G. and Challies, C. N. 1970, Summary report on the vegetation and introduced mammals of northern Fiordland, Protection Forestry Branch Report, no. 91, (unpublished).

Other sources include the following newspapers and periodicals:

'West Coast News', various issues, February 1900;

'Southland Times', 2 December 1912, 1 May 1971, 18 April 1972; and various issues 1920–1955;

'Christchurch Press', April 1972;

'Timaru Herald', 1978;

'New Zealand Fishing and Shooting Gazette', 1928–1950;

'Weekly Press', 15 February 1923; 30 July 1927.

Ken Tustin

Ken Tustin's love affair with mountains and wildlife grew from tramping and hunting in the Ruahine and Kaweka Ranges during his schoolboy days. Later, he spent summers as a professional hunter in the Southern Alps and Fiordland while pursuing university degrees at the University of Victoria, in Wellington, and the University of British Columbia, in Canada.

After ten years as a research scientist with the Forest Research Institute, specialising in studies of deer in Fiordland and tahr in the mountains of Canterbury, Ken launched into a second career—still in his beloved mountains—as a helicopter pilot. Since then he has lived and worked in Burma and Laos as well as New Zealand and has spent five summers in Antarctica. With Marg, he lives in Wanaka and works as a contract helicopter pilot and wild game animal consultant.